PRAISE FOR
My Ishmael

"*My Ishmael* isn't just a sequel to the original. Instead, the original must be seen as a springboard for this new penetrating look into the machinery of our own culture, with all the drama and intrigue that a culture's history has to offer."

—Lance Pierce, Editor, *Illusions Magazine*

"[An] intellectually dynamic tale . . . Quinn's intention is to stimulate discussion, and he succeeds."

—*Booklist*

'I'm crazy about any book that can get people, especially young people, excited about ideas. And that's just what Quinn has done with his writing. . . . [He] has an amazing story to tell."

—Lois Blinkhorn, *Milwaukee Journal Sentinel*

"*My Ishmael* . . . is a lesson in the evolution of modern society."

—*The Rocky Mountain News*

"Quinn engagingly presents an antidote to a fundamental flaw of our culture, invoking a law in human history that can halt our civilization's plunge toward planetary catastrophe."

—*Lit Notes*

PRAISE FOR
The Story of B

"The author writes a facile, clear prose, and the ideas he wants to discuss are admittedly important. Quinn is a provocative thinker."

—*Kirkus Reviews*

"Continuing the thought-provoking philosophical construct that he set up in *Ishmael,* Quinn provides an even deeper and more wide-ranging story. *The Story of B* is enormously readable, with several shocking plot twists that help mold what could have been just a treatise into a good story. A must for fans of *Ishmael,* this disturbing, intelligent book will also attract new readers."

—*Booklist*

"One of the most important storytellers of our age, Daniel Quinn, in *The Story of B,* continues the journey begun so beautifully with *Ishmael.* Whether or not you agree with every word, there is no doubt that 'B' offers us a unique opportunity—to think together about the unquestioned beliefs and assumptions that have shaped our culture over the past 10,000 years and that will, if they *remain* unquestioned, keep us on a path that seems increasingly unsustainable."

—Peter Senge, author of *The Fifth Discipline*

PRAISE FOR
Ishmael

"From now on I will divide the books I have read into two categories—the ones I read before *Ishmael* and those read after."

—Jim Britell, *Whole Earth Review*

"A thoughtful, fearlessly low-key novel about the role of our species on the planet . . . laid out for us with an originality and a clarity few would deny."

—*The New York Times Book Review*

BOOKS BY DANIEL QUINN

Ishmael

My Ishmael

Providence: The Story of a Fifty-Year Vision Quest

The Story of B

A Newcomer's Guide to the Afterlife
(with Tom Whalen)

MY ISHMAEL

Daniel Quinn

BANTAM BOOKS

New York London Toronto Sydney Auckland

MY ISHMAEL

A Bantam Book

PUBLISHING HISTORY

Bantam hardcover edition published December 1997
Bantam trade paperback edition / October 1998

ISBN 0-553-37965-8

Published simultaneously in the United States and Canada

Bantam Books are published by Bantam Books, a division of Bantam
Doubleday Dell Publishing Group, Inc. Its trademark, consisting of the
words "Bantam Books" and the portrayal of a rooster, is Registered in U.S.
Patent and Trademark Office and in other countries. Marca Registrada.
Bantam Books, 1540 Broadway, New York, New York 10036.

PRINTED IN THE UNITED STATES OF AMERICA

FFG   10

Many persons, inspired by *Ishmael,* have inspired me.
This book is dedicated to three of them:
Rachel Rosenthal, Ray C. Anderson, and Alan Thornhill
(with special thanks to Howie Richey,
the architect of Mokonzi Nkemi's revolution,
and to author James Burke, whose books and columns
brought to my attention some of the connections noted
in the chapter entitled "Revolutionaries").

Readers familiar with the work of Richard Dawkins,
especially in *The Selfish Gene,* will easily recognize
the debt owed to him in these pages—a debt I most
humbly and gratefully acknowledge here.

MY ISHMAEL

Hello There

I think it's pretty lousy to wake up at age sixteen and realize you've already been screwed. Not that there's anything terrifically unusual about getting screwed at this age. It seems like everyone inside fifty miles is bent on doing you in. But not many sixteen-year-olds get screwed in this particular way. Not many have the *opportunity* to get screwed this way.

I'm grateful, I really am.

But this story is not about me at age sixteen. This is about something that happened when I was twelve. That was a painful time in my life.

My mother was deciding she might as well go ahead and be a drunk. In the previous three or four years she wanted me to think she was just a social drinker. But she figured I must know the truth by now, so why go on pretending? She didn't ask my opinion about it. If she had, I would've said, "Please go on pretending, Mom. Especially in front of me, okay?"

But this isn't a story about my mother. It's just that you have to understand some of this if you want to understand the rest.

My parents were divorced when I was five, but I won't bore you with that story. I don't even *know* that story, really, because Mom tells it one way and Dad tells it another. (Sound familiar?)

Anyway, Dad remarried when I was eight. Mom almost did the same, but the guy turned out to be a creep, so she skipped it. Along about in there, she started putting on weight big time. Luckily, she already had a good job. She heads up the word-processing operation at a big law firm downtown. And then she took to "stopping for a drink after work." This got to be a pretty long stop.

All the same, she rolled out of bed every morning at seven-thirty, no matter what. And I think she made it a rule not to start drinking before the end of the business day. Except on weekends, of course—but I won't go into that either.

I was not a happy girl.

In those days I thought it might help if I played the Dutiful Daughter. When I got home from school, I tried to put the house back to the way Mom would have wanted it if she cared anymore. Mostly this meant cleaning up the kitchen. The rest of the house stayed pretty neat. But neither of us had time to tackle the kitchen before heading off to work and school.

Anyway, one day as I was gathering up the newspaper, something in the want-ad section caught my eye. It read:

**TEACHER seeks pupil. Must have an earnest
desire to save the world. Apply in person.**

This was followed by a room number and the name of a
ratty old office building downtown.

It struck me as weird that a teacher would be seeking a
pupil. It just didn't make any sense. The teachers I know,
seeking a pupil would be like a dog seeking a flea.

Then I took another look at the second sentence, *Must
have an earnest desire to save the world.* I thought, Wow, this
guy doesn't want much.

The crazy thing was that this teacher ought to be pitching
his services like everyone else, and he wasn't. It was like a
help-wanted ad. It was like the teacher needed the pupil, not
the other way around. A shiver started at the back of my
neck, and the hair stood up all over my head.

"Wow," I said, "I could *do* this. I could be this guy's
pupil. I could be *useful!*"

Something like that. It sounds silly now, but this ad
hooked into my dreams. I knew where the building was, and
all I had to remember was the room number. But I tore the
ad out anyway and put it in a drawer in my room. That way
if I fell down, hit my head, and became an amnesiac, I'd still
find it sitting there someday.

It must have been a Friday night, because the next morning I lay in bed thinking about it. Having a daydream about
it, actually.

I'll get to the daydream later.

Room 105

The good news was that Mom didn't try to keep me on a short leash. She didn't keep *herself* on a short leash, so maybe she figured she had no business keeping *me* on one. Anyway . . .

After breakfast I told her, "I'm going out," and she said, "Okay."

Not "Where're you going?" Or "When'll you be back?" Just "Okay."

I took a bus downtown.

We live in a pretty decent little city. (I'm not going to say where exactly.) You can stop at a red light without getting car-jacked. Drive-by shootings are rare. No snipers on the roofs. Like that. So I didn't give a second thought to going downtown on a Saturday morning by myself.

I knew the building mentioned in the ad. It was the Fair-field. A loser uncle of mine once had an office there. He chose it because it was in a good location but cheap. In other words, crummy.

The lobby brought back memories. It looked just the way it smelled, like wet dogs and cigars. It took me a while to figure out where to go. There was just one bank of offices on the ground floor, and Room 105 wasn't in it. I finally found it at the back, by the loading dock, facing the freight elevator.

I said to myself, This can't be right. But there it was, Room 105.

I said to myself, What am I doing here, anyway? This door's not going to be unlocked on a Saturday. But it was.

I walked into this huge, empty room. Then I took in a lungful of air and was almost knocked down. It wasn't wet dogs and cigars this time. It was *zoo*. I didn't mind that. I like zoos.

But, as I said, the place was empty. There was one sag-ging bookcase over at the left and one overstuffed chair over at the right. They looked like leftovers from a garage sale or something.

I said to myself, The guy has moved out.

I looked around again. At the high dirty windows over-looking the alley. At the dusty industrial lights hanging from the ceiling. At the peeling walls the color of pus.

Then I said to myself, Okay, I'll move in.

I think I meant it. Nobody could possibly want this place, could they? So why shouldn't I have it? I mean, it already had a chair, didn't it? I could do without the rest for a while.

There was one feature I hadn't figured out. The chair was facing a big sheet of dark glass in the middle of the right-hand wall. It reminded me of the kind of window witnesses look through to identify suspects in a police lineup. There had to be a room behind it, because there was a door beside the window.

I went over to have a look. I put my nose up against the glass and used my hands to block out the light, and . . .

I thought it was a movie.

About ten feet back from the glass there was sitting this great huge fat gorilla, munching on a tree twig. He was staring right back at me, and I suddenly knew it was not a movie.

"Yow," I said, and jumped back.

I was startled but not exactly scared. It seemed like I *should* be scared. I mean, I knew I'd be screaming my head off if I was a character in a movie. But the gorilla was just sitting there. I don't know, maybe I was just too dumb to be scared. All the same, I did look over my shoulder to make sure I had a clear shot at the door.

Then I slanted my eyes in to see if the gorilla was staying put. He was. He wasn't even quivering, or I would have been out of there.

All right. I had to put all this together.

The teacher had not moved out. I mean, no one could move out of a place and forget to take his gorilla along. So the teacher had not moved out. Maybe he had just *stepped* out. For lunch or something.

And forgot to lock his door. Or something.

The teacher would soon be back. Probably. Maybe.

I looked around again, still trying to figure out what the deal was here.

The room I was in was not a living space—no bed, no kitchen facilities, no storage space for clothes or anything. So the teacher didn't live there. But obviously the *gorilla* lived there, in the room on the other side of the glass.

Why? How come?

Well, what the hell, I guess you can keep a gorilla if you want to.

But why keep a gorilla this particular way?

I looked in again and noticed something I'd missed the first time. It was a poster on the wall behind the gorilla. It said:

> WITH MAN GONE,
> WILL THERE BE HOPE
> FOR GORILLA?

Well, I said to myself, that's an interesting question. It didn't seem like a very hard one, though. Even at age twelve I knew what was going on in the world. The way we were going, gorillas were not going to be around for very much longer. So the answer was yes. With Man gone, there *would* be hope for Gorilla.

The ape in the next room grunted, just as if he didn't think much of my reasoning.

I wondered if the poster was part of the course. The ad in the newspaper said *Must have an earnest desire to save the world.* That made sense. Saving the world would certainly mean saving gorillas.

But not saving people? That's what popped into my head. You know what it's like to have ideas pop into your head. It's like they come from out of the blue. But this one came from outer space. I mean, I can tell strangers from friends. This was a stranger.

I gave the ape a look. The ape gave me a look—and I *knew*.

I vanished from that place. That's how fast I got out of there. One second I was eyeing the gorilla, and the next I was standing out on the sidewalk, breathing hard.

I wasn't far from the center of town, where a couple of department stores are still hanging on by their fingernails. I headed there, where I'd find some people. I wanted to be around people while I thought about this.

The gorilla had *talked to me*—inside my own head.

That was what I had to think about.

I didn't have to wonder if it happened. It happened. I couldn't make up something like that. And why *would* I make up something like that? To fool *myself*?

I went over all this while riding the escalators at Pearson's. Six floors up. Six floors down. Very soothing. Nobody cares. Nobody bothers you. Nobody notices. At the bottom you have to switch from down to up. Jewelry and notions. Women's clothing. Men's clothing. Housewares. Toys. Furniture. At the top you have to switch from up to down. Furniture. Toys. Housewares. Men's clothing. Women's clothing. Jewelry and notions. All coming at you in restful slow motion.

Teacher seeks pupil. Must have an earnest desire to save the world.

I say, *You mean, save the world, as in gorillas.*

And the gorilla says, *But not people?*

Where was the teacher while all this was going on?

And what would have gone on if the teacher had been there?

What was the plan? What was the idea?

I could see an exotic teacher having an exotic pet.

A mind-talking ape. Pretty exotic. Yeah.

Teacher seeks pupil. Must have an earnest desire to save the world and be able to put up with a telepathic ape.

Hey—that was *me*, down to a tee.

I stopped for a Coke. It wasn't even noon yet.

I Take on The Ape

When I got back to Room 105, I put a hand to the door-knob and an ear to the wood.

And heard a man's voice.

I couldn't make out what he was saying. He was yards from the door—and facing the wrong way. At least that was the way I pictured it.

"Mumble umble bumble," he said. "Bum bum umble mumble."

Silence. A full minute of silence.

"Um bumble umble bum," the man went on. "Bum bum mumble um bumble."

Silence. Only half a minute this time.

"Umble?" the man asked. "Umble bumble um mum-blebum."

And so on. Exciting listening. It went on and on.

I thought of just walking in. It was an appealing idea—as an idea.

I thought of coming back later, but that wasn't even an appealing idea. Who knew what I might miss?

I hung in. The minutes dragged by like rainy afternoons. (I put that in a writing assignment once. *The minutes dragged by like rainy afternoons.* The teacher wrote *Good!!* in the margin. What a creep.)

Suddenly the man's voice was right by the door.

"I don't know," he was saying. "I really don't. But I'll give it a try."

I scurried across the hall and put my back against the freight-elevator door.

Another minute passed. Then the man said, "Okay," and opened the door.

He stepped out into the hall, saw me, and froze for a second as if I was a cobra poised to strike. Then he decided to pretend I wasn't there. He closed the door behind him and started to walk away.

I said, "Are you the teacher?"

From the way he frowned at me, you would've thought this was a real hard question. Finally he got his wits together and figured out what he wanted to say. He drew himself up and said . . . no.

Obviously he wanted to say a lot more—maybe thousands of words more. But that was all he could manage at the moment: no.

I said, very politely, "Thank you."

He frowned some more, turned away, and stomped off.

At school any guy you don't like is a dork, but *dork* isn't a word I use all that much. I guess I like to save it up for special people, like this guy. This guy was a dork. I took an instant dislike to him, I don't know why. About my mother's age, dressed cheap and ugly. One of those dark, intense types, if you know what I mean. I swear I never knew what a bad haircut looked like till I saw his. He had "intellectual—keep your distance" written all over him.

I gave my attention to the door in front of me. I couldn't think of anything that needed thinking about, so I just went through it.

Nothing had changed, but it was all different now, because I understood what the deal was. What I'd heard through the door was a conversation between the dork and the ape. Naturally I only heard the dork's side, because the ape wasn't talking out loud.

The dork wasn't the teacher. Therefore the ape was the teacher.

There was one thing more. The dork wasn't *afraid*. This was important. It meant the ape wasn't dangerous. If a dork didn't have to be afraid, *I* didn't have to be afraid.

Now that I knew he was there, it was easy to spot the gorilla behind the glass. He was right where I'd left him.

I said to him, "I came because of the ad."

Silence.

I thought maybe he hadn't heard me. I moved up to the chair and said it again.

The ape stared at me in silence.

"What's the matter?" I said. "You talked to me before."

He closed his eyes, very, very slowly. It's not easy to close your eyes that slowly. I thought maybe he was falling asleep or something.

"What's the matter?" I said again.

The ape sighed. I don't know how to describe a sigh like that. I expected to see the walls bending under the weight of that sigh. I waited. I figured he was getting ready to speak. But after a full minute he was still just sitting there.

I said, "Didn't you put the ad in the paper?"

He squeezed his eyes shut as if to blot out all this unpleasantness. All the same, he finally opened his eyes and spoke. As before, I heard it in my head, not in my ears.

"I put the ad in the paper," he admitted. "But not for you."

"What do you mean, not for me? I didn't see anything there that said, 'This ad is for everyone but Julie Gerchak.' "

"I'm sorry," he said. "I should say I didn't put the ad in the paper for children."

"Children!" This really made me mad. "You call me children? I'm twelve years old. I'm old enough to steal cars. I'm old enough to have an abortion. I'm old enough to deal crack."

This great huge fat ape began to writhe, I swear to God. Wow, I was really getting off on this. I was beating up on a thousand-pound gorilla.

He writhed for a while. Then he began to get a new grip on things. He calmed down and started talking.

"I'm sorry I tried to dismiss you so easily," he said. "Clearly you're not a dismissible person. However, the fact that you're old enough to steal cars is not relevant here."

"Go on," I told him.

"I'm a teacher," he said.

"I know that."

"As a teacher, I'm able to help certain kinds of pupils. Not every kind. I can't help someone with chemistry or algebra or French or geology."

"I didn't come here for anything like that."

"These are examples only. What I mean is that I can offer only a certain kind of teaching."

"So what are you saying? Are you saying I don't want that 'certain kind of teaching'?"

He nodded. "That's what I'm saying. The teaching I'm able to offer isn't a kind that will be helpful to you . . . just yet."

In a split second my eyes were burning with tears, but I certainly wasn't going to let him see them.

"You're just like everyone else," I told him. "You're a liar."

That made his eyebrows shoot up. "A liar?"

"Yes. Why don't you tell the truth? Why don't you say, 'You're just a kid—no use to anybody. Come back in ten years. Then maybe you'll be worth my time.' Say that, and you won't hear another word out of me. Say that, and I'll turn around and go home."

He sighed again, even deeper than before. Then he nodded, just once.

"You're perfectly correct," he said. "I was telling a lie. And I was expecting you not to see through it. Please accept my apology."

I nodded back.

"But the truth may not please you much either," he went on.

"What is the truth?"

"We'll have to see. Your name is Julie?"

"That's right."

"And you don't like being treated like a child."

"That's right."

"Then sit down and I'll question you as if you were an adult."

I sat down.

"What brought you here, Julie? And please don't tell me my ad brought you. We're past that. What do you want? What are you doing here?"

I opened my mouth, but nothing flew out, not a single syllable. I sat there gaping for half a minute or so. Then I said, "What about the guy who was just here? Did you ask *him* what he wanted? Did you ask *him* what he was doing here?"

The gorilla did the strangest thing then. He took his right

hand and put it straight across his eyes. It looked like he was going to start counting for a game of hide-and-seek. The funny thing was, he wasn't actually touching his face. He was just holding his hand one inch from his nose, as if reading some tiny message written in his palm.

I waited.

After about two minutes he lowered his hand and said, "No, I did *not* ask him these things."

I just sat there batting my eyelashes at him.

The gorilla licked his lips—nervously, it seemed to me. "I think we can safely say that I'm not prepared to deal with the needs of a person your age. I think that can be safely said. Yes."

"You mean you give up. Is that what you're telling me? You want me to go away because you give up."

The gorilla stared at me. I couldn't tell whether he was staring hopefully or angrily or what.

I said, "Don't you think a twelve-year-old girl can have an earnest desire to save the world?"

"I don't doubt it," he said, though it sounded like the words were pretty hard to get out.

"Then why won't you talk to me? Your ad in the paper said you need a pupil. Isn't that what it said?"

"That's what it said."

"Well, you've got one. Here I am."

We Lurch To The Starting Line

A long moment passed. I read that in a book once: *A long moment passed*. But this was a *really* long moment. Finally the gorilla spoke again. "Very well," he said with a nod. "We'll begin and see where it takes us. My name is Ishmael."

He seemed to expect a reaction of some kind, but to me this was just a noise. It would have been the same if he'd said his name was whizbang. He already knew my name, so I just waited. Finally he went on again.

"Referring to the young man who was just here—his name is Alan Lomax, by the way—I said I didn't ask what he wanted. But I did ask him to tell a story that would explain why he was here."

"A story?"

"Yes. I asked for his story. Now I ask for yours."

"I don't know what you mean by a story."

Ishmael frowned as if he suspected I might be playing dumb. Maybe I *was,* a little.

He went on: "Your classmates are doing something else this afternoon, aren't they? Whatever they're doing, you're not doing it."

"Yeah, that's right."

"So. Explain to me why you're not doing what your classmates are doing. How does your story differ from theirs that it brings you to this room on a Saturday afternoon?"

Now I knew what he meant, but it didn't help. What story was he talking about? Did he want to hear about my folks' divorce? About my mom's adventures in boozing? About the problems I was having with Mrs. Monstro at school? About my former boyfriend Donnie, the famous Guy Who Wasn't?

"I want to understand what you're looking for," he said, answering these questions as if I'd spoken them aloud.

"I don't get it," I told him. "The teachers I'm used to don't ask what you're looking for. They just teach what they teach."

"And is that what you were hoping to find here? A teacher like the ones you're used to?"

"No, it wasn't."

"Then you're in luck, Julie, because I'm not like them. I'm what is called a maieutic teacher. A maieutic teacher is one who acts as a midwife to his pupils—or, of course, *her* pupils. Do you know what a midwife is?"

"A midwife is . . . someone who helps at childbirth. Isn't that right?"

"That's right. A midwife helps bring into the light an infant that has been growing inside its mother. A maieutic teacher helps bring into the light ideas that have been growing inside his pupils." The gorilla stared at me intently while

I thought about this. At last he went on. "Do you think there are any ideas growing inside of you?"

"I don't know," I told him. It was the truth.

"Do you think *something* is growing inside of you?"

I looked at him as blankly as I could. He was beginning to frighten me.

"Tell me this, Julie. Would you have come here two years ago if you'd seen my advertisement?"

That was easy. I told him no.

"So something has changed," he went on. "Something inside of you. This is what I want to know about. I must understand what brought you here."

I stared at him for a while, then I said, "Do you know what I say to myself all the time? I mean *all* the time— twenty times a day. I say to myself, 'I've got to get out of here.'"

Ishmael frowned, puzzling over this.

"I'll be taking a shower or washing the dishes or waiting for the bus, and that's what'll pop into my head: 'I've got to get out of here.'"

"What does it mean?"

"I don't know."

He grunted. "Of course you know."

"It means . . . *Run for your life.*"

"Is your life in danger?"

"Yes."

"From what?"

"From everything. From people walking into school-rooms with machine guns. From people bombing airplanes and hospitals. From people pumping nerve gas into subways. From people dumping poison in the water we drink. From people cutting down the forests. From people destroying the ozone layer. I don't really know all this stuff, because I don't want to listen. Do you know what I mean?"

"I'm not sure."

"I mean, do you think I know what an ozone layer is? I don't. But they say we're poking holes in it, and if the holes get big enough, we're going to start dying like flies. They say the rain forests are like the planet's lungs, and if we cut them down, we'll suffocate. Do you think I know if this is right? I don't. One of my teachers said that as many as two hundred species of plants and animals go extinct every day because of what we're doing to this planet. I remembered that—I've got a good memory for stuff like that—but do you think I know if it's true? I don't, but I believe it. This same teacher says we're adding fifteen million tons of carbon dioxide to the air every day. Do you think I know what this means? I don't. All I know is that carbon dioxide is a poison. I don't know where I saw it or heard it, but the suicide rate among teenagers has tripled in the last forty years. Do you think I go looking for this stuff? I don't. But it jumps out at me anyway. People are eating the world alive."

Ishmael nodded. "So you've got to get out of here."

"That's right."

Ishmael gave me a few seconds to think about that, then he said, "But this doesn't explain why you've come to see *me*. My ad doesn't say anything about getting out of here."

"Yeah, I know. It sounds like I'm not making any sense."

Ishmael cocked an eyebrow at me.

"I've got to think about this," I told him.

I got up and turned away to face the rest of the room. There wasn't much scope for sightseeing. Just those high, dusty windows, those pus-colored walls, and that tired-looking little bookcase at the other end. I headed for the bookcase. I could have saved myself the trip. There were a bunch of books on evolution, a bunch on history and prehistory, and a bunch on primitive peoples. There was a book on chimpanzee culture that looked interesting—but nothing on gorillas. There were a couple of archaeological atlases. There was a book with the longest title I'd ever seen, something like *Man's Rise to Civilization As Shown by the Aboriginal Peoples of the New World from Prehistoric Times to the Coming of the Industrial State.* There were three translations of the Bible, which seemed excessive, for an ape. There was nothing I could curl up with in front of the fireplace, even if I had a fireplace. I poked around for as long as I could then went back and sat down.

"You wanted me to tell you a story. I don't have a story to tell, but I've got a daydream."

"A daydream?" Ishmael said, half a question.

I nodded, and he said a daydream would do very well.

"Okay. This is what I was daydreaming about this morning. I was thinking, wouldn't it be great if I got down to Room 105 of the Fairfield Building, and I went in and there was this woman at the reception desk, and she looked at me and—"

"Wait," Ishmael said. "Excuse me for interrupting."

"Yes?"

"You're . . . plunging."

"Plunging?"

"Hurtling. Charging ahead, rushing."

"You mean I'm going too fast?"

"Yes, much too fast. We're not working under a deadline here, Julie. If you intend to share this story with me, then please let it unfold leisurely—as leisurely as it unfolded in your head this morning."

"Okay," I said. "I see what you mean. You want me to start over?"

"Yes, please. But no plunging this time. Take a moment to gather your thoughts. Relax, and let it come back to you. Don't summarize it for me. Tell it as it happened."

Take a moment? Relax? Let it come back to me? He didn't seem to realize what he was asking for. I was sitting down, sure, but I couldn't sit back and be comfortable, because if I did that, my feet would dangle over the edge and I'd feel like a six-year-old. I had to have my feet on the floor, because I had to be ready to get out of there in half a second—and if you think you wouldn't feel that way, I suggest you sit down toe-to-toe with a full-grown gorilla and try it. The only way for me to relax and let the daydream come back was to curl up in a corner of the chair and close my eyes—and I just wasn't quite ready to do that in the presence of a thousand-pound ape.

I gave Ishmael a sort of snooty, impatient scowl intended to convey all that. He took it in, mulled it over for a bit, and then did something that almost made me laugh out loud.

He used two fingers to do a little swish over his heart and then solemnly held them up for my inspection, just like a Boy Scout: *Cross my heart and hope to die.*

What the hell, I *did* laugh out loud.

The Daydream

In my daydream I didn't dress carefully for my visit to the Fairfield Building—any more than I did when I went there in real life. That would have been uncool. It would have been equally uncool to dress in my grubbiest, so I just split the difference. There are plenty of girls prettier than me, uglier than me, taller than me, shorter than me, fatter than me, thinner than me—and maybe it makes sense for them to knock themselves out over what they wear, but not me.

The Fairfield Building of my daydream was spruced up a bit and no longer the near slum of real life. And, in my daydream, Room 105 wasn't on the ground floor beside a loading dock, it was an elevator ride up from the lobby (and someone had taken a good stiff brush to the elevator as well, uncovering some handsome brass metalwork).

The door to Room 105 said . . . nothing. I worked on that some. I wanted it to bear some intriguing legend like GLOBAL POSSIBILITIES or COSMIC VENTURES, but no, it remained stubbornly blank. I went in. A young woman looked up from a desk in the front. Not a receptionist. She wasn't wearing secretary clothes but rather something more casual and chic. And she wasn't sitting at the desk, she was bending over it, packing a box.

She glanced up curiously, as if strangers seldom came through that door, and asked if she could help me.

"I'm here about the ad," I told her.

"The ad," she said, straightening up to give me a more serious inspection. "I didn't realize the ad was still running."

I couldn't think of anything to say to that, so I just stood there.

"Wait a second," she said, and disappeared down a hall. She returned a minute later in the company of a man the same age as her, twenty or twenty-five. He was dressed the same way, not in a suit but casually—more a hiker than a businessman. They stared at me blankly till I began to feel like a piece of furniture that had been delivered on approval.

At last the man said, "You came because of the ad?"

"That's right."

The woman said to him, "You know they'd really like to have one more." Obviously I had no idea who "they" were.

"I'm aware of that," he said. Then: "Come back to my office and we'll talk about it. I'm Phil, by the way, and this is Andrea." Back in his office we sat down, and he said, "The reason we're hesitating is that we need people who can go away for a while. For a good *long* while, actually."

"That's no problem," I told him.

"You don't understand," Andrea said. "We're talking about years, maybe even decades."

"Really?"

"Really."

"Well, I wouldn't mind that," I told them. "Honestly."

("Now you notice," I said to Ishmael, "that neither of them said I was too young or it'd be better if I was a boy or I should really stay home and take care of my mother or finish school or anything like that." He nodded to show he hadn't missed that important point.)

The two of them exchanged another look, then Phil asked how long it would take me to get ready.

"You mean to leave?" He nodded. "I'm ready *now*. I *came* ready."

"That's great," Andrea said. "As you can see, we're just packing up here. If you'd come an hour later, you'd have missed us."

Now you notice that they both referred to the ad, but neither one of them had uttered even one syllable of its main word, which was *teacher*. This worried me a little. I wondered if the teacher angle was just some kind of lure, but I kept it to myself. Adults get real cranky if you quiz them about the scams they're running on you. So I kept my mouth shut and helped carry boxes down to a huge Suburban parked in the alley behind the building.

An hour's drive took us out into the middle of nowhere (an unspecified nowhere that will not be found in any maps of this region). It looked like the spot where they shot all those goofy old horror–sci-fi movies with giant spiders and killer shrews. I guess you could say it *was* the spot. This was *my* daydream, after all.

Our destination was like a small military camp with no soldiers. We drove in, and folks waved and went on with what they were doing. It was easy to see there were two groups—the Staff, who were sort of khaki and uniform, like Phil and Andrea, and the Recruits, who were sort of miscellaneous, like mall walkers on a Saturday afternoon.

Phil and Andrea dropped me off at a barracks, where some recruits took me in and assigned me a bed and so on.

No one offered to explain anything, and I didn't ask. I figured it would all come clear eventually. What actually happened, however, was that I finally said something that made it clear I was totally clueless. They were shocked that Phil and Andrea hadn't spelled it out for me, and I said, so why don't *you* spell it out? Well, they had to scratch their heads and do some hemming and hawing, but one of them finally took charge and said, "Why go looking for a *teacher* if you want to save the world?"

"Because I don't know how to do it myself, obviously."

"But what kind of teacher *would* know how to do it, do you think?"

"I have no idea," I told her. This was a woman in her forties named Gammaen.

"Do you think it might be some government official or other?"

I told her I didn't think so, and when she asked why, I said, "Because if somebody in the government knew how to do it, then they'd be *doing* it, wouldn't they?"

"Why do you think people *in general* don't know how to save the world?"

"I don't know."

"Do you think no one in the whole *universe* knows how to live without destroying the world?"

"I have no idea," I told her.

They got stuck at this point for a while. Finally one of the guys had a shot at it. He said, "There are people all over the universe who know how to live in the world without destroying it."

"Oh yeah?" I said. I wasn't being smart. This was the first I'd heard of it—and that's what I told him.

"Well, that's the case," he said. "There are thousands of inhabited planets all over the universe—maybe millions—and the people who live on them do just fine."

"They do?"

"They do. They don't wreck them or strip them bare or fill them up with poisons."

"Well, that's great," I said. "But how does that help *us*?"

"It would help us if we knew how they did it, wouldn't it?"

"Certainly."

For a second it looked like they were going to get stuck again, but then Gammaen found a way to carry on.

"We're going out there to learn," she said.

"Who is?"

"*We* are. All the recruits—you, us."

"Going out *where*?" I asked, still not able to take in what she was getting at.

"Out into the universe," she said.

Finally it got spelled out: *We were waiting to be picked up.*

It was expected that we'd be gone for decades. We wouldn't be going to school. We'd be visiting planets, observing—figuring it out.

And what we learned we'd bring back to the people of earth.

That was the program.

And that was the daydream.

Meet Mother Culture

Stupid, huh?"

Ishmael frowned. "Why do you say that?"

"Well, I mean, it's a daydream. It's meringue. Fluff. Twaddle."

He shook his head. "No story is devoid of meaning, if you know how to look for it. This is as true of nursery rhymes and daydreams as it is of novels and epic poems."

"Okay."

"Your daydream isn't fluff or twaddle, Julie, I can assure you of that. And what's more, it's done what I wanted it to do. I asked for a story that would explain what you're doing here, and you've given me that. I now understand what you're looking for. Or to put it more precisely, I now understand what you're prepared to learn—and without that I couldn't proceed at all."

I didn't really understand what he was getting at, but I told him I was glad to hear it.

"Even so," he went on, "I'm not sure as yet how to go on with you. Whether you know it or not, you present me with a special problem."

"Why is that?"

"I'm not like the teachers at your school, Julie, who merely teach you subjects that your elders have decided you should know—things like mathematics, geography, history, biology, and so on. As I explained earlier, I'm a teacher who acts as a midwife to his pupils, bringing out into the open air the ideas that are growing inside of them." Ishmael paused for a moment to think, then asked what I thought the difference was between me and Alan Lomax—educationally speaking.

"Well, I suppose he's finished high school and probably college."

"That's right. And so?"

"So he knows some things I don't know."

"That's true," Ishmael said. "Nevertheless, the same ideas are growing inside of both of you."

"How do you know that?"

His lip twitched into a smile. "Because you've both been listening to the same mother from the day of your birth. I'm not referring to your biological mother, of course, but rather to your cultural mother. Mother Culture speaks to you through the voice of your parents—who likewise have been listening to her voice from the day of their own birth. She speaks to you through cartoon characters and storybook characters and comic-book characters. She speaks to you through newscasters and schoolteachers and presidential candidates. You've listened to her on talk shows. You've heard her in popular songs, advertising jingles, lectures, political speeches, sermons, and jokes. You've read her thoughts in newspaper articles, textbooks, and comic strips."

"Okay," I said. "I guess I see what you mean."

"This is, of course, not peculiar to your particular culture, Julie. Every culture has its own nurturing and sustaining educational mother. The ideas being nurtured in you and Alan are very different from those being nurtured in tribal peoples who are still living the way their ancestors lived ten thousand years ago—the Huli of Papua New Guinea, for example, or the Macuna Indians of eastern Colombia."

"Yes, I see."

"The things to be brought forth from you and Alan are the same, but they're at different stages of development. Alan's been listening to Mother Culture for twenty years longer than you, so what is to be found in him is naturally more fully fixed and articulated."

"Yeah, I can see that. Like the way a fetus is more filled out at seven months than at two months."

"Exactly."

"Okay. So now what?"

"So now I'd like you to go away and let me think about how I'm to proceed with you."

"Go away where?"

"Anywhere. Wherever you like. Home, if you have one."

This made it my turn to frown. "If I *have* one? What makes you think I don't have one?"

"I think nothing," Ishmael replied coolly. "You bridled at my calling you a child, and you tell me you're old enough to steal cars, have an abortion, or deal crack cocaine. Therefore I thought it best to make no assumptions about your living arrangement."

"Wow," I said. "Do you take everything so literally?"

Ishmael took a moment to scratch the side of his jaw. "Yes, I suppose I do. You'll find that I have a certain sense of humor, but statements of comical exaggeration tend to be lost on me."

I told him I'd keep that in mind—indulging in some comical exaggeration. Then I asked him when I should come back.

"Come back whenever you please."

"Tomorrow?"

"By all means," he said. "Sundays are not days off for me."

The little twitch around his mouth told me this was meant to be a joke of some kind.

Mom was in a comfortable haze by the time I got back. I guess she feels it's her motherly duty to take an interest in how I spend my time away from home, so she asked where I'd been. I told her the lie I'd prepared, that I'd been with Sharon Spaley, a friend.

Did anyone think I was going to tell her the truth? That I was having a cozy little chat with an ape?

Gimme a break.

The People of The Curse

When I got to Room 105 the following morning, I put my ear to the door. I wanted to know if Alan the dork was ahead of me. When I was sure he wasn't, I went in.

Nothing had changed. This means I was knocked down by the smell, which I now knew was gorilla smell. I don't mean I disliked it. I didn't. I wish I had a bottle of it. You know, put on a dab before going to parties. *That* would make folks sit up and take an interest in things.

Ishmael was where I'd left him. I wondered if there was anywhere else for him to be in that joint. I figured there had to be a room behind the one I could see into. The room behind the glass was too small for anyone to live in, much less a gorilla.

I sat down, and we looked at each other.

I said, "What'll you do if Alan comes while I'm here?"

He made a face. I guess he thought this was an unnecessary question. All the same, he answered it—by asking me what I *wanted* him to do.

"I guess I want you to tell him to come back later."

"I see. And is that what I should tell *you* if you come while Alan's here?"

"Yes."

"If Alan's here when you arrive, I should tell you to come back later?"

"That's right."

He shook his head, bemused. "I'll have to talk to him about it. I can tell *you* to come back later, but I can't tell *him* to come back later. Not without discussing it first."

"I don't want you to do that," I told him. "If Alan comes while I'm here, I'll just leave."

"But why? What have you got against him?"

"I don't know. I just don't want him to know about me."

"What is it you don't want him to know?"

"I don't want him to know *anything*. I don't even want him to know I exist."

"I can't guarantee such a thing, Julie. If he walks through the door right now, he obviously *will* know you exist."

"I realize that. But that's just my first choice," I told him. "If I can't get that, then I'll get the next best thing."

"And what's the next best thing?"

"Whatever I get just by walking out, that's the next best thing."

Ishmael suddenly lifted his upper lip, exposing a row of golden-brown teeth as big as thumbs. It took me a second to recognize this as a smile.

He said, "I'm beginning to think you have a character very like my own, Julie."

I gaped at him.

"If you don't understand what I mean by that right now, you'll understand it someday."

He was right, I didn't understand it then. Now, four years later, I *think* I understand it. Maybe.

Anyway, when the chitchat was over, Ishmael settled back into his brushy bed and started in. "You believe that *someone* in the universe must know how to live in the world without destroying it. This is what your daydream seems to indicate."

"Well . . . I don't exactly *believe* it."

"Let's say rather that it makes sense to you. It seems reasonable to you that, if there is intelligent life elsewhere in the universe, some people somewhere must know how to live sustainably on their world."

"That's right."

"Why does this seem reasonable, Julie?"

"I don't know."

The ape frowned. "Before saying, 'I don't know,' I'd appreciate it if you'd take a moment to see if perhaps you *do* know. And even if you find you truly *don't* know, please take a stab at the answer."

"Okay. You want to know why it seems reasonable that people on other planets would know how to live sustainably."

"That's right."

I thought about it for a while and told him it was a good question.

"The whole art consists of asking good questions, Julie. This is information I need to draw from you right at the beginning. It will be the basis of all our later work."

"I see," I said, and went back to thinking. After another while I said, "It's hard to explain."

"Simple things are almost always the hardest to explain,

Julie. Showing someone how to tie a shoelace is easy. Explaining it is almost impossible."

"Yeah," I told him. "That's so." I worked on it some more. Finally I said, "I don't know why this example works, but it does work a little bit. Let's say you have a dozen ice-makers put out by a dozen different companies. One or two of these ice-makers will turn out to be not worth a damn. But most of them will work pretty well."

"Why is that?"

"I guess because you wouldn't expect every single one of these companies to be incompetent. Most of them have to be sort of averagely competent to be in business at all."

"In other words, if you lived on a world where a lot of people made ice-makers, but not a single one of them worked, you'd figure your world was exceptional. If you visited other worlds, you'd expect to find people who knew how to make viable ice-makers. In still other words, it seems to you that there's something abnormal about dysfunctionality. What's normal is for things to work. What's *not* normal is for things to fail."

"Yeah, that's right."

"Where do you get this impression, Julie? Where do you get the impression that what's normal is for things to work?"

"Wow," I said. Where *did* I get that impression? "Maybe this is it. Every other thing in the whole universe seems to work. The air works, the clouds work, the trees work, the turtles work, the germs work, the atoms work, the mushrooms work, the birds work, the lions work, the worms work, the sun works, the moon works—the whole universe works! Every single thing in it works—except for us. Why? What makes us so special?"

"You know what makes you special, Julie."

"I do?"

"Yes. This will be the first piece of knowledge I tease out

into the light from you. What does Mother Culture have to
say about this? What makes you different from turtles and
clouds and worms and suns and mushrooms? They all work,
and you don't. Why don't you work, Julie? What makes you
special?"

"We're special because everything else works. And it's
because we're special that we don't work."

"I agree that there is a circularity in what you learn from
Mother Culture on this point. But it will be useful if you
define that specialness."

I squinted at him for a while, then I said, "There's noth-
ing wrong with turtles and clouds and worms and suns.
That's why *they* work. But there *is* something wrong with *us*.
And that's why we don't work."

"Good. But what *is* that, Julie? What's wrong with you?"

I spent some time on it. Finally I said, "Is this what
maieutic teaching is like?"

Ishmael nodded.

"I'm impressed. I like it. No one has ever done this with
me before. Anyway, what's wrong with us is that we're civilized. I think that's it." But as I went on thinking about it
that answer lost some of its certainty. "That's part of it," I
told him, "that we're civilized. But there's also something
about the *way* we're civilized. We're not civilized *enough*."

"And why is that?"

"Wow," I said. "The reason we're not civilized enough is
that there's something wrong with us. It's like there's a drop
of poison in us, and this one drop of poison is all it takes to
ruin everything we do." I guess I was sitting there with my
mouth open, because finally Ishmael told me to go on. I went
on.

"Here's what I hear, Ishmael. Is it okay to call you Ishmael?"

The gorilla nodded, saying, "That *is* how I'm called."

"Here's what I hear: *We've got to evolve to a higher form in order to survive.* I'm not exactly sure where I hear this. It's like it's something in the air."

"I understand."

"This form we're in right now is just too primitive. *We're* just too primitive. We have to evolve into some higher, more angelic form."

"In order to work as well as mushrooms and turtles and worms."

I laughed and said, "Yeah, that's funny. But that's the perception, I think. We don't work as well as mushrooms and turtles and worms because we're too intelligent, and we don't work as well as angels and gods because we're not intelligent enough. We're in an awkward stage. We were all right when we were *less* than human and we'll be all right when we're *more* than human, but we're washouts as we are right now. Humans are just no good. The form itself is no good. I think that's what Mother Culture has to say."

"So the flaw is intelligence itself, then—according to Mother Culture."

"That's right. Intelligence is what makes us special, isn't it? Moths can't screw up the world. Catfish can't screw up the world. It takes intelligence to do that."

"In that case, what do you make of your daydream quest? As you head into the universe to learn how to live, are you looking for angels?"

"No. That's funny."

Ishmael cocked his head on one side and gave me a quizzical look.

"I'm looking for intelligent races just like us—but they know how to live without destroying their worlds. We're even more special than I thought."

"Go on."

"It's like we're specially *cursed.* The people of this one planet."

Ishmael nodded. "This is how it's generally understood,

among the people of your culture, that humanity is specially cursed—somehow badly made or fundamentally flawed or even literally divinely cursed."

"That's right."

"This is why, in your daydream, it's necessary to look elsewhere in the universe for the knowledge you seek. You can't find it amongst yourselves, because you're a cursed race. To find the knowledge you need to live sustainably, you need to find a race that *isn't* cursed. And there's no reason to suppose that *everyone's* cursed. You feel that *someone* out there *must* know how to live sustainably."

"That's right."

"So you see, Julie, your daydream was very far from being twaddle. And I'm sure that the journey you dreamed of, if it could be taken, would in fact put you in contact with thousands of peoples who live sustainably without difficulty."

"You are? Why?"

"Because the curse under which you operate is very, very localized—despite what Mother Culture teaches. It doesn't even remotely extend to the whole of humanity. Thousands of peoples have lived here sustainably, Julie. Without difficulty. Without effort."

Well, naturally I blinked at that one. "You mean like . . . Atlantis?"

"I mean nothing remotely like Atlantis, Julie. Atlantis is a fairy tale."

"Then I have no idea what you're talking about. None."

Ishmael nodded slowly. "I realize that. Very few of you would know what I'm talking about."

I waited for him to drop the other shoe, and when it didn't drop, I said, "Aren't you going to tell me who these people are?"

"I'd rather not, Julie. You see, you definitely *have* this information, and if I were to reach inside you and drag it out, then you'd be impressed, but you'd learn nothing. The midwife is there to help her client bring forth the child, not to bring it forth herself."

"You're saying I already know who these people are?"

"I haven't the slightest doubt of it, Julie."

I shrugged and crossed my eyes and did all the usual things, then told him to go ahead.

"Your Culture"

Ishmael said, "It is your culture's deep-seated perception that wisdom is not to be found among you. This is what your daydream reveals. You know how to build marvelous electronic gadgets, you know how to send ships into space, you know how to peer into the depths of atoms. But the simplest and most needful knowledge of all—the knowledge of how to live—simply doesn't exist among you."

"Yes, that's the way it seems."

"This isn't a new perception by any means, Julie. It's been extant in your culture for millennia."

"Excuse me," I said. "You keep saying that—'the people of your culture'—and I keep not being sure what you mean by it. Why don't you just say 'you humans' or 'you Americans'?"

"Because I'm not talking about humans or Americans. I'm talking about the people of your culture."

"Well, I guess you're going to have to explain that."

"Do you know what a culture is?"

"To be honest, I'm not sure."

"The word *culture* is like a chameleon, Julie. It has no color of its own but rather takes color from its setting. It means one thing when you talk about the culture of chimpanzees, another when you talk about the culture of General Motors. It's valid to say there are only two fundamentally different human cultures. It's also valid to say there are thousands of human cultures. Instead of trying to explain what *culture* means when it's all by itself (which is almost impossible), I'm just going to explain what I mean when I say 'your culture.' All right?"

"That's fine," I said.

"In fact, I'm going to make it even easier than that. I'm going to give you two rules of thumb by which you can identify the people of your culture. Here's one of them. You'll know you're among the people of your culture if the food is all *owned,* if it's all under lock and key."

"Hmm," I said. "It's hard to imagine it being any other way."

"But of course it once was another way. It was once no more owned than the air or the sunshine are owned. I'm sure you must realize that."

"Yeah, I guess so."

"You seem unimpressed, Julie, but putting food under lock and key was one of the great innovations of your culture. No other culture in history has ever put food under lock and key—and putting it there is the cornerstone of your economy."

"How is that?" I asked. "Why is it the cornerstone?"

"Because, if the food wasn't under lock and key, Julie, who would work?"

"Oh. Yeah. Right. Wow."

"If you go to Singapore or Amsterdam or Seoul or Buenos Aires or Islamabad or Johannesburg or Tampa or Istanbul or Kyoto, you'll find that the people differ wildly in the way they dress, in their marriage customs, in the holidays they observe, in their religious rituals, and so on, but they all expect the food to be under lock and key. It's all owned, and if you want some, you'll have to buy it."

"I see. So you're saying these people all belong to one culture."

"Clearly I'm talking about fundamentals, and nothing is more fundamental than food. I'm sure it's difficult for you to realize how very bizarre you are in this respect. You think it makes complete sense to have to work for what's free for the taking to every other creature on earth. You alone lock food away from yourselves and then toil to get it back—and imagine that nothing could possibly make better sense."

"Yes, it *is* bizarre if you put it like that. But it isn't just our culture that has done that. It's *humanity,* isn't it?"

"No, Julie. I know Mother Culture teaches that this is something humanity did, but that's a lie. It was only you, a single culture, not the whole of humanity. By the time we're finished, you'll have no doubt about that at all."

"Okay."

"Another rule of thumb you can use to identify the people of your culture is this: They perceive themselves to be members of a race that is fundamentally flawed and inherently doomed to suffering and misery. Because they're fundamentally flawed, they expect wisdom to be a rare commodity, difficult to acquire. Because they're inherently doomed, they're not surprised to be living in the midst of poverty, injustice, and crime, not surprised that their rulers are self-serving and corrupt, not surprised to be rendering the world uninhabitable for themselves. They may be indignant about these things, but they're not surprised by them, because this is how they expect things to be. This makes as much sense to them as having their food under lock and key."

"Do you mind if I play devil's advocate for a minute?"

"Not at all."

"There's a teacher at school who's always giving us pitying looks because he's a Buddhist, which means he's miles ahead of us in terms of awareness and spiritual enlightenment and so on. For him, the people of 'our culture' are the people of the West, and the people of the East belong to an entirely different culture."

"I take it this person is himself a Westerner."

"Yes, he is. What does that have to do with it?"

Ishmael shrugged. "Westerners often think the East is one vast Buddhist temple, which is rather like thinking the West is one vast Carthusian monastery. If the teacher you mention were to visit the East, he'd certainly experience many new things, but he'd find, first, that the food is all under lock and key and, second, that humans are considered to be a miserable, destructive, greedy lot, just as they are in the West. These are the things that qualify them to be named people of your culture."

"Are there really people in the world who *don't* think they're a miserable, destructive, greedy lot?"

Ishmael considered this for a moment and said, "Let me turn that question back to you in this way. In your fantasied journey into the universe, were you planning to look for other cursed races?"

"No."

"Is it your expectation that every intelligent species in the universe is accursed?"

"No."

Ishmael studied me for a moment and said, "I see that your question remains unanswered. Let me answer it this way. Even at your age, you've probably already met a certain kind of person who is convinced that anything bad that happens in his life is someone else's fault—never his own. If you haven't met such a person, I can guarantee that you will do so someday. Such a person never learns from his mistakes, because as far as he's concerned, he *makes* no mistakes. He never discovers the sources of his difficulties, because he believes those sources lie in others who are beyond his control. To put it very simply, everything that goes wrong in his life he blames on others. He never says to himself, 'The problem is something I'm doing.' He says, 'The problem is something other people are doing. Other people are to blame for all my troubles—and I can't change them, so I'm helpless.' "

"Yeah, I know someone like that," I told him. I didn't see any reason to tell him it was my mother.

"Your entire culture has adopted this way of dealing with your difficulties. You don't say, 'The problem is something we're doing.' You say, 'The problem is human nature itself. Human nature is to blame for all our troubles—and we can't change that, so we're helpless.' "

"Yow," I said. "I get it."

"I too get it, Julie," Ishmael said. "Teachers need pupils to help them continue their own journey of discovery."

I raised my brows at him.

"You've heard me say a dozen times that the people of your culture think of themselves as belonging to a flawed, doomed race."

"That's right," I told him.

"Now, thanks to you, I have a much better way of saying this: *The people of your culture blame human nature for their troubles.* It's still true that you think of yourselves as belonging to a flawed, doomed race, but now we both have a better understanding of *why* you think of yourselves this way. It

serves a purpose. It enables you to shift blame from yourselves to something that is beyond your control—human nature. You are blameless. The fault is in human nature itself,
which you cannot change."

"Right. I see that."

"Let me take a moment to state that 'human nature' is
something the people of your culture claim to know about.
It's not something I claim to know about. Whenever I use
the term, it will be as it comes from the mouth of Mother
Culture. The very concept is foreign to me. It belongs to an
epistemological framework unique to your culture. Don't
make faces. It won't hurt you to hear a new word. Episte-
mology is the study of what is knowable. To the people of
your culture, 'human nature' is a knowable object. To me,
it's a fabulous object, an object invented to be searched for,
like the Holy Grail or the philosopher's stone."

"Okay," I told him. "But I don't know why you're insisting on all this."

His face twisted into a smile. "I'm talking to posterity
through you, Julie."

"Come again?"

"Teachers live on through their pupils. That's another
reason why they need them. You seem to have an unusual
memory. You remember what you hear with unusual clarity."

"Yes, I guess that's true."

"You're going to be my rememberer. You'll carry my
words beyond the walls of this room."

"Carry them where?"

"Wherever you go—wherever that may be."

Well, I spent some time frowning over all this. Then I
said, "What about Alan? Is he a rememberer too?"

Ishmael shrugged. "I suppose I may as well go into this
now, Julie. I've had many pupils. Some have taken nothing

from me, some have taken a little, and some have taken a lot. But none has taken all. Each takes as much as he or she can carry away. Do you understand?"

"I think so."

"What they do with what they take is obviously beyond my control. For the most part, I have no idea what they do with it—or if they do anything at all. One recently wrote to me with his own strange notion of what to do. He intends to immigrate to Europe and set himself up as a sort of itinerant lecturer or preacher there."

"What did *you* want him to do?"

"Oh, it isn't at all a matter of what I want. Each must do what is within his or her compass. I call the notion strange only because it's inconceivable to me. I know only how to bring people along in *this* context—through dialogue. I simply can't imagine doing it in a lecture hall. My deficiency, not his."

"I'm feeling lost, Ishmael. What's this got to do with Alan and me?"

"When I called you my rememberer, you asked if Alan is also a rememberer. I wanted you to understand that what I'm giving you to remember is very different from what I'm giving him to remember. No two journeys are ever alike, because no two pupils are ever alike."

"Okay. That makes sense."

"We've taken a small side trip here to show you how to recognize members of your culture. Now let's see if we can get back to the main road we left. . . . I was saying that it's your culture's deep-seated perception that wisdom is not to be found among you, and that this perception has been extant in your culture for millennia."

"Yeah, I remember."

"Do you understand why I'm bringing this up?"

"No, not really."

"Your daydream takes it for granted that wisdom must be found elsewhere—billions of miles away from this planet. This is why it was necessary for you to construct a daydream in the first place. You know in your bones that the secret you're looking for is not to be found here."

"Yeah, that's right. I see what you're saying."

"What I'd like you to see next is that the loss of this secret was an event in your history. It isn't something missing from your genes. Humanity wasn't born deficient. This was something that happened uniquely among the people of your culture."

"Okay. But why do you want me to see that?"

"Because . . . Have you ever lost anything? A key, a book, a tool, a letter?"

"Sure."

"Can you remember how you went about trying to find it?"

"I tried to remember where I was when I had it last."

"Of course. If you know where you lost something, then you know where to look for it, don't you?"

"Yes."

"This is what I want to show you now: where and when you lost the secret that is known to every other species on this planet—and to every other intelligent species in the universe, if there are such."

"Wow," I told him. "We must really be special, if every other species in the universe knows something we don't."

"You are indeed special, Julie. On this point, your Mother Culture and I are in complete agreement."

The History of Man in 17 Seconds

Ishmael said, "There's only one place to begin with any pupil, Julie, and that place is where the pupil is. Do you see what I mean?"

"I think so."

"For the most part, the only way I can know where you are is if you tell me. And that's what you must do now. I need you to tell me what you know of human history."

I groaned, and Ishmael asked me why. "History is not my favorite subject," I told him.

"I can understand that," he said, "knowing how the teachers in your schools are forced to teach it. But I'm not asking you to recite what you've learned (or failed to learn) in school. Even if you'd never spent a single day in school, you would have a general impression of what's happened here, just by having your eyes and ears open in this culture for twelve years. Even someone who has done nothing but read the Sunday funnies has that."

"Okay," I said, and then made a connection. "Is this Mother Culture's version of human history? Is that what you're asking for?"

Ishmael nodded. "That's what I'm asking for. I need to know how much of it you've taken in. Even more to the point, *you* need to know how much of it you've taken in."

"I see," I told him, and started to work on it. After about three minutes he started to squirm, which in his size made an impressive sight. I gave him an inquiring look.

"Keep it simple, Julie. This isn't a term paper on which you're going to be graded. Just give me the general outline that everyone understands. I don't want a thousand words or even five hundred. Fifty words will do it."

"I guess I'm trying to figure out how to work in the Pyramids and World War Two."

"Let's begin with the framework. Once we have that, we can 'work in' anything we please."

"All right. Humans appeared here about what—five million years ago?"

"Three million is a widely accepted estimate."

"Okay, three million. Humans appeared about three million years ago. They were scavengers. Is that the right word?"

"They may well have been scavengers originally. But I think the word you're looking for is foragers."

"Yeah, that's right, they were foragers. Nomads. They lived off the land, like Native Americans used to do."

"Good. Go on."

"Well, they went on living off the land right up to about ten thousand years ago. Then for some reason they gave up the nomadic life and started farming. Is that right—ten thousand years?"

Ishmael nodded. "New findings might push it back, but until they do, ten thousand is the generally accepted figure."

"Okay, so they settled down and started farming, and that was basically the beginning of civilization. All this stuff. Cities, nations, wars, steamboats, bicycles, rockets to the moon, atomic bombs, nerve gas, and so on."

"Excellent," the gorilla said. "Alan had to perform the same feat for me, but it took him almost two hours."

"Really? Why?"

"Partly because he's male and must show off a bit. And partly because he's been listening to the voice of Mother Culture for so long that he thinks it's his own voice. He has a hard time distinguishing one from the other."

"I see," I said, trying not to sound smug.

"In any event, the basic lie is now in place: Around ten thousand years ago people gave up the foraging life and settled down to become farmers."

I looked at it for a minute then asked him which part of it was wrong. "The date is right, isn't it?"

He nodded.

"The foraging part is right, too, isn't it? I mean, before people were farmers, they were foragers, right?"

He nodded again.

"Then they started farming. That's what they did, wasn't it?"

"Yes."

"Then where's the lie?"

"The lie's hidden in the only part of the statement you haven't thought about."

"Will you repeat it for me?"

" 'Around ten thousand years ago people gave up the foraging life and settled down to become farmers.' "

"Wow," I said. "I don't even see any *room* in there for a lie."

"Nor would most people of your culture. It is, after all,

your culture's version of the story, so naturally it appears completely unexceptional to you. You'll see it (or some variation of it) repeated in all your textbooks. You'll see it repeated again and again in newspaper stories and magazine articles. If you keep your eyes open, you'll come across it in one form or another two or three times a week. You'll see it repeated routinely by historians, who would certainly recognize it as a lie if they weren't just repeating it routinely."

"But where's the lie?"

"The lie is in the word *people,* Julie. It wasn't *people* who did this, it was the people of your culture—one culture out of tens of thousands of cultures. The lie is that your actions are humanity's actions. The lie is that you are humanity itself, that your history is human history. The truth is that ten thousand years ago *one people* gave up the foraging life and settled down to become farmers. The rest of humanity— the other ninety-nine percent—went on exactly as before."

I went into a coma for a minute or two, then I said, "Here's the way it seems. It's like this was the next step in human evolution. *Homo forager* became extinct, and *Homo farmer* took over."

Ishmael nodded. "That's very perceptive, Julie. I hadn't seen that myself. It's exactly the impression one receives, but of course it isn't true."

"How do you know that?"

"First, because *Homo forager* did not become extinct—and is still not extinct. And second, because foragers and farmers don't belong to different species at all. They're biologically indistinguishable. The difference between them is strictly cultural. Bring a forager's baby up among farmers and he'll be a farmer. Bring a farmer's baby up among foragers and he'll be a forager."

"Okay. But even so, it was like . . . I don't know. It was like the band struck up a new tune and everyone started dancing to it all over the world."

Ishmael nodded and said, "I know this is how it sounds, Julie. Your history books have reduced it to a very simple story indeed. In fact, it's an extremely dense and complex story—and one that everyone in your culture vitally needs to know. Your future doesn't depend on understanding the fall of Rome or the rise of Napoléon or the American Civil War or even the World Wars. Your future does depend on understanding how you came to be the way you are, and this is the story I'm trying to reveal to you."

Ishmael stopped and went glassy-eyed for about ten minutes. Finally he scowled and shook his head, and I asked what was wrong.

"I was trying to think of a way to make the story comprehensible to you in a single telling, Julie, but I don't think it can be done that way. It has to be presented in several different tellings, each telling designed to bring out a different set of themes. Does that make any sense to you?"

"No, not much, to be honest. But I'm certainly willing to listen."

"Good. Here's a telling of the story based on your metaphor of the tune and the dancers. Although it may sound fanciful, it's not nearly as fanciful as the story told in your textbooks, which is about as useful, historically speaking, as the tales of Mother Goose."

Tunes & Dancers

Terpsichore is among the places you would enjoy visiting in the universe (Ishmael said). This was a planet (named, by the way, after the muse of dancing) where people emerged in the usual way in the community of life. For a time they lived as all others live, simply eating whatever came to hand. But after a couple of million years of living in this way, they noticed it was very easy to promote the regrowth of their favorite foods. You might say they found a few easy steps that would have this result. They didn't have to take these steps in order to stay alive, but if they took them, their favorite foods were always more readily available. These were, of course, the steps of a dance.

A few steps of the dance, performed just three or four days a month, enriched their lives greatly and took almost no effort. As here on earth, the people of this planet were not a single people but many peoples, and as time went on, each people developed its own approach to the dance. Some continued to dance just a few steps three or four days a month. Others found it made sense for them to have even more of their favorite foods, so they danced a few steps every second or third day. Still others saw no reason why they shouldn't live mostly on their favorite foods, so they danced a few steps every single day. Things went on this way for tens of thousands of years among the people of this planet, who thought of themselves as living in the hands of the gods and leaving everything to them. For this reason, they called themselves Leavers.

But one group of Leavers eventually said to themselves, "Why should we just live *partially* on the foods we favor? Why don't we live *entirely* on the foods we favor? All we have to do is devote a lot more time to dancing." So this one particular group took to dancing several hours a day. Because they thought of themselves as taking their welfare into their own hands, we'll call them Takers. The results were spectacular. The Takers were inundated with their favorite foods. A manager class soon emerged to look after the accumulation and storage of surpluses—something that had never been necessary when everyone was just dancing a few hours a week. The members of this manager class were far too busy to do any dancing themselves, and since their work was so critical, they soon came to be regarded as social and political leaders. But after a few years these leaders of the Takers began to notice that food production was dropping, and they went out to see what was going wrong. What they found was that the dancers were slacking off. They weren't dancing several hours a day, they were dancing only an hour or two and sometimes not even that much. The leaders asked why.

"What's the point of all this dancing?" the dancers said.

"It isn't necessary to dance seven or eight hours a day to get the food we need. There's plenty of food even if we just dance an hour a day. We're never hungry. So why shouldn't we relax and take life easy, the way we used to do?"

The leaders saw things very differently, of course. If the dancers went back to living the way they used to, then the leaders would soon have to do the same, and that didn't appeal to them at all. They considered and tried many different schemes to encourage or cajole or tempt or shame or force the dancers into dancing longer hours, but nothing worked until one of them came up with the idea of locking up the food.

"What good will that do?" he was asked.

"The reason the dancers aren't dancing right now is that they just have to reach out and take the food they want. If we lock it away, they won't be able to do that."

"But if we lock the food away, the dancers will starve to death!"

"No, no, you don't understand," the other said with a smile. "We'll link dancing to receiving food—so much food for so much dancing. So if the dancers dance a little, they'll get a little food, and if they dance a lot, they'll get a lot. This way, slackers will always be hungry, and dancers who dance for long hours will have full stomachs."

"They'll never put up with such an arrangement," he was told.

"They'll have no choice. We'll lock the food away in storehouses, and the dancers will either dance or they'll starve."

"The dancers will just break into the storehouses."

"We'll recruit guards from among the dancers. We'll excuse them from dancing and have them guard the storehouses instead. We'll pay them the same way we pay the dancers, with food—so much food for so many hours of guarding."

"It will never work," he was told.

But oddly enough it did work. It worked even better than before, for now, with the food under lock and key, there were always plenty of dancers willing to dance, and many were glad to be allowed to dance ten hours, twelve hours, even fourteen hours every single day.

Putting the food under lock and key had other consequences as well. For example, in the past, ordinary baskets had been good enough to hold the surplus food being produced. But these proved to be too flimsy for the huge surpluses now being produced. Potters had to take over for basket-makers, and they had to learn how to make bigger pots than ever before, which meant building larger and more efficient kilns. And because not all dancers took kindly to the idea of food being locked away, the guards had to be equipped with better weapons than before, which meant that toolmakers began looking at new materials to replace the stone weapons of the past—copper, bronze, and so on. As metals became available for use in weapons, other artisans found uses for them. Each new craft gave birth to others.

But forcing the dancers to dance for ten or twelve hours a day had an even more important consequence. Population growth is inherently a function of food availability. If you increase the food available to any population of any species, that population will grow—provided it has space into which to grow. And of course the Takers had plenty of space into which to grow—their neighbors' space.

They were perfectly willing to grow peacefully into their neighbors' space. They said to the Leavers around them, "Look, why don't you start dancing the way we do? Look at how far we've come dancing this way. We have things you can't even dream of having. The way you dance is terribly inefficient and unproductive. The way we dance is the way people were *meant* to dance. So let us move into your territory, and we'll show you how it's done."

Some of the folks around them thought this sounded like a good idea, and they embraced the Taker way. But others said, "We're doing fine the way we are. We dance a few hours a week, and that's all we care to dance. We think you're crazy to knock yourselves out dancing fifty and sixty hours a week, but that's your business. If you like it, you do it. But we're not going to do it."

The Takers expanded around the holdouts and eventually isolated them. One of these holdout peoples were the Singe, who were used to dancing a couple hours a day to produce the foods they favored. At first they lived as before. But then their children began to be jealous of the things Taker children had, and they started offering to dance a few hours a day for the Takers and to help guard the food storehouses. After a few generations the Singe were completely assimilated into the Taker lifestyle and forgot that they had ever been the Singe.

Another holdout people were the Kemke, who were used to dancing just a few hours a week and who loved the leisure this lifestyle gave them. They were resolved not to let happen to them what happened to the Singe, and they stuck to their resolve. But soon the Takers came to them and said, "Look, we can't let you have all this land in the middle of our territory. You're not making efficient use of it. Either start dancing the way we dance or we're going to have to move you into one corner of your territory so we can put the rest to good use." But the Kemke refused to dance like the Takers, so the Takers came and moved them into one corner of their land, which they called a "reservation," meaning it was "reserved" for the Kemke. But the Kemke were used to getting most of their food by foraging, and their little reservation just wasn't big enough to sustain a foraging people. The Takers said to them, "That's all right, we'll keep you supplied with food. All we want you to do is stay out of the way on your reservation." So the Takers began supplying them with food. Gradually the Kemke forgot how to do their own hunting and gathering, and of course the more they forgot, the more dependent they became on the Takers. They began to feel like worthless beggars, lost all sense of self-respect, and fell into alcoholism and suicidal depression. In the end their children saw nothing on the reservation worth staying for and drifted off to start dancing ten hours a day for the Takers.

Another holdout people were the Waddi, who spent only a few hours a month dancing and were perfectly happy with that lifestyle. They'd seen what happened to the Singe and the Kemke and were determined that it wouldn't happen to them. They figured they had even more to lose than the Singe and the Kemke, who were already used to doing a lot of dancing for the sake of having their favorite foods on hand. So when the Takers invited them to become Takers, the Waddi just said no thanks, we're happy the way we are. Then, when the Takers finally came and told them they'd have to move onto a reservation, the Waddi said they didn't care to do that either. The Takers explained that they weren't being offered a choice in the matter. If they didn't move to the reservation willingly, they'd be moved by force. The Waddi replied that they would meet force with force and warned the Takers that they were prepared to fight to the death to preserve their way of life. They said, "Look, you have all the land in this part of the world. You don't need this little part that we're living in. All we ask is to be allowed to go on living the way we prefer. We won't bother you."

But the Takers said, "You don't understand. The way you live is not only inefficient and wasteful, it's wrong. People weren't meant to live the way you live. People were meant to live the way we Takers live."

"How can you possibly know such a thing?" the Waddi asked.

"It's obvious," the Takers said. "Just look at how successful we are. If we weren't living the way people were meant to live, then we wouldn't be so successful."

"To us, you don't look successful at all," the Waddi replied. "You force people to dance ten and twelve hours a day just to stay alive, and that's a terrible way to live. We dance just a few hours a month and never go hungry, because all the food in the world is right out there free for the taking. We have an easy, carefree life, and that's what success is all about."

The Takers said, "That's not what success is about at all. You'll see what success is about when we send in our troops to force you onto the land we've set aside for you."

And the Waddi did indeed learn about success—or at least what the Takers considered success—when their soldiers arrived to drive them from their homeland. The Taker soldiers weren't more courageous or more skillful, but they outnumbered the Waddi and could bring in replacements at will, which the Waddi couldn't. The invaders also had more advanced weapons and, most important of all, unlimited supplies of food, which the Waddi certainly did not. The Taker soldiers never had to worry about food, because fresh shipments arrived daily from back home, where it was being produced continuously and prodigiously. As the war dragged on, the Waddi force became smaller and smaller and weaker and weaker, and before long the invaders wiped them out completely.

This was the pattern not only for the years ahead but for the centuries and millennia ahead. Food production increased relentlessly and the Taker population increased endlessly, impelling them to expand into one land after another. Everywhere they went, they met peoples who danced a few hours weekly or monthly, and all these peoples were given the same choice that had been given to the Singe, the Kemke, and the Waddi: *Join us and let us put all your food under lock and key—or be destroyed.* In the end, however, this choice was only an illusion, because they were destroyed whatever they did, whether they chose to be assimilated, allowed themselves to be driven onto a reservation, or tried to repel the invaders by force. The Takers left nothing in their wake but Takers as they stormed across the world.

And it finally came to pass, after about ten thousand years, that almost the entire population of Terpsichore were Takers. There were just a few remnants of Leaver peoples hidden away in deserts and jungles that the Takers either didn't want or hadn't gotten around to yet. And there was none among the Takers who doubted that the Taker way was the way people were meant to live. What could be sweeter than having your food locked away and having to dance eight, ten, or twelve hours a day in order to stay alive?

In school, this was the history their children learned. People like them had been around for some three million years, but for most of that time they were unaware of the fact that dancing would encourage the regrowth of their favorite foods. This fact had been discovered only about ten thousand years ago, by the founders of their culture. Joyously locking away their food so that they couldn't get at it, the Takers immediately began dancing eight or ten hours a day. The people around them had never danced before, but they took it up enthusiastically, seeing at once that this was the way people were meant to live. Except for a few scattered peoples who were too dim-witted to perceive the obvious advantages of having their food locked away, the Great Dancing Revolution swept across the world without opposition.

The Parable Examined

Ishmael stopped talking, and I stared into the space in front of me like a bomb-blast victim. Finally I told him I had to go out and get some caffeine and think about this. Or maybe I just staggered out without a word, I don't really remember.

Actually, I went back to Pearson's department store and rode the escalators for a while. I don't know why this soothes me, but it does. Other people go for walks in the woods. I go for rides on department-store escalators.

Then I stopped for a Coke. Looking back, I see that this is the second time I've mentioned Coke. I wouldn't want anyone to think I was giving it a boost here. Everyone in the world should stop buying Coke as far as I'm concerned, but I'm afraid I do occasionally suck one down.

After forty-five minutes I was still feeling like a bomb-blast victim, except that I wasn't suffering or anything. I felt that I now understood what learning is. Of course, learning can be like looking up the meaning of a word. That's learning, for sure, sort of like planting a blade of grass in a lawn. But then there's learning that is like dynamiting the whole lawn and starting over, and that's what Ishmael's tale of the dancers did. Eventually some questions began to form in my mind, and I headed back to Room 105 to get them asked.

I said, "Let me see if I actually understand what I heard."

"That's a good plan," Ishmael agreed.

"By 'dancing' you mean the practice of agriculture."

He nodded.

"You're saying agriculture isn't just the full-scale, all-out farming we practice. You're saying agriculture is encouraging the regrowth of the foods you favor."

He nodded again. "What else could it be? If you're stranded on a desert island, you can't grow chickens and chickpeas—unless you find some already growing there. You can only regrow whatever is already growing."

"Right. And you're saying people were encouraging the regrowth of their favorite foods long before the Agricultural Revolution."

"Certainly. There's nothing mysterious about the process. People as smart as you had been around for as long as two hundred thousand years when your 'revolution' started. There were people in every generation smart enough to be rocket scientists, but you don't need to be a rocket scientist to figure out that plants grow from seeds. You don't need to be a rocket scientist to figure out that it makes sense to stick a couple of seeds in the ground when you leave an area. You don't need to be a rocket scientist to do a little weeding. You don't need to be a rocket scientist to know that when you're hunting game, it's always better to take a male than a female. Nomadic hunters are only a step away from being hunter/herders who follow the migrations of their favorite animals, and these are only a step away from being herder/hunters who exert some control over the migration of their favorite animals and chase off other predators. And these are only a step away from being true herders, who control their animals completely and breed them for docility."

"So you're saying that the revolution just consisted of doing something *full-time* that people had already been doing *part-time* for thousands of years."

"Of course. No invention ever comes into being fully developed in a single step, from nothing. Ten thousand inventions had to be in place before Edison could invent the electric lightbulb."

"Yeah. But you're also saying that the real innovation of our revolution wasn't growing the food, it was locking it up."

"Yes, that was certainly the key. Your revolution would have ground to a halt without that feature. It would grind to a halt *today* without that feature."

"That was the last thing I was going to bring up. You're saying the revolution never ended."

"That's right. It will end shortly, however. The revolution worked fine so long as there was always more space to expand into, but now there just isn't any more."

"I suppose we could export it to other planets."

Ishmael shook his head. "Even that would be a stopgap measure, Julie. Let's say that six billion inhabitants represents a reasonable planetary maximum for your species (though I suspect that six billion is actually much more than a healthy maximum). You'll reach that six billion well before the end of this century. And let's say that you had instantaneous access to every habitable planet in the universe, to which you could immediately begin exporting people. At present your population is doubling every thirty-five years or so, so in thirty-five years you'd fill a second planet. After seventy years four planets would be full. After a hundred and five years eight planets would be full. And so on. At this doubling rate a billion planets would be full by the year 3000 or thereabouts. I know that sounds incredible, but, trust me, the arithmetic is correct. By about 3300 a hundred billion planets would be full; this is the number you could occupy in this entire galaxy if each and every star had one habitable planet. If you continued to grow at your present rate, a second galaxy would be full in another thirty-five years. Four galaxies would be full thirty-five years later, and eight would be full thirty-five years after that. By the year 4000 the planets of a million galaxies would be full. By the year 5000 the planets of a trillion galaxies would be full—in other words, every planet in the universe. All in just three thousand years and working under the improbable assumption that every single star in the universe has a habitable planet."

I told him these numbers were hard to believe.

"Do the arithmetic yourself sometime, then you won't have to believe it, you'll know it. Whatever grows without limit must inevitably end by overwhelming the universe. The anthropologist Marvin Harris once calculated that if the human population doubled every generation—every twenty years, as opposed to every thirty-five—the entire universe would be converted into a solid mass of human protoplasm in less than two thousand years."

I sat there for a while trying to bring it all down to a manageable size. At last I told him about someone I knew, a girl who almost went off the deep end when someone finally got around to telling her where babies come from. "She must have grown up at the bottom of a well or something," I told him.

He rewarded me with a look of polite inquiry.

"I guess she felt betrayed by God first, that he would have come up with such a nasty method for human procreation. Then she felt betrayed by everyone around her who had known and hadn't told her. Then she felt humiliated to know that she was the last person on the face of the earth to hear this very simple fact."

"I take it this has some relevance to our conversation?"

"Yes. I'd like to know if I'm the last person on the face of the earth to hear what you've been telling me today in this story of the dancers."

"First, let's make sure we *know* what I've been telling you. What does the story accomplish?"

That wasn't too tough a question. This was what I'd been thinking about as I traveled the air inside Pearson's. I said, "It demolishes the lie that ten thousand years ago everyone gave up foraging and settled down to become farmers. It demolishes the lie that this was an event that everyone had been waiting for from the beginning of time. It demolishes the lie that, because our way has become the dominant way, this must prove it's the way people are 'meant' to live."

"So, are you the last person on the face of the earth to know all this? Hardly. There are many who, on hearing the story, would feel that they 'knew it all along' or suspected that it was 'something like that.' There are many who might have worked it out—who have all the facts at their disposal—but who didn't. The *will* to work it out isn't there for them."

"What do you mean by that?"

"I mean that people seldom look very hard for things they don't want to find. They avert their eyes from such things. I should add that this is not an observation of any great originality on my part."

"I'm lost," I told him after a bit. "I think we've wandered off the main road again."

"We weren't wandering, Julie—at least not aimlessly. Some of what you need to examine can't be seen from the

main road, so we have to take a secondary road now and
then. But these always lead back to the main road. Do you
see where it's leading?"

"I have a sense of it, but I'm not sure."

"The main road leads to why the people of your culture
have to look off-planet to find wisdom—into the heavens,
home of God and his angels; into outer space, home of 'advanced' alien races; into the Great Beyond, home of the spirits of the departed."

"Wow," I said. "Is *that* where we're heading! It never
occurred to me that my daydream fit this sort of pattern.
That's what you're saying, isn't it?"

"That's what I'm saying. You perceive yourselves to be
deprived of essential knowledge. You've always been so. It's
your nature to be so. The very inaccessibility of this knowledge makes it special. It's inaccessible because it's special, and
it's special because it's inaccessible. In fact, it's so special that
you can only access it through supernormal means—prayer,
séance, astrology, meditation, past-life reading, channeling,
crystal gazing, card reading, and so on."

"In other words, hoogy-moogy," I put in.

Ishmael glared at me for a moment, then blinked, twice.
"Hoogy-moogy?"

"Everything you just mentioned. Séances, astrology, channeling, angels, all that stuff."

He gave his head a little shake, the way you do a salt-
shaker to see if there's anything in it. Then he went on.
"What I want you to see is that the people of your culture
accept the fact that this knowledge is inaccessible. It doesn't
amaze them or even puzzle them. It needs no explanation.
They fully *expect* this knowledge to be difficult to come by.
You, for example, felt sure that nothing less than a galactic
tour could deliver it to you."

"Yeah, I do see that now."

Ishmael shook his head. "I still haven't quite managed to articulate what I'm getting at. Let me try again. Thinkers aren't limited by what they know, because they can always increase what they know. Rather they're limited by what puzzles them, because there's no way to become curious about something that doesn't puzzle you. If a thing falls outside the range of people's curiosity, then they simply *cannot* make inquiries about it. It constitutes a blind spot—a spot of blindness that you can't even know is there until someone draws your attention to it."

"Which is what you're trying to do here with me."

"Exactly. The two of us are exploring an unknown territory—a whole continent that lies inside your culture's blind spot." He paused for a moment, then said that this seemed like a good place to stop for the day. I guess I agreed. I wasn't exactly tired, but I did feel as though I'd just finished three pieces of pie.

I stood up and told him I'd see him next Saturday then. When this produced no reaction after about thirty seconds, I said, "Isn't that all right?"

"It's not exactly ideal," he said.

I told him school had just started, and I always tried to set a good example for myself during the first few weeks. Which meant being serious about homework on school nights.

"Let me explain the situation, Julie. I'm in a difficult position." He waved a hand at his surroundings. "Maintaining me in these quarters has been the undertaking of a friend of long standing, Rachel Sokolow. She died two months ago."

"I'm sorry to hear it," I said, the way people do.

"I called my position difficult, but it's much worse than that. In two weeks I'll be forced to vacate these premises."

"Where will you go?"

He shook his head. "I'm still working that out. What you

must understand just now is that I don't have much time left here. This means it isn't practical for you to think of coming just on weekends."

I picked at this for a minute, then asked if Alan Lomax was helping him.

"Why do you ask that?"

"I don't know. I guess I just figured you could hardly move out of here without help."

"Alan isn't helping me," Ishmael stated. "He knows nothing about it. There's no need for him to know about it. There *is* a need for you to know about it, because you were thinking we had all the time in the world." I guess he could see that I wasn't satisfied with what he was telling me, because he went on. "Alan has been with me for a couple of weeks already, almost daily, and we will soon have gone just about as far as we can go together."

Even so, there was obviously something he was carefully *not* explaining, which was why Alan was being kept in the dark. Even if he didn't *need* to know about Ishmael's forthcoming move, why *not* know about it?

It was then that Ishmael showed me he could "say" things without using words. He could sort of beam me an attitude, and the attitude he beamed at me was: *This is none of your business.*

It wasn't nearly as flat and gruff as it looks spelled out in words. And of course I already knew it was none of my business. Snoops always know exactly what is and isn't their business.

A Visit To Calliope

Ishmael seemed relieved to have his problem out in the
open. We were working under a deadline and could not
afford to shilly-shally. All the same, I did begin our next
session with a question that was probably superfluous:

"If you knew you had only a few weeks left here, why did
you put that ad in the newspaper?"

He grunted. "I put the ad in the newspaper precisely
because I have only a few weeks left here. This may well be
my last chance."

"Your last chance to do what?"

"To get someone to *take this away*."

" 'This' being what's in your head?" He nodded. "Excuse
me if I'm being dense, but I thought you'd already had lots
of pupils."

"That's right, but none of them has taken away what you'll take away, Julie. None of them has taken away what Alan will take away. Each of you encodes the message differently. Each of you has received a different telling and will transmit a different telling—of the same message."

"Alan hasn't heard the story of the dancers?"

"No, and you won't hear the story of the hapless airman. The stories you hear are stories created for you in particular, at particular times when you need to hear them, as the stories Alan hears are stories created for him in particular, at particular times when he needs to hear them. And with that as an introduction, I'll present another one I prepared for you last night. You remember I said that the story of how you came to be this way would take several tellings."

"Yes."

"The story of Terpsichore was the first telling. This, the story of Calliope (named after the muse of epic poetry), is the second."

"This is another planet you would definitely want to visit on your quest for enlightenment," Ishmael began. "Life emerged on Calliope in much the same way it did on earth. Those who wish to imagine that God called every species to life in a final, changeless form are welcome to do so, but I'm incapable of embracing such a primitive scenario. If one accepts the invitation to think of God as a parent, then one must wonder what sort of parent would actually care to bring his or her children into being as fully formed adults, all ready to soar like eagles, see like hawks, run like cheetahs, hunt like sharks, and think like computer scientists. Only a very unimaginative and insecure one, I feel.

"Be that as it may, the creatures of Calliope came into being by means of the process generally known as evolution. There's no reason to imagine that this process is unique to earth. On the contrary, for reasons that will become plain, it would be very surprising if it were so.

"There's no need or reason to go through the process in detail. It will be enough if you see and understand even a few of its results. For example, I would recommend to your attention a creature that made its appearance on Calliope some ten million years ago, a quilled lizard with a long snout suitable for browsing in anthills. When I say that it made its appearance, I don't mean that it had no predecessor. Of course it did—I trust you understand that."

I said I did.

"This quilled lizard (let's call it a porcuzard) was nevertheless a strange creature—or would certainly seem strange to you or me, as does the porcupine or the anteater. Now let me ask what your expectation is for this creature. Is it your expectation that it will be a successful addition to the community of life on Calliope?"

I said I didn't have any basis for an expectation. How could I? Ishmael nodded as if he could see the sense in this reply.

"Let's transpose the matter to a locale closer to home. Suppose biologists were to discover a porcuzard living in the deepest jungles of New Guinea. Such a thing is not at all impossible. New species are being discovered all the time."

"Okay."

"What would be your expectation in this case? Would you expect a creature like this to be a successful inhabitant of the jungles of New Guinea?"

"Certainly. Why wouldn't it be?"

"That's not the question I'm exploring here, Julie. The question I'm exploring is: What is your expectation? And you've answered that: You expect it to be successful. The next question is, why do you expect it to be successful?"

"Because . . . if it weren't successful, then it wouldn't be there at all."

"Where would it be?"

"It would be nowhere. It would have disappeared."

"Why?"

"Why? Because . . . Because failures disappear. Don't they?"

"In this case, Julie, I'd rather you answered this yourself. Do failures disappear or not?"

"They disappear. They *have* to. If a species is here, then it obviously can't be a failure."

"Exactly. No matter how strange it may look to us. Thus a flightless bird like the emu, improbable as it seems, is successful—where it is, for the time being. This doesn't constitute a guarantee for the lifetime of the planet. The dodo was a success—where it was, when it was. Then conditions changed, and it could no longer succeed—where it was, when it was—so it failed and disappeared."

"I understand."

"This is a fundamental fact: The community of life that we see here at any given time isn't just a random collection. It's a collection of *successes*. It's the remainder that is left over when the failures have disappeared."

"Right."

"Now let's return to Calliope. I'll ask again what your expectation is for the porcuzard."

"My expectation is that it's a success, because if it was a failure, it wouldn't be there at all."

"That's right. No species emerges by failing. What the community brings forth are successes—species that are able to cope with the conditions around them. This is why I say that the process we observe here is overwhelmingly likely to be the process observed everywhere. At any given moment communities anywhere will be largely composed of species that work."

"Yeah, I don't see how it could be any other way."

"At the same time, however, any given species in the

community might be declining. Come back in twenty years, and it may be gone. But that doesn't invalidate our general expectations. Any given species may go *out* of existence by failing, but it certainly didn't come *into* existence by failing. No species comes into existence by failing. That's simply unthinkable."

"Yes, I see that."

"Now back to Calliope again. Here is a picture of porcuzard reproductive life. They are entirely promiscuous. Neither males nor females recognize their young, but females recognize their home nest and will nurse any pup in that nest. If a female finds the unguarded nest of another porcuzard inside her home territory, she'll enter that nest and kill any pups she finds."

I asked why she would do that.

"Her intentions can't be known, of course, but killing these pups does in fact tend to increase her own reproductive success. With these pups gone, her own pups are more likely to carry her genes into the gene pool. Do you understand what I'm saying?"

"I think so. Maybe a little vaguely, but I think so."

"Good. The males follow a contrary practice. As I just explained, a female kills rivals to her pups *inside* her territory. A male kills pups *outside* his territory."

"Why outside rather than inside?"

"Because inside his territory, the pups may well be his own. Inside her territory, the female's pups are only in her nest. Inside his territory, the male's pups are all over the place."

"My head is beginning to swim a bit. How does killing pups outside his territory increase his reproductive success?"

"In a different way from the way that killing pups increases the female's chance of reproductive success. The male who is moving around outside his home territory is looking for opportunities to mate, and those opportunities will increase if the females he encounters are not currently nursing pups. If he kills off this generation of pups, the next generation of pups will carry his genes exclusively."

"Wow," I commented. "So this killing off of pups has nothing to do with population control."

"The individuals are acting in a way that improves their representation in the gene pool, but of course this way of acting has many other effects as well. When the population is dense in a female's home territory, she's more likely to encounter the nests of her rivals—and so is more likely to kill pups. On the other hand, when the population is sparse, the male has fewer mating possibilities in his home territory and so goes farther afield. And, going farther afield, he's more likely to encounter pups that he will kill. In other words, when the home territory is sparsely populated, the female kills few pups and the male kills many elsewhere. When the home territory is densely populated, the female kills many pups and the male kills few. The overall effect does tend to stabilize the population. Nothing can ultimately succeed if it has the opposite effect."

"Okay."

"Now, what is your expectation of this system? Do you expect it to be a success for porcuzards, or a failure?"

This question struck me as rather pointless, and I said so. "The way you've set it up, any system would be a success. You could make up anything, and I'd have to say that my expectation is that it works. You could make up a system in which porcuzards don't mate at all, and I'd have to say that it must work or it wouldn't be there, would it?"

"A valid objection," he conceded. "However, this isn't just some fantasy I've concocted. It's exactly what is observed among white-footed mice, *Peromyscus leucopus,* such as you might find in forests of the Allegheny Mountains. This isn't to say that it's unique to them. Similar patterns are found in meadow voles, gerbils, lemmings, and several species of monkeys."

"Okay. I guess I just don't quite see where you're headed with this."

"I'll try to point the way for you. The ways of the porcuzards (or white-footed mice) seem bizarre—until you understand how they contribute to the animals' success. Perhaps they even seem immoral, something that right-thinking people should put a stop to."

"Yes, that's true."

"I'd like you to see, however, that if you were to convert them to what might seem to you to be a higher, nobler standard of behavior, they would very probably become extinct within just a few generations. To use a bit of jargon, our examination of these strategies reveals them to be evolutionarily stable. Imagine that these species as we see them right now are the product of a hundred thousand experiments conducted over a ten-million-year period. During that time all sorts of reproductive strategies have been tested. Many of them have proved to be self-eliminating, like the one you suggested—not mating at all. Animals that don't mate at all obviously contribute nothing to the gene pool. Generation after generation, those with no tendency to mate do not reproduce. Generation after generation, less and less is seen of this tendency. Does that make sense to you?"

"Yes, of course."

"During this period dozens of strategies are tested, and those that tend to promote reproductive success are reinforced in every generation, and those that tend to diminish reproductive success are weakened. Does this still make sense?"

"Yes."

"At the end of this period, what is found is that a single set of strategies has prevailed. When the home territory starts to become crowded, females kill pups in rival nests. When reproductive opportunities start to become scarce, males move out of their home territory and kill pups wherever they find them. An analysis of these strategies will show you why they can't be improved upon by any others, but this is neither the time nor the place for such an analysis. In the absence of that analysis, I ask you to take my word for it. These two strategies are evolutionarily stable, which means that no others exist that can supplant them. Any other strategy will fail. Individuals that desist from killing pups in the circumstances I've described will not be as reproductively successful as individuals that do not desist. This means that any attack on these strategies constitutes an attack on the biological viability of these species."

"Okay, my head is swimming, but I think I've got that."

"These infanticidal patterns probably seem quite strange to you. I'd suggest that this isn't because they're inherently peculiar but rather because you haven't grown up with them the way you've grown up with other patterns. You'll never see a documentary about white-footed mice, because they're just not fascinating cinematic subjects. What you *will* see are documentaries about big, dramatic creatures like ibex, big-horn sheep, and elephant seals. And these will without fail show you behaviors that promote individuals' reproductive success. For example, in any film about ibex, you're bound to see footage of males bashing into each other head-on during the rut. In the same way, in any film about elephant seals, you're bound to see footage of giant males savagely thrashing one another to contest possession of a harem. People find an amusement in these spectacles that they would never find in the spectacle of a white-footed mouse biting the head of a helpless pup no bigger than a thumb."

"I can believe that."

"Nonetheless, the contests of the creatures I've just mentioned are no less deadly. They're just more exciting to watch."

"True, I guess. But I'm not sure what your point is."

"I'm trying to get you used to the fact that things that look strange to you are not in fact stranger than things that look ordinary. You're used to seeing animals being aggressive, so the aggressiveness of mountain goats and elephant seals seems unremarkable to you. But you're not used to seeing animals killing their rivals' young, so the infanticidal behavior of white-footed mice seems grotesque and perhaps even shocking to you. But in fact, both strategies are equally grotesque and equally ordinary. I guess you could say that I'm trying to get you to stop looking at your neighbors in the community of life as if they were characters in *Bambi* —humans in animal disguise. In a Disney animated feature, two male deer clashing heads in rut would be portrayed as courageous and heroic warriors. But a white-footed mouse sneaking into a rival's nest to kill a pup would surely be portrayed as a vile and cowardly villain."

"Yeah, I certainly see that."

Calliope, Part II

I find, Julie, that I have to make some general remarks about competition in the community of life."

"Okay."

"Alan and I are exploring the subject of *interspecies* competition—competition among different species. A certain set of rules or strategies have evolved in the community of life that assure a lively but limited competition among species. Roughly speaking, they can be summarized this way: 'Compete to the full extent of your capabilities, but don't hunt down your competitors, destroy their food, or deny them access to food.' You and I (in case you haven't noticed) are exploring another kind of competition, *intraspecies* competition—competition among members of the same species."

"Yeah," I said brightly. "Okay."

"As you can easily notice in the case of white-footed mice, the rules that apply to interspecies competition don't apply to intraspecies competition. A female white-footed mouse will go out of her way to kill a rival female's pups, but she would never go out of her way to kill a shrew's pups. I wonder if you can figure out why."

After working on it for a while, I said, "The way I understand it, by killing rival pups, the white-footed mouse is increasing the likelihood of her own reproductive success. It will be her genes that go into the gene pool, not her rivals'. Is that right?"

"Perfectly right."

"Then killing shrew pups won't give her that benefit."

"Why not?"

"Killing shrew pups would be irrelevant. The genes of shrews go into the shrew gene pool, don't they? Am I understanding that right?"

Ishmael nodded. "You're understanding it right. The genes of shrews go only into the shrew gene pool."

"Then killing shrews can no more increase her representation in the gene pool for white-footed mice than killing owls or alligators."

Ishmael stared at me for so long that I began to squirm. Finally I asked him what was wrong.

"Nothing's wrong, Julie. Your ability to give such an answer simply makes me wonder if you've already been studying in this area."

"No," I said. "I'm not even sure what 'this area' is."

"It doesn't matter. You're very quick. I'll have to be careful not to let you get a big head. Nevertheless, your conclusion is a bit too sweeping. The white-footed mouse would derive *some* benefit from killing shrew pups, because the shrew pups compete with her own pups for *some* resources."

"Then why not kill them?"

"Because there are thousands of species that compete with

her pups for *some* resources—and she can't kill them all. There is only one species that competes with her pups *totally*—for *all* resources."

For a second I didn't see it, then of course I did: "Other white-footed mice."

"Of course. Killing a nestful of shrews would be of very limited benefit to her. But killing a nestful of white-footed mice represents a clear and undoubted benefit."

"Yeah, I can see that."

"This is why the rules that govern competition *between* species are (and must be) very different from the rules that govern competition *within* species. Competition within species is always more arduous than competition between species. This is because the members of a given species are forever competing for the same resources. And this is especially true when it comes to mates. Many hundreds of species might compete with a white-footed mouse for a chance to grab a mulberry, but only another white-footed mouse will compete with it for a chance to mate with another white-footed mouse."

"Ah," I said.

" 'Ah' meaning what?"

" 'Ah' meaning . . . now we come back to the rutting battles of the elephant seals and the bighorn sheep. Am I right?"

"Not exactly," said the gorilla. "Our focus is on intraspecies competition in general—for all resources, not just the reproductive ones."

"Okay. But . . . is this really on the main road? Are we still headed toward an explanation of why we turn to spooks and angels and ufonauts to find out how to live?"

"Unlikely as it seems, we're definitely on that road."

"Good."

·   ·   ·

"Evolution brings forth what works. For example, we've already seen that killing rivals' pups works for white-footed mice. But of course it wouldn't work for them to kill their own pups. That strategy would never evolve. It *couldn't* evolve, because it's self-eliminating. I'm sure you see that."

"Yes."

"Now we're going to have a look at what works when it comes to conflict among conspecifics—members of the same species. Because conspecifics are constantly competing for the same resources, opportunities for conflict among them arise daily, even hourly. Obviously, therefore, evolution must have brought forth means of resolving these conflicts that are less than deadly. It wouldn't work to have every conflict over resources settled by mortal combat."

"Yes, I see that."

"There are a finite number of strategies that can be adopted by conspecifics in conflict, but it's not to our purpose for me to develop a complete list of them here and now. Rather, what I'd like to do is pay another visit to Calliope to study the Awks to see the strategies evolution has brought forth among them for dealing with conflict."

"What are Awks?"

"Awks are a sort of cross between monkeys and ostriches, if you can picture such a bizarre coupling. Originally they were birds, but they became so much at home in the trees that flight became superfluous for them. So they're rather like ostriches in that they have stunted little wings, and they're rather like monkeys in that they have very useful grabbing and swinging appendages like hands and tails that enable them to elude almost every sort of predator that comes after them. Unlike many species, in which the male is superfluous after impregnating the female, the male Awk must be on hand to help provide food for newborn offspring. And by the time he's no longer needed as a food collector for the young, the three or four females under his care are ready to mate again. So Awks have a recognizable sort of family life.

"When two Awks come face-to-face over a luscious piece of fruit, here's what generally happens. They glare at each other and bare their teeth and shriek. If one of them is distinctly smaller than the other, then it will probably give up rather quickly and slink away. But not always. Two out of five times (perhaps corresponding to how hungry it is), it will start bouncing up and down in a clearly threatening manner. When this happens, the other will usually back down, even if it's larger. But again, not always. Perhaps one out of five times, it will refuse to be intimidated and will try some intimidation of its own, bouncing up and down and snapping its teeth. This will usually send the other off with its tail between its legs—but again, not always. Perhaps one time in ten, the smaller will recklessly continue to threaten the larger, and they'll end up in a physical battle that will last twenty or thirty seconds and will result in a few minor cuts and bruises before the victor carries away the fruit.

"The strategy each Awk is following can be expressed roughly as follows. 'If confronted by an Awk competitor, be aggressive, but back down if the other is distinctly bigger—unless you really need the resource in contention, in which case you might occasionally try being a bit more aggressive just to see if the other will back down. If the other responds by becoming more aggressive, run away, unless you really need that resource and are feeling lucky.' Now of course I don't mean that this strategy is something reasoned out. But if it *were* to be reasoned out and articulated in words, then it would be something like that. The Awks *behave* as though they were following a consistent strategy, roughly as I've described it."

"I understand."

"Now this sort of behavior isn't at all unusual. Most earthly species resolve their conspecific conflicts over resources in just such a fashion. It doesn't pay to get into a serious battle over every acorn, but it also doesn't pay to back down over every acorn. It's important to be predictable to a certain extent, but it's also important not to be too predictable. For example, your opponent should know that when you start snapping your teeth at him, you're pretty likely to attack. On the other hand, your opponent shouldn't be able to count on your backing down just because he starts snapping his teeth at *you*."

"Right."

"Again, this sort of strategy evolves because it *works*—again and again, for all sorts of species, and very probably all over the universe."

"Yes, that makes sense."

Ishmael paused to think for a moment. "What I'm pointing out is that, if you were to take the journey you fantasized in your daydream, you'd find the same general evolutionary background everywhere, because everywhere (and not just on this planet) evolution is a process that intrinsically and invariably brings forth what works, and what works is not going to vary dramatically from one planet to the next. Wherever you go in the universe, you'll find species going *out* of existence by failing but never coming *into* existence by failing. Wherever you go in the universe, you'll find it *never* pays to fight to the death over every morsel of food."

I closed my eyes and settled back in my chair to ponder that for a while. When I came to, I said, "You're telling me something about the wisdom I would have found if I'd been able to take that galactic journey in fact."

He nodded. "Yes. In a sense, the two of us are taking that journey right here, without leaving the ground. To proceed . . . In my initial examination of the competition strategies of Awks, I felt it best to postpone the very important element of territoriality. I'd like to catch up on that now. Humans often misunderstand animal territoriality by thinking of it in human terms. A human group will tend to start out by finding a territory for themselves—a place to call their own. They carve out a piece of real estate and say, 'This territory is ours, and we'll defend everything in it.' People therefore assume that an animal is making the same sort of statement when it goes about marking a territory with its scent. This anthropomorphism leads to much confusion. This is not only because animals are incapable of this level of abstraction, but also because they know nothing about territories and have no interest in territories. To begin at the beginning, an animal never goes looking for territory as such —a place to call its own. It goes looking for food and mates, and when it finds them, it draws a circle around them that says to conspecific rivals, 'The resources inside this circle are taken and will be defended.' It doesn't give a hang about the acreage itself, and if the resources in it disappeared, the animal would walk away from it without a backward glance."

"That seems obvious enough," I offered.

Ishmael shrugged. "Every path is plain once it's been opened. However, having established that there is a difference, we can proceed as if it didn't matter. For the most part, animals defending their resources act exactly as if they were defending a territory. We can begin by noting that animals don't defend their territory against all the thousands of species that invade it—they couldn't and they don't need to. The only species they must defend it against is their own, for reasons we've already noted.

"Territoriality adds another dimension to conspecific conflict. Forty years ago the great Dutch zoologist Nikolaas Tinbergen constructed a marvelous demonstration of this, using two male sticklebacks that had built breeding nests at opposite ends of an aquarium. Tinbergen used two glass cylinders to trap the sticklebacks and move them around the aquarium. Let's call them Red and Blue. When he brought Red and Blue together in their cylinders at the center of the tank, they reacted with equal hostility to each other. But when he moved them toward Red's nest, their behavior began to change. Red tried to attack, and Blue tried to retreat. When he moved them to the vicinity of Blue's nest, their roles reversed: Blue tried to attack, and Red tried to retreat. (This, by the way, also demonstrates the 'territorial' fallacy; the sticklebacks are clearly not contesting *water*.) This is the element that territoriality adds to the strategy typically followed by conspecifics in conflict: 'If you're the resident, attack; if you're the intruder, withdraw.' If you have a dog or a cat, you will have seen this strategy enacted many times in the vicinity of your home."

"Yes—but speaking of cats and dogs raises a question about animals and territoriality. Cats and dogs will often insist on going back to an old home even after their human family has moved on to a new one."

Ishmael nodded. "You're absolutely right, Julie. I wasn't thinking about domesticated animals when I made those remarks. Domesticated animals display a very human attitude toward territory, and of course this is largely what makes them domesticated. The very term *to domesticate* means 'to attach or accustom to a home.' If they're abandoned and allowed to run wild, however, you'll see them quickly shed this attachment-to-home as utterly unworkable for them in the feral state."

"Yeah, I see that," I said.

"Let's get back to Calliope and the Awks," Ishmael said. "As it happens, some five million years have passed since our last visit, and important climatic changes have taken place. The unbroken forest canopy that once sheltered the Awks is gone, but it didn't disappear so quickly that the Awks were unable to adapt to the changes this brought about. What we see now is a species that lives on the ground rather than in the trees, and since they really constitute a distinct species, we should give them a new name. Let's call them Bawks. These Bawks are no longer able to elude predators by scattering nimbly into the forest canopy the way their ancestors did. Back then it was every animal for itself, and that worked perfectly. But now they must stand together and defend themselves as a troop, and an individual that takes off on its own is very probably going to be the very one that is picked off by a predator.

"The Bawks' ancestors ate whatever came to hand in the trees—fruits, nuts, leaves, and a wide variety of insects. They weren't quite nimble enough to catch adult birds, but unguarded nestlings were a favored treat. As they were gradually forced down out of the trees in search of food, they continued to eat whatever came to hand, but conditions were very different on the ground. To begin with, food didn't just fall into their hands the way it used to. And on the ground they had many more competitors for what was available. They had to become more adventurous eaters. Many of their competitors were perfectly good to eat, but they were also harder to catch, because Bawks were not nearly as nimble on the ground as they had been in the trees. The Bawks gradually developed something to compensate for their individual lack of speed, and that was the teamwork that would make them successful hunters—something their ancestors had never needed to be.

"The nature of competition among them has changed. Although individuals still compete with other individuals for resources, each individual's overall success also depends on cooperating with other individuals to assure the success of the troop. As I've mentioned, Awks just scattered into the forest canopy when attacked, but Bawks aren't fast enough on the ground to do that. They have to stand together and fight as a team. Awks were strictly individual foragers, which worked perfectly well in the trees, but Bawks, confined to the ground, have better success foraging in teams. Now we see that the state of competition isn't primarily individual against individual but rather troop against troop. Nevertheless, although the competitive unit has changed, the strategies are the same: 'If your troop is the resident, attack; if it's the intruder, retreat. If neither troop is resident or intruder, follow a mixed strategy. Threaten the other troop, and if it retreats, fine. But if it threatens back, then attack sometimes and back down sometimes. Or if threatened yourselves, threaten back sometimes and retreat sometimes.' These strategies enable troops of Bawks to live side by side without either overrunning each other or being overrun. At the same time they can compete for the resources they need without having to fight to the death for every little thing."

"Yes, I see," said I, bravely keeping up my end of things.

"We now leave Calliope and return five million years later. After doing a little exploring, we discover that the Bawks are still thriving, but one branch of them has evolved into a new species that we'll call Cawks. I won't try to theorize about what pressure prompted this evolutionary development. It should be enough for us that it has occurred. Cawks in most ways seem closer to Bawks than Bawks did to Awks, which you'll remember lived in trees, foraged as individuals, and scattered when attacked. Cawks are like Bawks in that they live on the ground, forage in teams, and fight shoulder to shoulder when attacked. Cawks have simply taken these tendencies a giant step forward. These are cultural beings. This means that the parents of every generation transmit to their children what they learned from their own parents, together with anything new they learn during their lifetime. What they transmit is an accumulation of material from various periods in their past. For example, every child learns that the branch of a certain tree can be stripped of leaves and used as a sort of fishing pole to gather ants from a nest. This technique dates back three or four million years. Every child learns how to cure the hide of an animal so that it can be used for strapping or clothing, and this technique is two or three million years old. Every child learns how to fabricate twine from the bark of a tree, how to start a fire, how to turn a stone into a cutting tool, how to make a spear and a spear thrower, and these techniques are all a million years old. Thousands of arts and techniques—of various ages—are transmitted from one generation to the next.

"Although the Cawks live in groups like their predecessors, the Bawks, it wouldn't be correct to call them troops, because troops are basically the same from one to another. The Cawks live in tribes—the Jays, the Kays, the Ells, the Emms, the Enns, and so on—each very different from all the others. Each tribe has its own distinctive cultural collection that it passes on from one generation to the next, along with the various techniques I mentioned a moment ago, which are the common heritage of all Awks. The tribal heritage includes songs, stories, myths, and customs that may be tens of thousands of years old or even hundreds of thousands of years old. When we come upon them in the present moment, these are not literate peoples, and even if they were, their records wouldn't go back tens of thousands of years. If you ask them how old these things are, they'd only be able to say that no one knows. These are things that, as far as they're concerned, go back to the dawn of time. As far as the Jays know, they've literally been around forever. The same is true of the Kays, the Ells, the Emms, and all the rest.

"There are certain differences between tribe and tribe that seem rather arbitrary. One tribe likes basket-weave pots, another likes corded pots. One tribe likes weavings that are primarily black and white, another likes more colorful weavings. But there are other differences that seem much more crucial. In one tribe, lineage is reckoned through the mother;

in another, it's reckoned through the father. In one tribe, elders have a special voice in tribal affairs; in another tribe, all adults have an equal voice. One tribe operates under hereditary rule, another has a chief who rules until he's bested in single combat. Among the Emms, your key relatives are your mother and your uncles on your mother's side, and your father is of no special importance. Among the Ells, men and women never cohabit as husbands and wives; men live together in one longhouse, and women live together in another. One tribe practices polyandry (many husbands), another polygyny (many wives). And so on and on.

"Even more important than all these things are tribal laws, which have only one thing in common: They're not lists of things that are prohibited but rather procedures for handling problems that inevitably arise in communal life. What do you do when someone is constantly disrupting the peace with his or her bad temper? What do you do when a spouse has been unfaithful? What do you do when someone has injured or killed another tribal member? Unlike the laws you know, Julie, these laws were never formulated by any committee. Rather, they grew up among the tribal members the way strategies for competition grew up—by a steady winnowing out of what didn't work, of what didn't accomplish what people wanted—over tens of thousands of years. In a very real sense, the Ells *are* the laws of the Ells. Or even better, the laws of each tribe represent the *will* of the tribe. Their laws make utter sense to them in the context of their entire culture. The laws of the Ells wouldn't make sense to the Emms, but what difference does that make? The Emms have their own laws, which make utter sense to them, though they're clearly very different from those of the Ells or anyone else.

"It will be hard for you to imagine such a thing, but the laws of each tribe are completely sufficient for them. Because they've been formulated over the entire lifetime of the tribe, thousands of years, it's almost inconceivable that some situation could arise that has never been faced before. Nothing is more important for each generation than to receive the law in its entirety. By becoming Enns or Emms, the youth of each generation are imbued with the will of the tribe. The tribal laws represent what it *means* to be an Ell or a Kay. These are not your laws, Julie, which are largely useless, widely ignored and despised, and forever subject to change. These are laws that do what laws are supposed to do, year after year, generation after generation, age after age."

"Well," I said, "that sounds great, I guess, but it also sounds sort of stagnant. To be honest."

Ishmael nodded. "Of course I want you to be honest, Julie. Always. Remember, however, that in every case these laws represent the will of the tribe, not the will of some outsider. No one forces them to embrace these laws. No court will send them to jail if they scrap their heritage. They're perfectly free to abandon it anytime they want to."

"Okay."

"Only one thing remains to be done before we quit for the day, and that is to examine competition among the Cawks. The patterns that have evolved among them are very similar to those that prevail among the Bawks. Within the tribe, what works best for every individual is to support and defend the tribe; even though each tribal member needs the same resources, his or her best way to get them is to cooperate with other tribal members. As with the Bawks, whose competition is troop against troop, competition among the Cawks is tribe against tribe. In this area we notice that a new strategy is in play in addition to the ones we're familiar with. This might be described as a strategy of erratic retaliation: 'Give as good as you get, but don't be too predictable.'

"In practice, *give as good as you get* means that if the

Emms aren't bothering you, don't bother them, but if the Emms *do* bother you, then be sure to return the favor. *Don't be too predictable* means that even if the Emms aren't bothering you, it will be no bad thing if you make a hostile move against them from time to time. They will of course retaliate, giving as good as they get, but this is just a price to be paid for letting them know that you're there and haven't gotten soft. Then, once the score is even between you, you can get together for a big reconciliation party to celebrate your undying friendship and do some matchmaking (because, of course, it doesn't do to breed endlessly within a single tribe).

"Although the strategy of the 'Erratic Retaliator' may sound rather combative, it's actually a peacekeeping strategy. Think of two people who are quarreling over whether to go to a movie or to a play. Instead of settling the argument with blows, they flip a coin, agreeing beforehand that they'll go to a movie if it's heads and to a play if it's tails. The same purpose is served by agreeing to attack if you're the resident and to flee if you're the intruder. Combat is avoided if both parties follow the same strategy. Even so, if you spend a year observing the Jays, the Kays, the Ells, the Emms, the Enns, the Ohhs, and so on, what you see is that they seem to be in a state of more or less constant but very low-level warfare with each other. I don't mean daily or even monthly warfare, though there will be border skirmishes as frequently as that. I mean that every tribe exists in a state of perpetual readiness. And once or twice a year every tribe will initiate a raid against one or more of its neighbors. To a person of your culture, this will seem puzzling. A person of your culture will want to know when the Cawks are at last going to settle their differences and learn to live in peace. And the answer is that the Cawks will settle their differences and learn to live in peace as soon as mountain sheep settle their differences and learn to live in peace and as soon as sticklebacks settle their differences and learn to live in peace and as soon as elephant seals settle their differences and learn to live in peace. In other words, the competitive strategies practiced among the Cawks mustn't be viewed as disorders, as character defects, as 'problems' to be solved, any more than the competitive strategies of white-footed mice, wolves, or elk are these things. Far from being defects to be eliminated, they are what is left over when all other strategies are eliminated. In short, they're evolutionarily stable. They work for the Cawks. They've been tested for millions of years, and every other strategy tested against them has been eliminated as a failure."

"Whew," I said. "That sounds like a climax."

"It is," Ishmael said. "One last point and we'll call it a day. Why do the Enns just retaliate to attacks from their neighbors and occasionally initiate an attack of their own? Why don't they just go ahead and annihilate their neighbors?"

"Why would they do that?"

Ishmael shook his head. "That's not the right question, Julie. It doesn't matter why they'd do it. The question is, why wouldn't it work? Or maybe it *would* work. Maybe it would work better than the other strategy. This time, instead of just raiding the Emms, the Jays go in there and wipe them out."

"That changes the game entirely," I said.

"Go on."

"That would be like agreeing to flip a coin and then refusing to abide by the call."

"Why is that, Julie?"

"Because Emms *can't* retaliate if you wipe them out. The game is, 'You know I'll retaliate if you attack me, and I know you'll retaliate if I attack you.' But if I wipe you out, then you can't retaliate. The game's off."

"That's right, but then what, Julie? Let's suppose the Jays

have annihilated the Emms. What are the Kays, the Ells, the Enns, and the Ohhs going to think about this?"

The light dawned at last. "I see where you're going now," I told him. "They're going to say, 'If the Jays are going to start annihilating opponents, then we've got to adopt a new strategy toward them. We can't afford to treat them as though they're still playing Erratic Retaliator, because they're not. We have to treat them as though they're playing Annihilator, otherwise they may just annihilate *us*.' "

"And how do they have to treat them if they're playing Annihilator?"

"I'd say it would depend. If the Jays go back to playing Erratic Retaliator, then they could probably just let it be. But if the Jays continue to play Annihilator, then the survivors are going to have to join forces against the Jays and annihilate *them*."

Ishmael nodded. "This is what the Native Americans did when the European settlers finally made it completely clear that they were never going to play anything but Annihilator with them. The Native Americans tried to put aside old intertribal grudges and join forces against the settlers—but they waited too long."

InTermission

Between sessions at Room 105 I feel like I should present a musical interlude or share some Deep Thoughts or something so folks can get up and stretch, visit the bathroom, and get a snack. I have to admit that Alan handled this sort of thing really well in his book, but he's a professional, right? He *should* handle it well. The best I can do is tap-dance around for ten or twenty seconds.

No, the truth is, I'm a little bit lazy. I don't want to think about what was happening to me in the forty-eight hours that passed between the session I've just described and the next.

No, that's not right. The real truth is, I don't want anyone to *know* what was happening to me. It was too important.

Ishmael was turning me inside out and upside down, and I couldn't share that with anyone. Still can't. Sorry.

I also admire the way Alan made every new visit into an event. As best as I can remember, however, the next time I went to Room 105, I just walked in and sat down, and Ishmael glanced up and shot me a questioning look.

I looked back and said politely, "Is that celery?"

He frowned down at the stalk in his hand. "It *is* celery," he replied solemnly.

"I think of celery as something served at bridge parties, spread with tuna salad."

Ishmael pondered this for a moment, then said, "I think of celery as something eaten by gorillas when they come across it growing in the wild, as they do from time to time. You didn't *invent* it, you know."

And that was the way we started *that* session.

When the hilarity died down, I said, "I'm not sure what I'm supposed to make out of your story about the Awks, the Bawks, and the Cawks. Shall I tell you what I *think* I'm supposed to make out of it?"

"Please do."

"The Cawks are a model of humans as they were living here ten thousand years ago."

Ishmael nodded. "And as they're living still, where the people of your culture haven't gotten around to destroying them."

"Okay. But why go through the business of Awks, Bawks, and Cawks?"

"I'll explain my reasoning and perhaps it'll make sense. The competitive strategy followed among tribal peoples as we know them today is roughly the one of erratic retaliation I attributed to the Cawks: 'Give as good as you get, but don't be too predictable.' What is observed among them is exactly what I described as observed among the Cawks: Every tribe lives in a state of perpetual readiness—and in a state of more or less constant but very low-level warfare with their neighbors. When Taker peoples—people of your culture—encounter them, they naturally aren't curious to know why they live this way or whether it makes sense in any frame of reference or whether it works for them. They simply say, 'This is not a nice way to live and we won't tolerate it.' It would never occur to them to try to stop white-footed mice from living the way they live or to stop mountain goats from living the way they live or to stop elephant seals from living the way they live, but they naturally consider themselves experts on the way humans ought to live."

"That's right," I said.

"The next question to be considered is, how long have tribal peoples been living this way? Here is the answer. There's no reason to suppose that this way of living is a novelty for tribal peoples—any more than there is to suppose that hibernation is a novelty for bears or that migration is a novelty for birds or that dam building is a novelty for beavers. On the contrary, what we see in the competitive strategy of tribal peoples is an evolutionarily stable strategy that developed over hundreds of thousands of years and perhaps even millions of years. I don't know how this strategy developed in fact. I offer instead a theoretical narrative about how it *might* have developed. The final state of the strategy is not in doubt, but how it *became* the final state may never be more than a conjecture. Does that help?"

"Yes, it does. But tell me again where we are on the main road."

"Here's where we are. When you go among tribal peoples, you'll find that they don't look into the heavens to find out how to live. They don't need an angel or a spaceman to enlighten them. They *know* how to live. Their laws and their customs give them a completely detailed and satisfactory guide. When I say this, I don't mean that the Akoa Pygmies of Africa think they know how all human beings should live or that the Ninivak Islanders of Alaska think they know how all human beings should live or that the Bindibu of Australia think they know how all human beings should live. Nothing of the kind. All they know is that they have a way that suits them completely. The idea that there might be some universally right way for everyone in the world to live would strike them as ludicrous."

"Okay," I said, "but where does that leave us?"

"It leaves us still on the main road, Julie. We're trying to find out why the people of your culture are different from these tribal peoples, who look to themselves to find out how to live. We're trying to find out how this knowledge came to be so difficult to obtain among the people of your culture, why they have to look to gods and angels and prophets and spacemen and spirits of the dead to find out how to live."

"Right. Okay."

"I should warn you that people will tell you that the impression I've given you of tribal peoples is a romanticized one. These people believe that Mother Culture speaks the undoubted truth when she teaches that humans are innately flawed and utterly doomed to misery. They're sure that there must be all sorts of things wrong with every tribal way of life, and of course they're correct—if you mean by 'wrong' something *you* don't like. There are things in every one of the cultures I've mentioned that you would find distasteful or immoral or repugnant. But the fact remains that whenever anthropologists encounter tribal peoples, they encounter people who show no signs of discontent, who do not complain of being miserable or ill-treated, who are not seething with rage, who are not perpetually struggling with depression, anxiety, and alienation.

"The people who imagine that I'm idealizing this life fail

to understand that every single extant tribal culture is extant because it has survived for thousands of years, and it has survived for thousands of years because its members are content with it. It may well be that tribal societies occasionally developed in ways that were intolerable to their members, but if so, these societies disappeared, for the very simple reason that people had no compelling reason to support them. There's only one way you can force people to accept an intolerable lifestyle."

"Yeah," I said. "You have to lock up the food."

The FerTile CrescenT

We're ready now for the third and last telling of the story, Julie, which is set this time in the Fertile Crescent ten thousand years ago. This was by no means an empty area of the world—I mean, empty of human habitation. In those days the Fertile Crescent was a garden spot, not the desert it is today, and humans had lived there for a hundred thousand years at least. Like modern hunter-gatherers, these people were all practicing agriculture to some extent, in the sense that they made a practice of encouraging the regrowth of their favorite foods. As on Terpsichore, each people had its own approach to agriculture. Some spent only minutes a week at it. Others liked having more of their favorite foods around, so they spent a couple of hours a week at it. Still others saw no reason why they shouldn't live mostly on their favorite foods, so they spent an hour or two a day at it. You'll recall that, in the story of Terpsichore, I called all these people Leavers. We may as well retain this name for their earthly counterparts, because they too thought of themselves as living in the hands of the gods and leaving everything to them.

"Eventually, just as on Terpsichore, one group of Leavers said to themselves, 'Why should we just live *partially* on the foods we favor? Why don't we live *entirely* on the foods we favor? All we have to do is devote a lot more time to planting, weeding, animal husbandry, and so on.' So this one particular group took to working in their fields several hours a day. Their decision to become full-time farmers needn't have been made in a single generation. It may have developed slowly over dozens of generations or it may have developed quickly over just three or four generations. Both scenarios can be written in a way that seems plausible. But, slowly or quickly, there was a tribal people of the Fertile Crescent who assuredly became full-time farmers. Now I want you to tell me how it stands with these various peoples."

"How do you mean?"

"When you were here last, we spent a lot of time examining intraspecies competition—various strategies that allow competitors to resolve conflicts without engaging in mortal combat over every little thing. For example, the territorial strategy says, 'Attack if you're the resident, run away if you're the intruder.' "

"Yes, I see that."

"So: Tell me how it stands with these peoples in the Fertile Crescent."

"I assume they've been playing Erratic Retaliator. 'Give as good as you get, but don't be too predictable.' "

"That's right. As I've pointed out, there's no reason at all to think that tribal people were living differently ten thousand years ago from the way they live today. They kept themselves combat-ready at all times, gave as good as they got, and occasionally instigated a little mischief of their own, just so no one would be tempted to take them for granted. Now the fact you live entirely by farming doesn't in itself render this strategy unworkable. There were full-time agriculturalists in the New World who got along just fine following this strategy—neither overrunning their neighbors nor being overrun by them. But at some point in the Near East ten thousand years ago, one group of full-time farmers did begin to overrun their neighbors.

"When I say they overran their neighbors, I mean they did to their neighbors what their European descendants eventually did to the native peoples of the New World. When European settlers began to arrive here, the natives were of course still following the Erratic Retaliator strategy. This had worked for them from the beginning of time, and they were careful to follow it with the newcomers, who were baffled by it, to say the least. Just when they got things nicely sorted out—as they thought!—the natives would suddenly lash out in brutal and unprovoked attacks (just as they were used to doing among themselves). This made perfect sense to the natives, and it actually worked very well for them for quite a long time. The white settlers learned to be very, very respectful of the natives' unpredictability. But eventually, of course, the settlers' numbers grew to the extent that they were able to override the native strategy. In some cases they moved in and absorbed the natives. In other cases they moved in and drove the natives out to live or die elsewhere. And in still other cases they just moved in and exterminated them. But in every case, they annihilated them as tribal entities. The Takers were not at all interested in being surrounded by tribal peoples playing Erratic Retaliator—in the New World or in the Fertile Crescent. You can see why."

I agreed that I could.

"Last time you were here, you worked out what would happen if one tribe of Erratic Retaliators suddenly started playing Annihilator. Do you remember?"

"Yes. Their neighbors would eventually join forces to stop them."

"That's right, and ordinarily this would work perfectly well. Why didn't it work against the Takers in the Fertile Crescent?"

"I assume it didn't work there for the same reason it didn't work here in the New World. The Takers were able to generate unlimited supplies of the stuff that wins wars. This made them unbeatable by tribal peoples, even working together."

"Yes, that's right. New circumstances can undermine any strategy, even if it's worked flawlessly for a million years, and a tribe with virtually unlimited agricultural resources playing Annihilator was certainly something new. The Takers were irresistible, and this led them to imagine themselves to be the agents of human destiny itself. It still does, of course."

"It sure does."

"What I want to look at now is the revolution in its fiftieth year. The Takers have overrun four tribes to the north of them, called, let's say, the Hullas, the Puala, the Cario, and the Albas. The Puala made most of their living by agriculture even before they were overrun by the Takers, so the change has been least stressful for them. The Hullas, by contrast, were hunter-gatherers who did only a minimum of what we would call agriculture. The Albas had been herder-collectors for some time. And the Cario had maintained a few staple crops that they supplemented by hunting and gathering. Before being overrun by the Takers, these tribes had coexisted in the usual way, giving as good as they got and occasionally initiating raids on one another. Just to be sure you haven't forgotten, what is this Erratic Retaliator strategy in aid of?"

"In aid of?"

"Why do they have it? Why do they need any strategy at all?"

"They're competitors. This strategy keeps them on an even footing with each other."

"But the Takers put an end to the Erratic Retaliator game among them, because the program here is that the Hullas, the Puala, the Cario, and the Albas are now going to be Takers. That's the way people are meant to live, isn't it?"

"Yes."

"So the Erratic Retaliator strategy is out the window for these peoples."

"Right."

"But what keeps them on an even footing with each other now?"

"Wow," I said. "That's a good question. . . . Maybe they don't have anything to compete over?"

Ishmael nodded enthusiastically. "That's a terribly interesting idea, Julie. How would that come about, do you suppose?"

"Well, they're sort of all on the same side now."

"In other words, perhaps tribalism was actually the *cause* of competition, rather than an evolved way of *handling* competition. With the disappearance of discrete tribes, competition just melts away, and peace on earth ensues."

I told him I didn't know about the peace-on-earth part.

"Let's say you're the Cario. It's been a dry summer, Julie, and your neighbors to the north, the Hullas, have dammed a stream you use to irrigate your crops. Since you're all on the same side now, do you just shrug and let your crops wither?"

"No."

"So evidently being all on the same side doesn't put an end to intraspecies competition after all. What do you do?"

"I guess I'd ask the Hullas to dismantle their dam."

"Certainly. And they say no thanks. They've dammed the stream in order to irrigate their own crops."

"Maybe they could sort of share the water."

"They say they don't care to. They need all the water they can get."

"I could appeal to their sense of fair play."

A heavy wheezing sound reached me through the glass and I looked up to see Ishmael enjoying a good laugh. When he was finished, he said, "I trust you're making a joke."

"That's right."

"Good. So what are you going to do about the dammed stream, Julie?"

"I guess we're going to go to war."

"That is, of course, a possibility."

"Something occurs to me, though. It seems to me that the Cario and the Hullas could have had this conflict before they became Takers."

"Absolutely possible," Ishmael said. "What was it I said the Hullas were before becoming full-time farmers? With your excellent memory, I'm sure you remember."

"They were hunter-gatherers."

"Why would hunter-gatherers dam a stream, Julie? They have no crops to irrigate."

"True, but, just for the sake of argument, let's say they were farmers."

"All right. But, as I recall, the Cario were only partly dependent on farming. Losing a stream wouldn't threaten their way of life."

"True also," I said, "but again, just for the sake of the argument, let's say they were full-time farmers."

"Very well. Then the Cario are going to engage in some very brutal and very erratic retaliation. In the face of this, the Hullas will have to decide if damming the stream is worthwhile to them."

"So it's war in either case," I told him. "Becoming Takers didn't make any difference."

Ishmael shook his head. "A moment ago you said that, speaking for the Cario, you were going to have to 'go to war' over the dammed stream. Is 'going to war' the same as retaliation?"

"No, I suppose it isn't."

"What's the difference, as you see it?"

"Retaliation is giving as good as you get, going to war is conquering people to make them do what you want."

"So, even though it's possible to say that it's 'war in either case,' it's different kinds of war, with different objectives. The object of retaliation is to show people that you can be nice or nasty, depending on whether *they're* nice or nasty. The object of going to war is to conquer them and bend them to your will. Very different things, and erratic retaliation was about the former, not the latter."

"Yes, I suppose that's true."

Ishmael was silent for a moment, then he asked if I saw erratic retaliation at work anywhere among the Takers of today. After thinking about it for a while, I told him I saw it at work in juvenile-gang warfare.

"That's very astute, Julie. Erratic retaliation is precisely the strategy they employ as a means of maintaining an equal footing among themselves. And what do the people of your culture want to do with juvenile gangs?"

"They want to suppress them, for sure. Do away with them."

"Naturally," Ishmael said, nodding. "But there are some other highly visible combatants pursuing a strategy of erratic retaliation right now, aren't there?"

"Oh," I said, "yeah, I guess so. You mean all those crazy people in Bosnia."

"That's right. And what do the people of your culture want to do with them?"

"They want to make them stop fighting."

"They want to make them stop acting like Erratic Retaliators."

"Exactly."

" 'Going to war' is acceptable to you, but erratic retaliation is not, and it never has been. Right from the beginning, the Takers have been unalterably hostile to this tribal strategy. I suspect it's because erratic retaliation is fundamentally self-controlling and fundamentally unsusceptible to outside management. And Takers don't trust anything that's self-controlling. They want to manage it all and can't stand having anything going on around them that is outside their control."

"Very true. But are you saying we should leave them alone to fight it out?"

"Not at all, Julie. You should know by now that I don't pretend to know what people 'should' do. Erratic retaliation isn't 'good' and the suppression of it 'evil.' What's happening in that part of the world is merely the latest calamity in a calamitous history that can't be made right by any means whatever."

"Yeah, that's the way it seems," I said.

"While we're momentarily off the track, I'd like to point out that we're in a position to observe something new here. I've shown you that competition among members of the same species is necessarily more comprehensive than competition among members of different species. Cardinals compete more comprehensively with other cardinals than they do with blue jays or sparrows, and humans compete more comprehensively with other humans than they do with bears or badgers."

"Yes."

"Now you're in a position to see that competition among peoples with the same lifestyle is necessarily more comprehensive than competition among peoples with different lifestyles. Farmers compete more comprehensively with other farmers than they do with hunter-gatherers."

"Wow, that's true," I said. "So that by creating a world full of farmers, we've heightened the level of competition to the max."

"This is indeed the situation among the Hullas, the Puala, the Cario, and the Albas, Julie. There was plenty of competition among them even when they were living in different ways. Now they're all living the same way, and so (far from having eliminated competition) they must compete even more intensely."

"Yes, I see that."

"In our examination of competitive strategies, we've seen that their effect is to make it possible for competitors to live side by side without having to engage in mortal combat over every little thing. The Hullas, the Puala, the Cario, and the Albas can no longer live side by side by playing Erratic Retaliator. That strategy has been thrown out. Without it, in the matter of the dammed stream, your only idea so far is: 'Let's go to war.' In other words, let's go straight to mortal combat. But I'm sure you can see that it's not going to work for the Hullas, the Puala, the Cario, and the Albas to go to war over every little thing."

"Right."

"The peacekeeping strategy of the past was 'Give as good as you get, but don't be too predictable.' The Takers discarded that. What did they come up with to replace it?"

I struggled with it for a few minutes and finally said, "I guess I have to say that what the Takers came up with was themselves. They made themselves the peacekeepers."

"They did indeed, Julie. They appointed themselves the

administrators of chaos, and they've been at it ever since, improvising generation after generation with varying degrees of success. They took the keeping of the peace into their hands at the beginning of their revolution, and it's been there ever since. When they arrived in the New World, no one was keeping the peace here, as you know. Rather, the peace was being kept in the traditional way, by people giving as good as they got and remaining unpredictable. The Takers put a stop to all that, and now the keeping of the peace is in their capable hands. Crime is a multibillion-dollar industry, children deal drugs on street corners, and maddened citizens vent their rage on each other with assault weapons."

The Crescent, Part II

Before the Hullas, the Puala, the Albas, and the Cario were overrun by the Takers, each tribe had its own way of dealing with things, the gift of tens of thousands of years of cultural experience. The Hulla way was not the Puala way, the Puala way was not the Alba way, and the Alba way was not the Cario way. The only thing these ways had in common was that they *worked*—the Hulla way for the Hullas, the Puala way for the Puala, the Alba way for the Albas, and the Cario way for the Cario.

"What was vitally important for all these peoples was to have ways of dealing with humans as they are. They didn't think of humans as flawed beings, but this doesn't mean that they thought of them as angels. They knew very well that humans are capable of being troublesome, disruptive, selfish, mean, cruel, greedy, violent, and so on. Humans are nothing if not passionate and inconsistent, and it doesn't take a giant intellect to figure this out. A system that works for tens of thousands of years is not going to be a system that works only for people who are invariably agreeable, helpful, selfless, generous, kind, and gentle. A system that works for tens of thousands of years is going to be a system that works for people who are always *capable* of being troublesome, disruptive, selfish, greedy, cruel, and violent. Does this make sense to you?"

"It makes perfect sense."

"Among tribal peoples, you don't find laws that *forbid* disruptive behavior. To the tribal mind, this would be supremely inane. Instead, you find laws that serve to minimize the damage of disruptive behavior. For example, no tribal people would ever frame a law forbidding adultery. Instead, what you find are laws that set forth what must happen when adultery occurs. The law prescribes steps that minimize the damage done by this act of infidelity, which has injured not only the spouse but the community itself by cheapening marriage in the eyes of the children. Again, the objective is not to punish but to make right, to promote healing, so that as far as possible, everything can return to normal. The same would be true of assault. To the tribal mind, it's futile to say to people, 'You must never fight.' What is not futile is to know exactly what must be done for the best when there's been a fight, so that everyone sustains the least damage possible. I want you to see how very different this is from the effect of your own laws, which, instead of reducing damage, actually magnify and multiply damage all across the social landscape, destroying families, ruining lives, and leaving victims to heal their own wounds."

"I do see it," I told him.

"As I think is clear from what I've said so far, there was one imperative that was common to all tribes: *Attack other tribes, defend each other.* In other words, despite all internal squabbles and vendettas, it was the tribe against the world. If you're a Hulla, it's fine to attack Cario or Puala, but attacking other Hullas is not the idea. If you're a Cario, it's fine to attack Hullas or Puala, but attacking other Cario is not the idea. Do you see why this must be so?"

"I think so. If Cario law encouraged the Cario to attack each other, then the Cario would eventually disappear as a tribe. And if Cario law prohibited Cario from attacking Hullas or Puala, then the Erratic Retaliator strategy would be out the window, and the Cario would also eventually disappear as a tribe."

"Exactly. At the beginning of your revolution, your own tribe, which I've called the Takers, was exactly like the Hullas, the Puala, the Albas, and the Cario—and indeed all the tens of thousands of others that were extant in the world at that time. I mean that they had a way of living that worked well for them and a set of laws that enabled them to deal effectively with disruptive behavior in their midst. What do you suppose happened to that original way of living that worked well for the Takers?"

"I can't imagine," I said.

"We'll have to see if we can imagine it together, Julie. Here's one thing we can be sure of: Nothing in the tribal way of the Takers prepared them for the responsibility they undertook when they overran their neighbors at the beginning of the revolution."

"How can you know that?"

"Tribal culture showed people how to cope with things that had been happening from the beginning of time. It didn't show people how to cope with things that had never happened before in the entire history of the world—and your revolution was just such a thing. People had been competing and conflicting from the beginning of time. They knew how to hold their own by playing the Erratic Retaliator strategy. But now one tribe, under an impetus never felt before among humans, was ready to wield a kind of power that had never been wielded before. Their population expanding in front of an abundance of food, the Takers were no longer interested in merely holding their own against their neighbors. They had more people to feed, needed more land, and had the power to overrun their neighbors—assimilating them, running them off, or exterminating them (it didn't matter which). But once they'd overrun their neighbors, they were in uncharted territory. What were they to do with them? They were certainly not going to go back to playing Erratic Retaliator with them. That would have made no sense at all. And they were also not going to allow them to go on playing Erratic Retaliator among themselves. That too would make no sense. Do you see why?"

"Yes, I think so. Erratic retaliation is a way of maintaining your independence on an equal footing with your neighbors. The Takers were against that. They didn't want the Hullas and the Puala and the Cario to be independent entities, constantly fighting among themselves."

"What was the old Taker law about fighting? I mean the law they followed before the revolution." Seeing my blank look, he added, "This is the law all tribal people follow in common about fighting."

"Oh. You mean 'Fight your neighbors, not yourselves.' "

"That's right. This was the law that was being followed by every tribe in the Fertile Crescent, every tribe in the Near East, and every tribe in the world."

"I've got that," I told him.

"But when the Takers began to overrun their neighbors, they had to create a new law. They didn't want the tribes they overran to go on fighting each other."

"I've got that too."

"So what was the new law, Julie?"

"The new law had to be 'Don't fight *anybody*.' "

"Of course. And as you pointed out a minute ago, this meant that the Erratic Retaliator strategy went out the window—and tribal independence went out with it. The Takers wanted to administer a world where people worked, not a world where people wasted energy playing Erratic Retaliator."

"Yes, that's obvious."

"The old tribal boundaries were meaningless now—geographically and culturally—not only for the Hullas, the Puala, the Cario, and the Alba, but for the Takers themselves. The Takers didn't bring to the new mix their old tribal ways. These would have been meaningless to the others. All the old tribal ways were equally meaningless in the new world order being built by the Takers. It was pointless for the Hullas to teach their children what had worked for Hullas for tens of thousands of years, because they were no longer Hullas. It was pointless for the Cario to teach their children what had worked for Cario for tens of thousands of years, because they were no longer Cario.

"But though they belonged to a new world order, people didn't stop being troublesome, disruptive, selfish, cruel, greedy, and violent, did they? The same old behavior continued—but without tribal law to moderate its effects. Even if the old tribal laws were remembered, the Takers would find them impossible to administer. The Hulla way of dealing with disruptive behavior might be fine for Hullas, but it wouldn't be acceptable to the Cario. I'm sure you can see that."

"Yes."

"So how are the Takers going to deal with disruptive behavior among the people they rule? What are they going to do about adultery, assault, rape, thievery, murder, and so on?"

"They're going to outlaw them."

"Of course. Under the tribal order, outlawing things was

never the idea. Instead, the laws of each tribe served to mini-mize the damage and put people back together. Tribal laws didn't say, 'Such things must *never* happen,' because they knew for an absolute fact that such things *will* happen. Rather, they said, 'When such things happen, here's what must be done in order to put things right as far as they can be put right.' "

"I understand."

"We're near the end here, Julie. There's only one last thing to see. To the tribal mind, it's asinine to formulate a law that you *know* is going to be disobeyed. To formulate a law that you *know* is going to be disobeyed is to bring the whole concept of law into disrepute. A prime example of a law that you *know* is going to be disobeyed is a law in the form *thou shalt not.* It doesn't matter what you follow those words with. Thou shalt not kill, thou shalt not lie, thou shalt not commit adultery, thou shalt not steal, thou shalt not in-jure—every single one of these is a law that you *know* is going to be disobeyed. Because tribal peoples didn't waste time with laws they knew would be disobeyed, disobedience was not a problem for them. Tribal law didn't outlaw mis-chief, it spelled out ways to *undo* mischief, so people were glad to obey it. The law did something good for them, so why would they break it? But from the very beginning Taker law was a body of laws that you *knew* would be bro-ken—and (not surprisingly) they've been broken day in and day out for ten thousand years."

"Yes. That's amazing—an amazing way to look at it."

"And because your laws were formulated with the under-standing that they would be broken from the very first day, you had to have a way of dealing with lawbreakers."

"Yes. Lawbreakers had to be punished."

"That's right. What else can you do with them? Having saddled yourselves with laws that you *assume* will be broken, you've never found anything to do that makes better sense than punishing people for doing exactly what you expected them to do in the first place. For ten thousand years you've been making and multiplying laws that you fully expect to be broken, until now I suppose you must have literally millions of them, many of them broken millions of times a day. Do you personally know a single person who isn't a law-breaker?"

"No."

"I'm sure that even at your age you've broken dozens."

"Hundreds," I said confidently.

"The very officials you elect to uphold the laws break them. And at the same time your pillars of society somehow find it possible to become indignant over the fact that some people have little respect for the law."

"It *is* amazing," I told him.

"The destruction of tribal law and the Erratic Retaliator strategy was not something that could have happened gradually, over hundreds or thousands of years. It had to begin immediately, at the site of the very first Taker encroachment. Tribal law and the Erratic Retaliator strategy were barricades that had to come down right at the outset. Whatever their real names were, the Hullas, the Cario, the Albas, and the Puala had to disappear as tribal entities. Within a few decades the surrounding tribes had to fall in the same way, willingly or unwillingly exchanging tribal independence for Taker power. The revolution spread outward from this center, like a circle of fire burning away a cultural heritage that reached all the way back to your primate origins.

"The memory of having been Hullas, Cario, Albas, and Puala didn't vanish in a single generation, of course, but neither did it plausibly survive for more than four or five generations—but say even ten generations and this is only two centuries. At the end of a thousand years here at the

center, the descendants of the Hullas, Cario, Albas, and Puala wouldn't even remember that such a thing as the tribal
life had ever existed. It would obviously still be remembered
at the perimeter of Taker expansion, but by now that perimeter enclosed Persia, Anatolia, Syria, Palestine, and Egypt. A
thousand years later that perimeter would extend well into
the Far East, Russia, and Europe. Tribal peoples were still
being encountered and engulfed at the perimeter of Taker
expansion, but this was eight thousand years ago, Julie.

"The revolutionary heartland was still the Near East and
indeed the Fertile Crescent. Mesopotamia, the land between
the Tigris and Euphrates, was the New York City of this era.
Here your culture's most powerful innovation (after totali-
tarian agriculture and locking up the food) was just being
tinkered with—writing. But another five thousand years
would pass before the logographers of classical Greece began
to think of using this tool to make a record of the human
past. When they did at last begin to record the human past,
this is the picture that began to emerge: *The human race was
born just a few thousand years ago in the vicinity of the Fertile
Crescent. It was born dependent on crops, and planted them as
instinctively as bees build hives. It also had an instinct for civilization. So, as soon as it was born, the human race began planting
crops and building civilization.* There was, of course, utterly
no memory left of humanity's tribal past, extending back
hundreds of thousands of years. That had disappeared without a trace in what one of my pupils whimsically (but quite
usefully) calls the Great Forgetting.

"For hundreds of thousands of years, people as smart as
you had had a way of life that worked well for them. The
descendants of these people can today still be found here and
there, and wherever they're found in an untouched state,
they give every evidence of being perfectly content with their
way of life. They're not at war with each other, generation
against generation or class against class. They're not plagued

by anguish, anxiety, depression, self-hatred, crime, madness, alcoholism, and drug addiction. They don't complain of oppression and injustice. They don't describe their lives as meaningless and empty. They're not seething with hatred and rage. They don't look into the sky, yearning for contact with gods and angels and prophets and alien spacemen and spirits of the dead. And they don't wish someone would come along and tell them how to live. This is because they already know how to live, as ten thousand years ago humans everywhere knew how to live. But knowing how to live was something the people of your culture had to destroy in order to make themselves the rulers of the world.

"They were sure they'd be able to replace what they destroyed with something just as good, and they've been at it ever since, trying one thing after another, giving the people anything they can think of that might fill the void. Archaeology and history tell a tale five thousand years long of one Taker society after another groping for something to placate and inspire, something to amuse and distract, something to make people forget a misery that for some strange reason simply will not go away. Festivals, revels, pageants, temple solemnities, pomp and circumstance, bread and circuses, the ever-present hope of attaining power, riches, and luxury, games, dramas, contests, sports, wars, crusades, political intrigue, knightly quests, world exploration, honors, titles, alcohol, drugs, gambling, prostitution, opera, theater, the arts, government, politics, careers, political advantage, mountain climbing, radio, television, movies, show business, video games, computers, the information superhighway, money, pornography, the conquest of space—something here for everyone, surely, something to make life seem worth living, something to fill the vacancy, something to inspire and console. And of course it did fill the vacancy for many of you. But only a fraction of you could hope to attain the good things that were available at any one time, as today only a small percentage of you can hope to live like people who must (surely must!) have a life worth living—billionaires and movie stars and sports heroes and supermodels. Always the vast majority of you have been relative have-nots. Is this expression familiar to you?"

"Have-nots? Yes."

"The tribal life wasn't an arrangement of haves and have-nots. Why would people put up with such an arrangement unless they were forced to? And until you put food under lock and key, there was no way to force people to put up with it. But the Taker life has always been an arrangement of haves and have-nots. The have-nots have always been the majority, and how were they supposed to discover the source of their misery? Who were they going to ask to explain why the world is ordered as it is, in a way that favors a handful, leaving the vast majority toiling just in order to be hungry, naked, and homeless? Were they going to ask their rulers? Their slave masters? Their bosses? Certainly not.

"About twenty-five hundred years ago, four distinct explanatory theories began to evolve. Probably the oldest theory was this, that the world is the work of two eternally warring gods, one a god of goodness and light, the other a god of evil and darkness. Certainly this made sense of a world that seemed to be forever divided between those who live in the light and those who live in the darkness; this theory was embodied in Zoroastrianism, Manichaeism, and other religions. Another theory had it that the world was the work of a community of gods who, absorbed in their own affairs, ran it to suit themselves, and when humans came into it, they might be befriended, used, destroyed, ravished, or ignored, entirely at the gods' whim; this, of course, was the theory embraced by classical Greece and Rome. Another theory had it that suffering is intrinsic to life, that it's the inevitable fate of those who live, and that peace can only be attained by those who relinquish desire of every kind. This was the theory given to the world by Gautama Buddha. Another theory had it that the very first man, Adam, living back there in Mesopotamia a few thousand years ago, had disobeyed God, fallen from grace, and been driven from paradise to live forevermore by the sweat of his brow, miserable, alienated from God, and prone to sin. Christianity built on this Hebraic base, providing a messiah who taught that in the Kingdom of God the first will be last and the last first—meaning that the haves and the have-nots will change places. During Christ's lifetime and in the decades following, most thought the Kingdom of God would be an earthly kingdom ruled by God directly. When this failed to materialize, however, it came to be understood that the Kingdom of God was heaven, accessible only after death. Islam too built on the Hebraic base, rejecting Jesus as a messiah but affirming that good works will be rewarded in the afterlife.

"But, as you well know, these theories have never entirely satisfied you, especially in recent centuries, and perhaps even more especially in recent decades, when the vast emptiness at the center of your lives swallows down an endless outpouring of religions, spiritual fads, gurus, prophets, cults, therapies, and mystical healings—without ever being satisfied."

"That's for sure," I told him.

Ishmael gave me a long, somber look. "Perhaps you now understand why so many people of your culture look into the sky, yearning for contact with gods and angels and prophets and alien spacemen and spirits of the dead. Perhaps you now understand why so many people in your culture have daydreams like the one you described to me during your first visit."

"I do understand it."

"Now you know where the main road leads. Though of course it doesn't end here."

"Well, I'm glad to hear *that* at least," I said.

A Goddamned Pride Thing

I hope you know I have a million questions," I told him when I arrived on Saturday, two days later.

"I expected a few, yes," Ishmael said.

"A lot of people, hearing what you've taught me so far, would say, 'Oh my God, then there's no hope at all for us!' "

"Why is that?"

"Well, we can't go back to living in caves, can we?"

"Very few tribal peoples lived in caves, Julie."

"You know what I mean. We can't go back to living *tribally*."

Ishmael frowned. "Actually, I'm not sure that *is* what you mean."

"Okay. What I mean is, we can't go back and start over.

We can't go back to living the way we lived before we became Takers."

"But what do you mean by that, Julie? Do you mean that
you can't go back to living in a way that works for people?"

"No. I guess I mean we can't go back to being hunter-
gatherers."

"Of course you can't. Have you ever heard me make such
a proposal? Have you heard me make even the slightest
beginning of the slightest hint of such a proposal?"

"No."

"And you never will. A dozen planets this size couldn't
accommodate the six billion of you as hunter-gatherers. The
idea is completely absurd."

"Then what?" I asked.

"You've forgotten what you came to me for, Julie. You
came to me to learn how people elsewhere in the universe
manage to live without devouring their worlds."

"That's right."

"Now you know how that's done, don't you? You just
didn't have to board a spaceship to learn it. The aliens you
were seeking were merely your own ancestors, who managed
very nicely to live here for hundreds of thousands of years
without devouring the world—your ancestors and their cultural descendants, tribal peoples who are still extant here
today. What's confusing you is that you imagine I've shown
you what the answers are, when in fact I've shown you only
where to *look* for answers. You think I'm saying, 'Adopt the
Hulla lifestyle,' when in fact I'm saying, 'Understand why
the Hulla lifestyle *worked*—and continues to work as well as
ever wherever it still exists.' As Takers, you've been struggling for ten thousand years to *invent* a lifestyle that works,
and have failed utterly so far. You've invented millions of
things that *have* worked—airplanes and toasters and computers and pipe organs and steamships and videocassette re-

corders and clocks and atom bombs and carousels and water pumps and electric lights and toenail clippers and ballpoint pens—but a lifestyle that works has always eluded you. And the more people you have, the more manifest, widespread, and painful this failure becomes. You're having a hard time building enough prisons to hold all your criminals. The nuclear family is staggering into oblivion. The incidence of drug addiction, suicide, mental illness, divorce, child abuse, rape, and serial murder continues to climb.

"The fact that you've never been able to invent a lifestyle that works isn't surprising. From the first, you underestimated the difficulty of such a task. Why *did* the tribal lifestyle work, Julie? I don't mean the mechanism, I mean how did it come about that such a lifestyle worked?"

"I guess it worked because it was tested from the time when people began. What worked survived, and what didn't work didn't survive."

"Of course. It worked because it was subject to the same evolutionary process that produced workable lifestyles for chimpanzees and lions and deer and bees and beavers. You can't just slap something together and expect it to work as well as a system that has been tested and refined for three million years."

"Yes, I can see that now."

"But, oddly enough, almost any of your improvisations would have worked *if* . . ."

"If what?"

"That's what I want *you* to answer, Julie. I think you can do this. The Mesopotamian empire would have worked under the code of Hammurabi *if* . . . what? The Eighteenth Dynasty of Egypt would have worked under the inspired religious leadership of Akhenaton *if* . . . what? Judah and Israel would have worked under the rule of the kings *if* . . . what? The vast Persian empire would have worked when Alexander swept across it *if* . . . what? The even more extensive Roman empire would have worked under the Pax Romana of Augustus Caesar *if* . . . what? I won't go through it all era by era, improvisation by improvisation. The world you know best, the United States of America, under what is presumably the most enlightened constitution in human history would work *if* . . . what?"

"If people were better."

"Of course. All of this would work beautifully, Julie, if people would just be better than people have ever been. You'd be just one big happy family, if only you would be better than people have ever been. The warring factions in the Balkans would hug and make up. Saddam Hussein would dismantle his war machine and enter a monastery. Crime would disappear overnight. No one would break any law. You could dispense with courts, police, prisons. Everyone would abandon self-interest and work together to improve the lot of the poor and to rid the world of hunger, racism, hatred, and injustice. I could spend hours listing all the wonderful things that would happen . . . if only people would just be better than people have ever been."

"Yeah, I'm sure of that."

"This was the tremendous strength of the tribal way, that its success didn't depend on people being better. It worked for people the way they are—unimproved, unenlightened, troublesome, disruptive, selfish, mean, cruel, greedy, and violent. And that triumph the Takers have never come close to matching. In fact, they never even made the attempt. Instead, they counted on being able to *improve* people, as if they were badly designed products. They counted on being able to punish them into being better, on being able to inspire them into being better, on being able to educate them into being better. And after ten thousand years of trying to improve people— without a trace of success—they wouldn't dream of turning their attention elsewhere."

"No, that's true. I'm pretty sure that most people, hearing

what I've heard here, would still say, 'Yes, well, that's all well and good, but we really do have an obligation to go on trying to make people better. They *can* be made better. We just haven't quite figured out how to do it yet.' Or they'd say, 'It's still something to work for. Just think how much *worse* people would be if we weren't constantly trying to make them better.'"

"I'm afraid you're right, Julie."

"Even so," I said, "I still feel stuck. What are we supposed to *do* with this? You're not expecting us to reinstate the Erratic Retaliator strategy, are you?"

Ishmael glared at me for a solid two minutes, but I wasn't intimidated. I knew he wasn't displeased with me, he was just working on something. When he finally had it worked out to his satisfaction, he went on to tell another of his stories.

"From time out of mind, a wooden bridge connected two peoples who had been allies from ancient times. It was built over a river that at every other point was too wide to be bridged. The spot seemed to have been designed for just this use, for a massive rock shelf presented itself as an abutment on each side of the river. After many centuries, however, it was felt that something more advanced than a wooden bridge was needed to join the two countries, and a team of engineers drew up plans for a metal bridge to replace it. This bridge was duly built, but after a few decades quite suddenly collapsed. Studying the wreckage, another panel of engineers decided that the evident metal fatigue they saw was a sign that an inferior grade of steel had been used by the builders. The bridge was rebuilt, using the best materials available, but it collapsed again after just forty years. Another panel of engineers convened to study the problem, and this time they focused on the original building plans, which they considered to be flawed in several fundamental ways. They drew up another set of plans, and the new bridge went up—and collapsed again, this time after only thirty years.

"Up till now, they'd been working with a continuous beam bridge supported by two pier foundations in the river. They decided to replace this with a multiple-span beam bridge, which they felt sure would fix the problem. When it too failed after just thirty years, they decided to try building a half-through arch bridge. This seemed like an improvement, so when it failed after forty years, they tried building a full-through arch bridge. This lasted only twenty-five years, so they next tried a deck arch bridge, then a portal bridge, each of which collapsed after only twenty-five years.

"The builders of the original wooden bridge had been gone for centuries, of course, but there was in that land a student of their works who now came forward to explain why the engineers' metal bridges were proving to be so short-lived. 'The traffic on the bridge naturally causes the metal to vibrate,' he said. 'That's only to be expected. This vibration is transmitted to the rocks you're using as abutments, a thing which, again, is only to be expected. What is not to be expected is the powerful resonance that this vibration wakens in these particular rocks. This resonance, carried back to the bridge by the metal, is what's causing them to disintegrate so quickly. The original bridge, being made of wood, transmitted almost no vibration to the rocks, so no answering resonance was created in them. This is why the original bridge lasted so long, and why it would actually still be here and working as well as ever if you hadn't torn it down.'

"Needless to say, the engineers were less than delighted to have this explanation. Far from expressing gratitude to their informant, they said: 'Well, what are you proposing we do about this? Are you suggesting that we should go back to building this bridge out of *wood*?'"

Ishmael gave me a long, inquiring look, which I returned for a couple of minutes as I thought about this. Finally I said, "Well, *wasn't* he suggesting that they go back to building the bridge out of wood?"

"Certainly not, Julie. He was trying to supply the missing piece of the puzzle that was baffling these engineers, so that they could begin to think productively. I should add, by the way, that real-life engineers would be very unlikely to go on building bridge after bridge in this feebleminded way. Nor would they react to this new information the way these engineers did. On the contrary, I'd expect real-life engineers to be positively inspired by this information, the lack of which had blocked all possibility of success. This information opens up to exploration all sorts of avenues that never would have been explored otherwise."

"I can see that. I guess I don't see what avenues of exploration you've opened up for *me*—or as you keep saying, for the people of my culture."

Ishmael pondered this for a while, then said, "Suppose, Julie, that we'd been able to take the galactic journey you daydreamed about. And suppose we found a planet where people very similar to you had a very satisfying and sustainable lifestyle that had worked for them for hundreds of thousands of years. And suppose we were able to throw a lasso around this planet and drag it back here to earth, where any and all of you would be free to study it to your heart's content and at your leisure. Would you look at this and still see nothing to explore?"

"No."

"Please explain the difference to me."

"I guess I just don't want to live the way people lived ten thousand years ago."

His right eyebrow shot up. "Forgive me if I stare, Julie. You've been so rational up to now."

"I'm not being irrational, I'm just being honest."

He shook his head. "You're turning down a suggestion that has never been made to you, Julie—and that's hardly rational. I've never asked you to live the way people lived ten thousand years ago. I've never even hinted at such a thing. If I told you that biochemists at a Jesuit university had discovered a cure for cancer, would you reject it on the grounds that you don't want to become a Roman Catholic?"

"No."

"Then again, please explain the difference to me."

"I don't see that what you're talking about is anything like a cure for cancer."

He studied me gravely for a few moments, then said, "Maybe you should go spend an hour studying wallpaper or whatever it is you do when you need a break."

I jumped up out of the chair and stomped to the back of the room to glare at the books in Ishmael's sagging old bookcase. I even opened a couple volumes hoping some brilliant quote would leap off the page at me, but nothing leaped. After ten minutes I went back and sat down.

"It's some sort of goddamned pride thing," I told him.

"Go on."

"If we had a planet hitched up next door that was inhabited by members of an alien race—I started to say *advanced* alien race—that would be one thing. It would be *tolerable* if they knew something we don't know. What is *not* tolerable is to have these goddamned *savages* know something we don't know."

"I understand, Julie. At least I think I do. But here's what you must understand. We're not exploring here what these people *knew.* You could sit down and talk to every tribal person on this planet about tribal life, and not one of them would spontaneously articulate the Erratic Retaliator strategy for you. But once you articulate it for *them,* they will of course recognize it immediately and will probably say something like, 'Well, we all know *that.* We didn't say it because it's just too obvious to need saying'—and I agree. It took one of the great scientific minds of all time to articulate the fact that unsupported objects fall toward the center of the earth, something any normal five-year-old knows—or would certainly imagine he knew if you pointed it out to him."

"I'm not quite sure what point you're making."

"I'm not quite sure either, Julie, to be honest. You'll have to be patient as I grope for answers that will satisfy you. . . . Scientists of many different kinds are interested in bioluminescence—the production of light by living creatures—but none of them is trying to find out what these creatures *know* about producing light. What they *know* about producing light is beside the point. Not long ago we studied a behavior that enables white-footed mice to be successful. But we weren't trying to find out what white-footed mice *know* about being successful. Is that clear?"

"Yes."

"The same applies to our study here. We're not interested in what Leavers *know* about living, any more than we're interested in what bioluminescent creatures know about light. Their knowledge is not our study. Their *success* is our study."

"Okay. I see that. What I don't see is how their success has anything to do with *us*."

Ishmael nodded. "This is precisely why it's never been studied by you, Julie. It's never seemed relevant to study people whose only accomplishment was to live on a planet for three million years without devouring it. But as you approach a point of no return in your plunge toward extinction, this study will soon seem very relevant indeed."

"Yeah, I see what you mean. Sort of."

"It's well known that the Vikings visited the New World five hundred years before Columbus did. But the Vikings' contemporaries weren't electrified by their discovery, because it was irrelevant to them. You could have proclaimed it from every housetop, and people would have been puzzled to know why you bothered. But when Columbus made his discovery five hundred years later, *his* contemporaries were electrified. The discovery of a new continent was now very relevant indeed. Until now, Julie, I've been like Leif Eriksson tromping around alone on a vast, marvelous continent that absolutely no one cares about and no one wants to hear about. This continent has been open and available for study by your philosophers, your educators, your economists, your political scientists for more than a century, but not one of them has given it more than a bored look. Its existence inspires in them nothing but yawns. But I sense that things are beginning to change. Your appearance here in this room is a sign of that change—and as you recall, I nearly missed it myself. I sense that more and more of you are becoming alarmed about your headlong plunge toward catastrophe. I sense that more and more of you are casting about for new ideas."

"Yeah. But unfortunately more and more of us are also casting about for more and more exotic forms of hoogy-moogy."

"That's only to be expected, Julie. What you're experiencing is tantamount to cultural collapse. For ten thousand years you've believed that you have the one right way for people to live. But for the last three decades or so, that belief has become more and more untenable with every passing year. You may think it odd that this is so, but it's the men of your culture who are being hit the hardest by the failure of your cultural mythology. They have (and have always had) a much greater investment in the righteousness of your revolution. In coming years, as the signs of collapse become more and more unmistakable, you'll see them withdraw ever more completely into the surrogate world of male success, the world of sports. And, much worse, you'll see them taking ever more violent revenge for their disappointment on the world around them—and particularly on the women around them."

"Why on women?"

"The Taker dream has always been a man's dream, Julie, and the men of your culture imagine that the collapse of this dream will devastate them while leaving women relatively untouched."

"And won't it?"

Ishmael thought for a moment before answering. "The inmates of the Taker prison build the prison anew for themselves in every generation, Julie. Your mother and father did their part and are doing it still. You personally, as you dutifully go to school and prepare to take your place in the world of work, are even now engaged in building the prison for your own generation to occupy. When it's all done, it'll be the work of all of you, men and women alike. Even so, the women of your culture have never been as enthusiastic about prison life as the men—have rarely gotten as much out of it as men have."

"Are you saying that men run the prison?"

"No. As long as the food remains under lock and key, the prison runs itself. The governing that you see is the prisoners governing themselves. They're allowed to do that and to live as they please within the prison. For the most part, the prisoners have chosen to be governed by men—or allowed themselves to be governed by men—but these men don't run the prison itself."

"What's the prison then?"

"The prison is your culture, which you sustain generation after generation. You yourself are learning from your parents how to be a prisoner. Your parents learned from their parents how to be a prisoner. Their parents learned from their parents how to be a prisoner. And so on, back to the beginning in the Fertile Crescent ten thousand years ago."

"How do we stop that?"

"By learning something different, Julie. By refusing to teach your children how to be prisoners. By breaking the pattern. This is why, when people ask me what they should do, I tell them, 'Teach others what you've learned here.' All too often, however, they reply by saying, 'Yes, that's fine, but what should we *do*?' When six billion of you refuse to teach your children how to be prisoners of Taker culture, this awful dream of yours will be over—in a single generation. It can only continue for as long as you perpetuate it. Your culture has no independent existence—no existence outside of you—and if you cease to perpetuate it, then it will vanish. Must vanish, like a flame with nothing to feed on."

"Yeah, but what would happen then? You can't just stop teaching your children *anything,* can you?"

"Of course not, Julie. You can't just stop teaching them anything. Rather, you must teach them something *new.* And if you're going to teach them something new, then of course you must first learn something new yourself. And that's what you're here to do."

"I get it," I said.

School Daze

I do realize, Julie, that I have to show you how to explore this new continent that I've led you to."

"I'm glad to hear that," I told him.

"Perhaps you'd like to hear how I first began to explore it myself."

"I'd like that very much."

"Last Sunday I mentioned the name Rachel Sokolow as the person who made it possible for me to maintain this establishment. You don't need to know how this came about, but I knew Rachel from infancy—was in communication with her as you and I are in communication. I'd had no experience of your educational system when Rachel started school. Not having any reason to, I'd never given it even a passing thought. Like most five-year-olds, she was thrilled to be going off to school at last, and I was thrilled for her, imagining (as she did) that some truly wonderful experience must be awaiting her. It was only after several months that I began to notice that her excitement was fading—and continued to fade month after month and year after year, until, by the time she was in the third grade she was thoroughly bored and glad for any opportunity to miss a day of school. Does this all come as strange news to you?"

"Yeah," I said with a bitter laugh. "Only about eighty million kids went to bed last night praying for six feet of snow to fall so the schools would have to close."

"Through Rachel, I became a student of your educational system. In effect, I went to school with her. Most of the adults in your society seem to have forgotten what went on when they were in school as small children. If, as adults, they were forced to see it all again through the eyes of their children, I think they'd be astounded and horrified."

"Yeah, I think so too."

"What one sees first is how far short real schooling falls from the ideal of 'young minds being awakened.' Teachers for the most part would be delighted to awaken young minds, but the system within which they must work fundamentally frustrates that desire by insisting that all minds must be opened in the same order, using the same tools, and at the same pace, on a certain schedule. The teacher is charged with getting the class as a whole to a certain predetermined point in the curriculum by a certain predetermined time, and the individuals that make up the class soon learn how to help the teacher with this task. This is, in a sense, the first thing they must learn. Some learn it quickly and easily and others learn it slowly and painfully, but all eventually learn it. Do you have any idea what I'm talking about?"

"I think so."

"What have you personally learned to do to help teachers with their task?"

"Don't ask questions."

"Expand on that a bit, Julie."

"If you raise your hand and say, 'Gee, Ms. Smith, I haven't understood a single word you've said all day,' Ms. Smith is going to hate you. If you raise your hand and say, 'Gee, Ms. Smith, I haven't understood a single word you've said all week,' Ms. Smith is going to hate you five times as much. And if you raise your hand and say, 'Gee, Ms. Smith, I haven't understood a single word you've said all year,' Ms. Smith is going to pull out a gun and shoot you."

"So the idea is to give the impression that you understand everything, whether you do or not."

"That's right. The last thing the teacher wants to hear is that you haven't understood something."

"But you began by giving me the rule against asking questions. You haven't really addressed that."

"Don't ask questions means . . . don't bring up things just because you wonder about them. I mean, like, suppose you're studying tidal forces. You don't raise your hand to ask if it's true that crazy people tend to be crazier during the full moon. I can imagine doing something like that in kindergarten, but by the time you're my age, that would be taboo. On the other hand, some teachers like to be distracted by certain kinds of questions. If they've got a hobbyhorse, they'll always accept an invitation to ride it, and kids pick up on that right away."

"Why would you want to have the teacher riding a hobbyhorse?"

"Because it's better than listening to him explain how a bill passes Congress."

"How else do you help teachers with their task?"

"Never disagree. Never point out inconsistencies. Never ask questions that go beyond what's being taught. Never let on that you're lost. Always try to look like you're getting every word. It all comes to pretty much the same thing."

"I understand," Ishmael said. "Again, I stress that this is a defect of the system itself and not of the teachers, whose overriding obligation is to 'get through the material.' You understand that, in spite of all this, yours is the most advanced educational system in the world. It works very badly, but it's still the most advanced there is."

"Yeah, that's what I understand. I wish you'd smirk or something to show when you're being ironical."

"I'm not sure I could even manage such an expression, Julie. . . . To return to my story, I watched Rachel being marched through the grades (and I should add that she went to a very expensive private school—the most advanced of the advanced). As I did so I began to put what I was seeing together with what I already knew of the workings of your culture and what I already knew of the working of those cultures that you are so far in advance of. At this point, I had developed none of the theories you've heard here so far. In societies you consider primitive, youngsters 'graduate' from childhood at age thirteen or fourteen, and by this age have basically learned all they need in order to function as adults in their community. They've learned so much, in fact, that if the rest of the community were simply to vanish overnight, they'd be able to survive without the least difficulty. They'd know how to make the tools needed for hunting and fishing. They'd know how to shelter and clothe themselves. At age thirteen or fourteen, their survival value is one hundred percent. I assume you know what I mean by that."

"Of course."

"In your vastly more advanced system, youngsters graduate from your school system at age eighteen, and their survival value is virtually zero. If the rest of the community were to vanish overnight and they were left entirely to their own resources, they'd have to be very lucky to survive at all.

Without tools—and without even tools for *making* tools, they wouldn't be able to hunt or fish very effectively (if at all). And most wouldn't have any idea what wild-growing plants are edible. They wouldn't know how to clothe themselves or build a shelter."

"That's right."

"When the youngsters of your culture graduate from school (unless their families continue to take care of them), they must immediately find someone to give them money to buy the things they need in order to survive. In other words, they have to find jobs. You should be able to explain why this is so."

I nodded. "Because the food is under lock and key."

"Precisely. I want you to see the connection between these two things. *Because* they have no survival value on their own, they *must* get jobs. This isn't something that's optional for them, unless they're independently wealthy. It's either get a job or go hungry."

"Yeah, I see that."

"I'm sure you realize that adults in your society are forever saying that your schools are doing a terrible job. They're the most advanced in the history of the world, but they're still doing a terrible job. How do your schools fall short of what people expect of them, Julie?"

"God, I don't know. This isn't something that interests me very much. I just tune out when people start talking about stuff like that."

"Come on, Julie. You don't have to listen very hard to know this."

I groaned. "Test scores are lousy. The schools don't prepare people for jobs. The schools don't prepare people to have a good life. I suppose some people would say that the schools *should* give us some survival value. We *should* be able to be successful when we graduate."

"That's what your schools are there for, isn't it? They're

there to prepare children to have a successful life in your society."

"That's right."

Ishmael nodded. "This is what Mother Culture teaches, Julie. It's truly one of her most elegant deceptions. Because of course this isn't at all what your schools are there for."

"What are they there for, then?"

"It took me several years to work it out. At that stage I wasn't used to uncovering these deceptions. This was my first attempt, and I was a little slow at it. The schools are there, Julie, to regulate the flow of young competitors into the job market."

"Wow," I said. "I see that."

"A hundred and fifty years ago, when the United States was still a largely agrarian society, there was no reason to keep young people off the job market past the age of eight or ten, and it was not uncommon for children to leave school at that age. Only a small minority went on to college to study for the professions. With increasing urbanization and industrialization, however, this began to change. By the end of the nineteenth century, eight years of schooling were becoming the rule rather than the exception. As urbanization and industrialization continued to accelerate through the 1920s and 1930s, twelve years of schooling became the rule. After World War Two, dropping out of school before the end of twelve years began to be strongly discouraged, and it was put about that an additional four years of college should no longer be considered something only for the elite. Everyone should go to college, at least for a couple of years. Yes?"

I was waving my hand in the air. "I have a question. It seems to me like urbanization and industrialization would have the opposite effect. Instead of keeping young people *off* the job market, the system would have been trying to put them *on* the job market."

Ishmael nodded. "Yes, on the surface that sounds plausible. But imagine what would happen here today if your educators suddenly decided that a high-school education was no longer needed."

I gave that a few seconds of consideration and said, "Yeah, I see what you mean. There would suddenly be twenty million kids out there competing for jobs that don't exist. The jobless rate would go through the roof."

"It would literally be catastrophic, Julie. You see, it's not only essential to keep these fourteen-to-eighteen-year-olds off the job market, it's also essential to keep them at home as non-wage-earning consumers."

"What does *that* mean?"

"This age group pulls an enormous amount of money—two hundred *billion* dollars a year, it's estimated—out of their parents' pockets to be spent on books, clothes, games, novelties, compact discs, and similar things that are designed *specifically* for them and no one else. Many enormous industries depend on teenage consumers. You must be aware of that."

"Yeah, I guess so. I just never thought of it in these terms."

"If these teenagers were suddenly expected to be wage earners and no longer at liberty to pull billions of dollars from their parents' pockets, these youth-oriented industries would vanish overnight, pitching more millions out onto the job market."

"I see what you mean. If fourteen-year-olds had to support themselves, they wouldn't be spending their money on Nike shoes, arcade games, and CDs."

"Fifty years ago, Julie, teenagers went to movies made for adults and wore clothing designed for adults. The music they listened to was not music written and performed for them, it was music written and performed for adults—*by* adults like

Cole Porter, Glenn Miller, and Benny Goodman. To be in on the first big postwar clothing fad, teenage girls scavenged their fathers' white business shirts. Such a thing would never happen today."

"That's for sure."

Ishmael fell silent for a few minutes. Then he said, "A while ago you mentioned listening to a teacher explain how a bill passes Congress. I assume you have in fact studied this in school."

"That's right. In civics."

"Do you actually know how a bill passes Congress?"

"I haven't a clue, Ishmael."

"Were you tested on it?"

"I'm sure I was."

"Did you pass?"

"Of course. I never fail tests."

"So you supposedly 'learned' how a bill passes Congress, passed a test on the subject, and promptly forgot all about it."

"That's right."

"Can you divide one fractional number by another?"

"I think so, yeah."

"Give me an example."

"Well, let's see. You've got half a pie and you want to divide it into thirds. Each piece will be a sixth."

"That's an example of multiplication, Julie. One-half times one-third equals one-sixth."

"Yeah, you're right."

"You studied division of fractional numbers in the fourth grade, probably."

"I remember it vaguely."

"Try again to see if you can think of an example in which you would divide one fractional number by another."

I gave it a shot and had to admit it was beyond me.

"If you divide half a pie by three, you get a sixth of a pie.

That's clear enough. If you divide half a pie by two, you get a fourth of a pie. If you divide half a pie by one, what do you get?"

I stared at him blankly.

"If you divide half a pie by one, you get half a pie, of course. Any number divided by one is that number."

"Right."

"So what do you get if you divide half a pie by a half?"

"Oh wow. One whole pie?"

"Of course. And what do you get if you divide half a pie by a third?"

"Three halves. I think. One and a half pies."

"That's right. In the fourth grade, you spent weeks trying to master this concept, but of course it's far too abstract for fourth graders. But presumably you passed the test."

"I'm sure I did."

"So you learned as much as you needed to pass the test, then promptly forgot all about it. Do you know why you forgot about it?"

"I forgot about it because, who cares?"

"Exactly. You forgot about it for the same reason that you forgot how a bill passes Congress, because you had no use for it in your life. In actual fact, people seldom remember things they have no use for."

"That's true."

"How much do you remember from what you learned in school last year?"

"Almost nothing, I'd say."

"Do you think you're different from your classmates in this regard?"

"Not at all."

"So most of you remember almost nothing from what you learn in school from one year to the next."

"That's right. Obviously we all know how to read and write and do simple arithmetic—or most of us do."

"Which pretty well proves the point, doesn't it. Reading, writing, and arithmetic are things you actually have use for in your lives."

"Yes, that's certainly true."

"Here's an interesting question for you, Julie. Do your teachers expect you to remember everything you learned last year?"

"No, I don't think so. They expect you to remember having *heard* about it. If the teacher says 'tidal forces,' she expects everyone to nod and say, 'Yeah, we studied those last year.' "

"Do you understand the operation of tidal forces, Julie?"

"Well, I know what they are. Why the oceans bulge out on both sides of the earth at the same time makes utterly no sense to me."

"But you didn't mention this to your teacher."

"Of course not. I think I got a 97 on the quiz. I remember the grade better than the subject."

"But now you're in a position to understand why you spend literally years of your life in school learning things you instantly forget once you've passed the test."

"I am?"

"You are. Give it a shot."

I gave it a shot. "They have to give us *something* to do during the years we're being kept off the job market. And they've got to make it look good. It's got to look like something r-e-e-e-a-l-l-y useful. They can't just let us smoke dope and rock 'n' roll for twelve years."

"Why not, Julie?"

"Because it wouldn't look right. The jig would be up. The secret would be out. Everyone would know we were just there to kill time."

"When you were listing things that people find wrong with your schools, you noted that they do a poor job of preparing people to get jobs. Why do you think they do such a poor job at this?"

"Why? I don't know. I'm not sure I even understand the question."

"I'm inviting you to think about this the way I would."

"Oh," I said. That was as far as I got for about three minutes. Then I admitted I didn't have any idea how to go about thinking about this the way he would.

"What do people think about this failure of the schools, Julie? This will give you a clue as to what Mother Culture teaches."

"People think the schools are incompetent. That's what I'd guess people think."

"Try to give me something you feel more confident in than a guess."

I worked on it for a while and said, "Kids are lazy, and the schools are incompetent and underfunded."

"Good. This is indeed what Mother Culture teaches. What would the schools do if they had more money?"

"If the schools had more money, they could get better teachers or pay teachers more, and I guess the theory is that the extra money would inspire teachers to do a better job."

"And what about the lazy kids?"

"Some of the more money would be spent buying new gadgets and better books and prettier wallpaper, and the kids would not be as lazy as before. Something like that."

"So let's suppose that these new and improved schools turn out new and improved graduates. What happens then?"

"I don't know. I guess they have an easier time getting jobs."

"Why, Julie?"

"Because they've got better skills. They know how to do things employers want."

"Excellent. So Johnny Smith isn't going to have to go to

work as a bagger in a grocery store, is he? He can apply for a job as an assistant manager."

"That's right."

"And that's wonderful, isn't it?"

"Yes, I'd think so."

"But you know, Johnny Smith's older brother graduated from school four years ago, before they were new and improved."

"So?"

"He too went to work for the grocery store. But of course, having no skills, he had to start as a bagger."

"Oh. Right."

"And now, after four years, he too wants to apply for that job as an assistant manager."

"Uh-oh," I said.

"And then there's Jennie Jones, another of your new and improved graduates. She doesn't have to take a job as a lowly administrative assistant at the accounting firm. She can go right in as office manager. And that's terrific, isn't it?"

"It is so far."

"But her mother went back into the workforce a few years ago, and having no skills, she had to start as a lowly administrative assistant at that accounting firm. Now she's ready to be promoted to office manager."

"Bad."

"How do you think people are going to like your new and improved schools that prepare graduates for good jobs?"

"They're not."

"Now do you know why schools do a poor job of preparing graduates for the workplace?"

"I sure do. Grads have to start at the bottom of the ladder."

"So you see that your schools are doing just what you *actually* want them to do. People *imagine* that they'd like to

see their children enter the workplace with really useful
business skills, but if they actually did so, they'd immediately
begin competing for jobs with their older siblings and their
parents, which would be catastrophic. And if graduates came
out of school with advanced skills, who would bag the groceries, Julie? Who would do the sweeping up? Who would
pump the gas? Who would do the filing? Who would flip
the burgers?"

"I suppose it would turn into an age thing."

"You mean you'd tell Johnny Smith and Jennie Jones that
they can't have the jobs they want, not because others are
more qualified but because others are older."

"That's right."

"Then what's the point of giving Johnny and Jennie skills
that would enable them to do these jobs?"

"I guess if they graduate with the skills, then at least
they'll have them when their time comes."

"Where did their older siblings and parents pick up these
skills?"

"On the job, I guess."

"You mean while bagging the groceries, sweeping up,
pumping the gas, doing the filing, and flipping the burgers."

"Yeah, I guess."

"And won't your improved graduates pick up the same
skills their older siblings and parents picked up by doing
these jobs?"

"Yes."

"Then what do they gain by learning them in advance,
since they'll be learning them on the job anyway?"

"I guess there's no advantage any which way," I said.

"Now let's see if you can figure out why your schools turn
out graduates with zero survival value."

"Okay . . . To begin with, Mother Culture says it would

be pointless to turn out graduates with a high survival value."

"Why is that, Julie?"

"Because they don't need it. Primitive people need it, sure, but not civilized people. It'd be a waste of time for people to learn how to survive on their own."

Ishmael told me to continue.

"I guess if you were conducting this conversation, you'd ask what would happen if we turned out a class of new and improved students with a hundred-percent survival value."

He nodded.

I sat there for a while working it through. "The first thing I thought of is that they'd go for jobs as wilderness guides or something. But that's completely stupid. The point is, if they had a hundred-percent survival value, they wouldn't need jobs *at all*."

"Go on."

"Locking up the food wouldn't keep them in the prison. They'd be *out*. They'd be *free!*"

Ishmael nodded again. "Of course a few of them would still elect to stay behind—but that would be a matter of choice. I daresay a Donald Trump or a George Bush or a Steven Spielberg wouldn't have any inclination to leave the Taker prison behind."

"I'll bet it would be more than a few. I'll bet half would stay."

"Go on. What would happen then?"

"Even if half stayed, the door would be open. People would come pouring out. A lot would stay in, but a lot would come out."

"You mean that, for a lot of you, getting a job and working until retirement age doesn't look like heaven."

"It sure doesn't," I said.

"So now you know why your schools turn out graduates with no survival value."

"That's right, I do. Since they don't have any survival value, they're forced to enter the Taker economy. Even if they'd rather opt out of that economy, they can't."

"Once again, the essential point to note is that, for all your complaining, your schools are doing just what you actually want them to do, which is to produce workers who have no choice but to enter your economic system, presorted into various grades. High-school graduates are generally destined for blue-collar jobs. They may be as intelligent and talented as college graduates, but they haven't demonstrated this by surviving a further four years of studies—studies that, for the most part, are no more useful in life than the studies of the previous twelve. Nonetheless, a college degree wins admittance to white-collar jobs that are generally off-limits to high-school graduates.

"What blue-collar and white-collar workers actually retain of their schooling doesn't much matter—in either their working lives or their private lives. Very, very few of them will ever be called upon to divide one fractional number by another, parse a sentence, dissect a frog, critique a poem, prove a theorem, discuss the economic policies of Jean-Baptiste Colbert, define the difference between Spenserian and Shakespearean sonnets, describe how a bill passes Congress, or explain why the oceans bulge on opposite sides of the world under the influence of tidal forces. Thus, if they graduate without being able to do these things, it really doesn't matter in the slightest. Postgraduate work is obviously different. Doctors, lawyers, scientists, scholars, and so on actually have to use in real life what they learn in graduate school, so for this small percentage of the population schooling actually does something besides keep them off the job market.

"Mother Culture's deception here is that schools exist to serve the needs of *people*. In fact, they exist to serve the needs of your economy. The schools turn out graduates who can't live without jobs but who have no job skills, and this suits your economic needs perfectly. What you're seeing at work in your schools isn't a system *defect,* it's a system *requirement,* and they meet that requirement with close to one hundred percent efficiency."

"Ishmael," I said, and our eyes met. "You worked this out all by yourself?"

"Yes, over several years, Julie. I'm a very slow thinker."

School Daze II

Ishmael asked if I'd watched any younger siblings grow up from infancy, and I told him no.

"Then you wouldn't know from experience that small children are the most powerful learning engines in the known universe. They effortlessly learn as many languages as are spoken in their households. No one has to sit them down in a classroom and drill them on grammar and vocabulary. They do no homework, they have no tests, no grades. Learning their native languages is no chore at all, because of course it's immensely and immediately useful and gratifying to them.

"Everything you learn during these early years is immensely and immediately useful and gratifying, even if it's only how to crawl or how to build a tower of blocks or how to bang a pot with a spoon or how to make your head buzz with a piercing screech. The learning of small children is limited only by what they're able to see, hear, smell, and get their hands on. This learning drive continues when they enter kindergarten, at least for a while. Do you remember the sort of things you learned in kindergarten?"

"No, I can't say that I do."

"These are things Rachel learned twenty years ago, but I doubt if they're any different nowadays. She learned the names of primary and secondary colors—red, blue, yellow, green, and so on. She learned the names of basic geometric shapes—square, circle, triangle. She learned how to tell time. She learned the days of the week. She learned to count. She learned the basic units of money—penny, nickel, dime, and so on. She learned the months and the seasons of the year. These are obviously things everyone would learn whether they studied them in school or not, but they're still somewhat useful and somewhat gratifying to know, so most children have no difficulty learning them in kindergarten. After re-viewing all this in grade one, Rachel went on to learn addi-tion and subtraction and to master beginning reading skills (though in fact she'd been reading since she was four years old at least). Again, children generally find these to be useful and gratifying studies. I don't intend to go through the entire curriculum in this way, however. The point I want to make is that, in grades K through three, most children master the skills that citizens need in order to get along in your culture, commonly characterized as the 'three R's'—reading, writing, and arithmetic. These are skills that, even at age seven and eight, children actually use and enjoy using. A hundred and fifty years ago this was the citizen's basic education. Grades four through twelve were added to the curriculum in order to keep youngsters off the job market, and the skills taught in these grades are the ones most students find to be neither useful in their lives nor gratifying to master. Addition, subtraction, multiplication, and division of fractional numbers exemplify these skills. No children at all (and very, very few adults) ever have occasion to use them, but they're available to be added to the curriculum, and so they have been. They take up months and months of time, and this is all to the good, since the whole point of the exercise is to take up the students' time. You've mentioned other subjects, like civics and earth sciences, which present plenty of opportunity for time-consuming activities. I remember that Rachel was required to memorize state capitals for some course or other. My favorite example of the tendency came to my notice when she was in the eighth grade. She actually learned to fill out a federal income-tax form, something she wouldn't need to do in actual life for at least five years, by which time she obviously would have forgotten the form, which would by then be substantially different anyway. And of course every child spends years studying history—national, state, and world, ancient, medieval, and modern—of which they retain about one percent."

I said, "I would have thought you would endorse the teaching of history."

"I do very much endorse it. I endorse the teaching of everything, because everything is what children want to know. What children very deeply want to know of history is *how things got to be this way*—but no one in your culture would think of teaching them that. Instead they're overwhelmed with ten million names, dates, and facts they 'should' know, but that vanish from their heads the moment they're no longer needed to pass a test. It's like handing a thousand-page medical text to a four-year-old who wants to know where babies come from."

"Yeah, that's absolutely true."

"You, here in these rooms, are learning the history that *matters* to you. Isn't that so?"

"Yes."

"Will you ever forget it?"

"No. Not possibly."

"Children will learn anything they *want* to learn. They'll fail at learning how to figure percentages in the classroom but will effortlessly learn how to figure batting averages (which are of course just percentages). They'll fail at learning science in the classroom but, working at their personal computers, will effortlessly defeat the most sophisticated computer security systems."

"True, true, true."

"If you monitor the right magazines, newspapers, or television programs, you'll see a report at least once a week of some new scheme or other designed to 'fix' your schools. What people mean by fixing the schools is making them work for people instead of just detaining them for twelve years, then releasing them unskilled onto the job market. In order to create something that works for people, the people of your culture think they have to invent something from scratch. It never occurs to them that they may be trying to reinvent the wheel. In case this expression is new to you, 'reinventing the wheel' means struggling very hard to duplicate a breakthrough that was actually made long ago.

"Among tribal peoples, the educational system works so well that it requires no effort on anyone's part, inflicts no hardship on learners, and produces graduates who are flawlessly educated to take their place in their particular society. To speak of it as a system will be misleading, however, if you expect to see huge buildings staffed by warders and their supervisors, under the direction of local and regional school boards. No such things exist. The system is completely invisible and immaterial, and if you were to ask a tribal people to explain it, they wouldn't even know what you were referring to. Education occurs among them constantly and effortlessly, which means they're no more aware of its functioning than they are of the functioning of gravity.

"Education occurs among them as constantly and effortlessly as education occurs in a household where there's a three-year-old. Unless you confine it to a crib or a playpen, there's simply no way to stop a three-year-old from learning. A three-year-old is a questing beast with a thousand arms probing everywhere. It must touch everything, smell everything, taste everything, turn everything upside down, see how it looks sailing through the air, see how it feels when swallowed or pressed into an ear. The four-year-old is no less thirsty for knowledge, but it no longer has to repeat the experiments of the three-year-old. It has already touched, smelled, tasted, turned upside down, flung, and swallowed everything it needs to. It's ready to move onward and outward—as is the five-year-old, the six-year-old, the seven-year-old, the eight-year-old, the nine-year-old, the ten-year-old, and so on. But it's not allowed to do this in your culture. This would be too messy. Starting with age five, the child must be restrained, confined, and compelled to learn not what it wants to learn but what your state legislators and curriculum writers agree it 'should' learn, in lockstep with all other children its age.

"Not so in tribal societies. In tribal societies, the three-year-old is free to explore the world around it as far as it likes, which is not as far as it will go when it's four, five, six, seven, or eight. There simply are no walls shutting the child in or out at any age, no doors closed against it. There is no age when it 'should' learn a given thing. Nor would anyone ever dream of giving thought to such a thing. Ultimately, all the things grown-ups do are fascinating to a child, and it eventually and inevitably wants to do them itself—not necessarily on the same day as every other child, nor in the same week or the same year. This process, Julie, isn't cultural, it's genetic. I mean that children don't *learn* to imitate their parents. How could such a thing be taught? It's *hardwired* into children to imitate their parents. They're *born* wanting to imitate them, in exactly the same way that ducks are born wanting to follow the first thing they see moving, which is usually their mother. And this hardwiring continues to operate within the child . . . until when, Julie?"

"What?"

"The child craves to learn how to do every single thing its parents do, but this craving eventually disappears. When?"

"Lord, how could I know that?"

"You know it perfectly well, Julie. This craving disappears with the onset of puberty."

"Wow," I said. "It sure does."

"The onset of puberty signals the end of the child's apprenticeship to its parents. It signals the end of childhood itself. Again, this isn't cultural, it's genetic. In tribal societies, the pubertal youth is understood to be ready for initiation into adulthood—and *must* be initiated into adulthood. You can no longer expect this person to want to imitate adults. That craving has vanished and that phase of life is over. In tribal societies, they make a ceremonial acknowledgment of this, so everyone is clear about it. 'Yesterday these people were children. Today they're adults. That's it.'

"The fact that this transformation is genetic is demonstrated by your own failure to abolish it through cultural means—legislation and education. In effect, you've passed a law extending childhood for an indefinite period and have redefined adulthood as a moral privilege that ultimately can only be self-awarded, on grounds that are far from clear. In tribal cultures, people are *made* adults just the way your presidents are made presidents, and they no more doubt that they're adults than George Bush doubts that he's the president. Most adults in your culture, however, are never absolutely sure when they've managed to cross the line—or even if they've *ever* managed to cross it."

"That seems to be true," I said. "I think all this has got to have something to do with gangs."

"Of course it does. You can work that out, I'm sure."

"I'd say that kids in gangs are rebelling against the law that extends childhood into an indefinite future."

"They are, but not consciously, of course. They simply find it intolerable to live under this law, intolerable to be asked to deny the genetic hardwiring that tells them they're adults. Of course, gangs flourish only in relatively disadvantaged groups. Other groups are well enough rewarded that they're willing to forgo adult privileges for a few more years. It's kids who are getting absolutely no reward for it—or at least no reward that they care about—who end up in gangs."

"Yeah, that's true."

"I've led us slightly off track here. I wanted to show you a model of education that works *for people*. It works very simply, without cost, without effort, without administration of any kind. Children simply go wherever they want and spend time with whomever they want in order to learn the things they want to learn when they actually want to learn them. Not every child's education is identical. Why on earth should it be? The idea is not that every child should receive the entire heritage but rather that every *generation* should receive it. And it is received, without fail; this is proved by the fact that the society continues to function, generation after generation, which it couldn't do if its heritage were not being transmitted faithfully and totally, generation after generation.

"Obviously many details are left behind from one generation to the next. Gossip isn't heritage. Events five hundred years old aren't remembered the way events fifty years old are remembered. Events fifty years old aren't remembered the way events last year are remembered. But everyone understands that anything not transmitted to the younger generation is simply lost, completely and irrevocably. But always the essential is transmitted, precisely because it *is* essential. For example, toolmaking skills that are needed on a daily basis can't possibly be lost—precisely because they're used on a daily basis, and children learn them as routinely as children of your culture learn to use telephones and remote controls. Present-day chimpanzees learn to prepare and use twigs to 'fish' for ants inside an anthill. Where the practice is found, it's transmitted unfailingly, generation after generation. The behavior isn't genetic, but the ability to *learn* it is genetic."

I told Ishmael that he seemed to be struggling very hard to say something that wasn't quite getting through to me. To my great surprise, he suddenly reached out for a stalk of celery that he bit into with a sound like a pistol shot. He munched for a moment before going on.

"Once upon a time a distinguished elder blue-winged teal by the name of Titi called a great conference of other distinguished elders to be held on the Isle of Wight in the English Channel. When they were at last gathered and settled down, one slightly less distinguished blue-winged teal by the name of Ooli stepped forward to make some introductory remarks.

" 'I'm sure you all know who Titi is,' he began, 'but in case you don't, I'll tell you. He is, without doubt, the greatest scientist of our age, and the world's foremost authority on avian migration, which he has studied longer and deeper than any other teal in history, blue-winged or otherwise. I don't know why he's called us together here at this time, but I don't doubt that his reasons are excellent.' And with that, Ooli turned the meeting over to Titi.

"Titi ruffled his feathers a bit to gather everyone's attention, then said, 'I've come here today to urge upon you a vitally important innovation in the rearing of our young.' Well, Titi certainly got everyone's attention with this announcement, and he was deluged with questions from teals who demanded to know what was supposed to be wrong with chick-rearing practices that had worked for blue-winged teals for more generations than any of them could count.

" 'I recognize and acknowledge your indignation,' Titi replied when he finally had them quieted down. 'But in order for you to understand my point, you'll have to recognize and acknowledge that I'm very different from you. As my old friend Ooli mentioned, I am the world's foremost authority on avian migration. This means I have a deep theoretical understanding of a process that you merely experience in an unthinking and routine manner. Very simply speaking, in the spring and fall of every year you experience a certain restlessness that is ultimately relieved by taking flight in one direction or the other over the English Channel. Isn't this so?'

"All his listeners had to agree that this was so, and Titi went on. 'I don't dispute the fact that your vague feelings of restlessness serve the essential purpose of getting you moving, but wouldn't you like to be able to see your children's lives guided by something more reliable than vague feelings of restlessness?'

"When he was asked to explain what he meant, he said, 'If you were making the sort of detailed observations that are made by scientists like me, you would know how amazingly often you dither about for a week or ten days, making one halfhearted start after another, flying this way and that, setting out as if you really meant to migrate, then turning back after five or ten or even twenty miles. You would know how many of you actually set out and make what amounts to the whole trip—flying in the wrong direction!'

"The teals in his audience waggled their wings in a nervous way and ruffled their feathers to hide their embarrassment. They knew that what Titi was saying was absolutely true (and indeed it *is* actually true—not only of teals but of migratory birds in general), but they were mortified to learn that this sloppy behavior had actually been *noticed* by someone. They asked what could be done to improve their performance.

" 'We must make our chicks aware of the elements of an ideal migrating schedule. We must prepare them to observe relevant conditions and to calculate the optimum moment to set out.'

" 'But it would seem that you, as a scientist, are already able to do that,' one of his listeners pointed out. 'Couldn't you just *tell* us when to migrate?'

" 'That would be supremely stupid,' Titi replied. 'There's no way I can be everywhere at once, making all the relevant calculations. You yourselves must make these calculations where you are, in reference to the specific conditions you individually face.'

"It's not easy to hear a teal groan in ordinary circumstances, but this flock of teals produced a mighty groan on hearing these words. But Titi went on, saying, 'Come, come, it's not as difficult as all that. You simply have to understand that migration becomes an advantage when the suitability of your present habitat is less than the suitability of the target habitat times what is known as the migration factor, which is just a measure of the extent to which the portion of your potential reproductive success that is under your active control would decrease as a result of this migration. I realize that this may sound like rather a beakful to you at the moment, but a few definitions and mathematical formulas will make it perfectly clear to you.'

"Well, these teals were mostly just ordinary birds, and they couldn't imagine opposing such a renowned and respected authority, who clearly knew a great deal more about migration than they did. They felt they had no choice but to go along with plans so obviously intended for their own good. Soon they were spending long evening hours with their chicks trying to comprehend and explain such things as track patterns, navigation mechanisms, degree of return, and degrees of dispersal and convergence. Instead of frolicking in the morning sunshine, chicks learned calculus, a mathematical tool developed in the seventeenth century by two famous blue wings named Leibniz and Newton that enables one to deal with the differentiation and integration of functions of one or more variables. Within just a few years every chick was expected to be able to calculate the migration-cost variables in both facultative and obligatory migrations. Weather conditions, wind direction and speed, even body weight and fat percentages enter into the calculation of migration thresholds.

"The initial failures of the new education system were spectacular but not unexpected. Titi had predicted that migratory success would actually be lower than normal for the first five years of the program but would return to and then surpass the norm within another five years. By the end of twenty years, he said, more teals would be migrating more successfully than ever before. But when teals eventually began to migrate with normal success once again, it was discovered that most were faking the calculations—merely following their instincts, matching data to behavior rather than behavior to data. When stringent new rules were enacted to prevent this form of cheating, migratory success dropped steeply. It was finally accepted that ordinary parents were not in fact qualified to teach their children anything as complex as migratory science. This was something only professionals could be expected to handle. Chicks were henceforth taken from the nest at an early age and turned over to a new cadre of specialists, who organized their young charges into brutally competitive units, imposing on them high standards, uniform testing, and harsh discipline. A certain amount of adverse reaction to the new regime was expected and soon materialized, in the form of chronic truancy, hostility, depression, and suicide among the young. New cadres of truancy officers, guards, psychotherapists, and counselors struggled to keep things under control, but before long members of the flock were streaking away like residents of a burning building (for Titi and Ooli were not quite mad enough to think they could keep the flock together by force).

"After the two old friends watched the last remnants of the flock scatter into the sky, Ooli shook his head and wondered where they'd gone wrong. Titi ruffled his feathers irritably and said, 'We went wrong by failing to take into account a great truth, namely that teals are stupid and lazy, and perfectly content to stay that way.' "

"The problems involved in migration—when to start, which way to go, how far to go, when to stop—are far beyond the power of any computer to solve, but they're routinely solved not only by relatively large-brained creatures like birds, tortoises, reindeer, bears, salamanders, and salmon but by plant lice, aphids, flatworms, mosquitoes, click beetles, and slugs. They don't need to be schooled in this. Do you understand?"

"Of course I understand."

"Millions of years of natural selection have produced creatures capable of solving these problems in a rough-and-ready way that isn't perfect but that does in fact work, because—behold!—these creatures are *here*. In the very same way, millions of years of natural selection have produced human creatures who are born with a ravenous desire to learn anything and everything their parents know and who are capable of feats of learning whose boundaries are literally beyond imagination. Toddlers growing up in a household in which four languages are spoken will learn those four languages flawlessly and effortlessly in a matter of months. They don't need to be schooled in this. But in two years—"

I held up a hand. "Let me help, Ishmael. I think I've got

it. Kids will learn anything they *want* to learn, anything they have a *use* for. But to make them learn things they *don't* have any use for, you have to send them to school. That's why we need schools. We need schools to force kids to learn things they have no use for."

"Which in fact they *do not* learn."

"Which in fact, when it's all over and the last bell rings, they *have not* learned."

Unschooling The World

B ut," I went on, "you don't actually think that the original system would work in the modern world, do you?"

Ishmael considered that for a while, then said, "Your schools would work perfectly if . . . what, Julie?"

"If people were better. If teachers were all brilliant and if kids were all attentive and obedient and hardworking and farsighted enough to know that learning everything in school would really be good for them."

"You've found that people won't be better, and you've failed to find a way to *make* them better, so you do what instead?"

"Spend money."

"More and more and more and more money. Because you

can't make people better, but you can always spend more money."

"That's right."

"What do you call a system that will only work if the people in it are better than people have ever been?"

"I don't know. Is there a special name for it?"

"What do you call a system that's built on the presumption that people in this system will be better than people have ever been? Everyone in this system is going to be kind and generous and considerate and selfless and obedient and compassionate and peaceable. What kind of system is that?"

"Utopian?"

"Utopian is right, Julie. Every one of your systems is a utopian system. Democracy would be heaven—if people would just be better than people have ever been. Of course, Soviet communism was supposed to have been heaven too— if people had just been better than people have ever been. Your justice system would work perfectly if people would just be better than people have ever been. And of course your schools would work perfectly under the same conditions."

"So? I'm not quite sure what you're getting at."

"I'm turning your question back to you, Julie. Do you actually think your utopian school system will work in the modern world?"

"I see what you mean. The system we *have* doesn't work. Except as a device to keep kids off the job market."

"The tribal system is a system that works with people the way they are, not the way you wish they were. It's a thoroughly practical system that has worked perfectly for people for hundreds of thousands of years, but you apparently think it a bizarre notion that it would work for you, now."

"I just don't see *how* it would work. How it could be *made* to work."

"First, tell me who your system works for and who it doesn't work for."

"Our system works for business but it doesn't work for people."

"And what are you looking for now?"

"A system that works for people."

Ishmael nodded. "During the early years of your children's lives, your system is indistinguishable from the tribal system. You simply interact with your children in a way that is mutually enjoyable, and you give them the freedom of the house—for the most part. You won't let them swing on the chandeliers or stick forks into electric light sockets, but otherwise they're free to explore what they want to explore. At age four or five, kids want to go farther afield, and for the most part they're allowed to do so within the immediate vicinity of the home. They're allowed to visit other kids down the hall or next door. In school, these would be social-studies lessons. At this stage, kids begin to learn that not all families are identical. They differ in membership, in manners, in style. After this point in your system, children are sent off to school, where all their movements are controlled for most of the waking day. But of course that doesn't happen in the tribal system. At age six and seven children begin to diverge widely in their interests. Some will continue to stick close to home, some will—"

I was waving my hand. "How are they going to learn to read?"

"Julie, for hundreds of thousands of years, children have managed to learn the things they want to learn and need to learn. They haven't changed."

"Yes, but how do they learn to read?"

"They learn to read the same way they learned how to see, by being around sighted people. The same way they learned how to speak, by being around speaking people. In other words, they learn to read by being around reading people. I know you've learned not to have any confidence in this process. I know you've been taught that this is something best left to 'the professionals,' but in fact the professionals have a very doubtful record of success. Remember that, one way or another, the people of your culture managed to learn to read for *thousands of years* without 'professionals' teaching them to do it. The fact is that children who grow up in reading households grow up reading."

"Yeah, but not all kids grow up in reading households."

"Let us posit, for the sake of argument, a child who is growing up in a household where the cooking instructions on food packages are not read, where the messages on television screens are not read, where telephone bills are not read, where the parents are totally, one hundred percent illiterate. Where the parents can't even tell whether they're holding a one-dollar bill or a five-dollar bill."

"Okay."

"At age four the child begins to widen his acquaintance of life. Are we going to posit one hundred percent illiteracy for all his neighbors? I think that would be going too far, but let's do it anyway. At age five the child's range extends even farther, and I think it's asking too much to suppose that his whole neighborhood is totally illiterate. He's surrounded by written messages, bombarded by written messages—all of which are intelligible to people around him, especially to his peers, who are not at all modest about flaunting their superior expertise. He may not instantly learn to read at graduate-school level, but at this age in your schools, he would only be learning the ABC's anyway. He learns enough. He learns what he needs to know. Without fail, Julie. I trust him to do this. I trust him to manage to do what human children have been doing effortlessly for hundreds of thousands of years. And what he needs right now is to be able to do anything his playmates do."

"Yeah, I can believe that."

"At age six and seven, as the child's range continues to expand, he's going to want to have a little money in his pockets, the way his playmates do. He won't need to go to school in order to learn the difference between pennies, nickels, and dimes. And he'll take in addition and subtraction like the air he breathes, not because he's 'good at mathematics,' but because he needs it as he moves farther and farther out into the world.

"Children are universally fascinated by the work their parents do outside the home. In our new tribal system, parents will understand that including their children in their working lives is their alternative to spending tens of billions of dollars annually on schools that are basically just detention centers. We're not talking about turning children into apprentices—that's something else entirely. We're just giving them access to what they want to know, and all children want to know what their parents are up to when they leave the house. Once they're loose in an office, children do the same things they did at home—they dig up all the secrets, investigate every closet, and of course learn how to work every machine, from the date-stamp machine to the copier, from the shredder to the computer. And if they don't know how to read yet, they'll certainly learn to read now, because there's very little they can do in an office without reading. This isn't to say that children would be prohibited from helping. There's nothing children like better at this age than feeling like they're helping Mommy and Daddy—and again, this isn't something learned, this is genetic.

"In tribal societies, it's taken for granted that children will want to work alongside their elders. The work circle is also the social circle. I'm not talking about sweatshops. There are no such things in tribal societies. Children aren't expected to behave like assembly-line workers, punching in and punching out. How else are they to learn to do things if they're not allowed to *do* them?

"But children will quickly exhaust the possibilities of their parents' workplace, especially if it's one where the same tasks are performed over and over. No child is going to be fascinated by stacking canned goods in a grocery store for long. The rest of the world is out there, and our supposition is that no door is closed to them. Imagine what a twelve-year-old with a musical bent could learn at a recording studio. Imagine what a twelve-year-old with an interest in animals could learn at a zoo. Imagine what a twelve-year-old with an interest in painting could learn in an artist's studio. Imagine what a twelve-year-old with an interest in performing could learn in a circus.

"Of course there would be no prohibition against schools, but the only ones that would actually attract students are the ones that attract them now—schools of fine arts, schools of music and dance, schools of martial arts, and so on. Schools of higher learning would doubtless attract older students as well—schools devoted to scholarly studies, the sciences, and the professions. The important thing to notice is that none of these are merely detention centers. All are dedicated to giving students knowledge they actually want and expect to use.

"I would expect a common objection to be that such an educational system would not produce 'rounded' students. But this objection merely reaffirms your culture's lack of confidence in your own children. Given free access to everything in your world, children would not become educationally rounded? I think the idea is absurd. They would become as rounded as they wanted to be, and there would be no presumption that education ends at age eighteen or twenty-two. Why would there be? These particular ages would become educationally meaningless. And in fact it would appear that very few people yearn to be Renaissance men and women. Why *should* they yearn for such a thing? If you're content to know nothing beyond chemistry or woodworking or computer science or forensic anthropology, whose business is it but your own? Every specialty that there is somehow manages to find candidates in every generation who want to pursue it. I've never heard of a single specialty disappearing for lack of candidates avid to pursue it. One way or another, every generation produces a few people who burn to study dead languages, who are fascinated by the effects of disease on bodies, who yearn to understand the secrets of rat behavior—and this would be as true under the tribal system as it presently is under your system.

"But, of course, having your children underfoot in the workplace would seriously reduce efficiency and productivity. Even though sending them to educational detention centers is terrible for children, it's unquestionably wonderful for business. The system I've outlined here will never be implemented among the people of your culture as long as you value business over people."

"So," I said, "you would be in favor of something like home schooling."

"I'm not in the least in favor of home schooling, Julie. It's not merely linguistic whimsy that connects the schooling of children with the schooling of fish. Schooling of any kind is unnecessary and counterproductive in human children. Children no more need schooling at age five or six or seven or eight than they need it at age two or three, when they effortlessly perform prodigies of learning. In recent years parents have seen the futility of sending their children to regular schools, and the schools have replied by saying, 'Well, all right, we'll permit you to keep your children at home, but of course you understand that your children still must be *schooled*, you can't just trust them to learn what they need to learn. We'll check up on you to make sure you're not just letting them learn what they *need* to learn but are learning what our state legislators and curriculum writers think they *should* learn.' At age five or six home schooling might be a lesser evil than regular schooling, but after that it's hardly even a lesser evil. Children don't need schooling. They need access to what they want to learn—and that means they need access to the world outside the home."

I told Ishmael I could think of another reason why people wouldn't go for the tribal system. "The world is too dangerous. People wouldn't let their kids wander around loose in a city these days."

"I'm not at all sure, Julie, that most urban business districts are any more dangerous than schools, these days. From what I read, children are much more inclined to go to school armed with deadly weapons than office workers are. Not many businesses need to have security guards in the hallways to protect executives from being attacked by workers and to protect workers from each other."

I had to admit that he had a bunch of points there.

"But the main thing I want you to see is that it's *your* system that is utopian. The tribal system isn't perfect, but it isn't a utopian scheme. It's completely feasible, and it would save you tens if not hundreds of billions of dollars every year."

"I don't suppose you'd get many votes from teachers, however."

Ishmael shrugged. "For half of what you're spending right now, you could retire every teacher in the system with a full pension."

"Yeah, they might go for that. But here's something I know people will say about all this: There's so much to learn in our fabulously terrific culture that we *have* to send them to school for all these years."

"You're right that it will be said, and those who say it will be right in the sense that there *is* a tremendous amount available to be learned in your culture that was not available to be learned in any tribal culture. But this misses the point I'm making here. Your basic citizen's education wasn't expanded from four grades to eight in order to include astronomy, microbiology, and zoology. It wasn't expanded from eight grades to twelve in order to include astrophysics, biochemistry, and paleontology. It wasn't expanded from twelve grades to sixteen in order to include exobiology, plasma physics, and heart surgery. Today's graduates don't leave school with all the advances of the past hundred years in their heads. Just like their great-great-grandparents a century ago, they leave with enough in their heads to start at the bottom of the job market, flipping burgers, pumping gas, and bagging groceries. It just takes today's graduates a whole lot longer to get there."

Wealth, Taker Style

The next day, Sunday, I wanted to get my weekend home-work out of the way before meeting again with Ishmael, so it was mid-afternoon by the time I got down to Room 105. I had my hand on the knob when I heard someone on the other side of the door say, very distinctly: "The gods would have it."

The dork had gotten in ahead of me.

For about ten seconds I considered hanging around for a while then decided against it. Feeling pretty bleak, I turned around and headed home.

The gods would have it.

I wondered what conversation *that* reply was part of. Certainly not one about school systems and teacher pensions. Not that the subject matter made any difference. I would've felt the same if what I'd overheard was "The supermarkets would have it" or "The Green Bay Packers would have it." You understand what I'm saying—I was jealous.

I suppose you think *you* wouldn't have been.

"I'd like you to see, Julie, if you can penetrate to the core of my message to you," Ishmael said when I was finally able to get back, on Wednesday. "See if you can discern what I'm saying to you again and again and again, every which way."

I gave it some thought and said, "You're trying to show me where the treasure is."

"That's it exactly, Julie. The people of your culture imagine that the treasury was completely empty when you came along and began to build civilization ten thousand years ago. You imagine that the first three million years of human life brought nothing of value to the store of human knowledge but fire and stone tools. In fact, however, you began by *emptying* the treasury of its most precious elements. You wanted to start with nothing and invent it all, and you did. Unfortunately, aside from the products (which work very well), you've been able to invent very little that works well—for people. Your system of writing laws that you *know* will be broken works very badly for people, but no matter where you look in *your* treasury you can't find a system to replace it with, because you started by throwing that system away. But it's still there, working perfectly, in the Leaver treasury I'm showing you. Your system of punishing people who break the laws invented to be broken works very badly for people, but no matter where you look in *your* treasury you can't find a system to replace it with, because you started by throwing that system away. But it's still there, working perfectly, in the Leaver treasury I'm showing you. Your educational system works very badly for people, but no matter where you look in *your* treasury you can't find a system to replace it with, because you started by throwing that system away. But it's still there, working perfectly, in the Leaver treasury I'm showing you. All the things I've shown you and will show you before we're finished were in the treasury of every Leaver people you've overrun and destroyed. Every one of those peoples knew how priceless these treasures were that you were trampling into the dirt. Many of them tried to make you see their value, but they never succeeded. Can you figure out why?"

"I think it would be because . . . We'd look at it this way: 'Well, sure the Sioux think their way of life is terrific. Big deal. Sure the Arapaho think they should be left alone. Why wouldn't they?' "

"That's right. If I succeed in showing the value of what you discarded, it won't be because I'm more brilliant than the Leavers of your own race but because *I'm not one of them*."

"I get it."

"What sack from the treasury shall I open for you today?" he asked.

"Wow," I told him. "That's not something I came prepared to answer."

"I didn't suppose you did, Julie. Think of a system you have that doesn't work well for people in general, though of course it may work well for some of you. Think of a system you've been tinkering with and fighting over right from the beginning. Think of another wheel you're sure you have to invent from scratch. Think of a problem you're sure you'll solve *someday*."

"Is this a particular system you have in mind, Ishmael?"

"No, I'm not trying to draw you into a guessing game. These are the characteristics of all the systems you've concocted to replace the systems discarded at the beginning of your revolution."

"Okay. There's one system I can think of that's like all those things, but I'm not sure there's a bag in the Leaver treasury that corresponds to it. In fact, I rather doubt it."

"Why is that, Julie?"

"Because this is the system we use to lock up the food."

"I see what you mean. Since Leaver peoples don't lock up their food, they wouldn't have a system for doing that."

"That's right."

"All the same, let's keep going in this direction for a bit. I'm not actually sure I know what system you're talking about."

"I guess I'm talking about the economic system."

"I see. So you don't think the Taker economic system works well for people in general."

"Well, it works terrifically for a few people, obviously. This is a cliché. There's a handful at the top who make out like bandits, then there's a lot in the middle who do pretty well, then there's a lot at the bottom who live in the toilet."

"It was or is the socialist dream to even this all out. To redistribute the wealth more equitably so that enormous amounts weren't concentrated in the hands of a few while the masses went hungry."

"I guess that's right. But I have to tell you that I know more about rocket science than I know about this stuff."

"You know enough, Julie. Don't worry about that. . . . When did you start having problems distributing the wealth? Let me ask that another way. When did dispropor-tionate amounts of wealth begin to be concentrated in the hands of a few people at the top of the heap?"

"God, I don't know. I have images of the very first potentates living in magnificent palaces while their subjects lived like pack animals."

"There's no doubt that this was indeed the case, Julie. The earliest Taker civilizations come to us fully formed in this mold. No developmental hesitancy to be seen here. As

soon as there's visible wealth—as opposed to just food on the
table, clothes on your back, and a roof over your head—it's
easy to predict how it will be distributed. There will be a few
ultrarich at the top, a more numerous wealthy class below
them, and a vastly more numerous class of tradesmen, merchants, soldiers, artisans, workers, servants, slaves, and paupers at the bottom. In other words, royalty, nobility, and
commoners. The size and membership of the classes has
changed over the centuries, but the way the available wealth
is distributed among them has not. Typically (and under-
standably) the top two classes feel the system is working
admirably well, and of course it is—for them. The system is
stable as long as the top two classes are fairly large, as they
are, say, in the United States. But in France in 1789 and in
Russia in 1917, the wealth was concentrated in just too few
hands. Do you understand what I'm saying?"

"I think so. You're not going to have a revolution if most
people feel they're making out pretty well."

"That's right. At this point in time the disparity between
the richest and the poorest of your culture is wider than any
Egyptian pharaoh could have imagined. The pharaohs could
own nothing remotely like the extravagances that are available to your billionaires. This is arguably one reason why
they built pyramids. What else were they going to do with
their money? They couldn't buy island paradises and travel
to them on private jets and three hundred-foot yachts."

"Very true."

"Among the wealthy of your culture, the collapse of the
Soviet empire is being perceived as a clear vindication of
capitalist greed. It's being taken as a statement from the poor
that they'd much rather live in a world where they can at
least dream of being rich than in a world where everyone is
poor but more or less *equally* poor. The ancient order has
been affirmed, and you can look forward to an unending
future of economic contentment, provided, as always, that

you're among the well-off. And if you aren't, the argument goes, you've no one to blame but yourself, because after all, under capitalism, anyone can be rich."

"Very persuasive," I said.

"The wealthy are always perfectly willing to leave things alone and not be troublemakers, and they don't see why others can't be as considerate as they are in this regard."

"Makes sense," I said.

"But now let's see if you can put your finger on the basic wealth-making mechanism of the Takers."

"It's not the same for everybody?"

"Oh no," Ishmael said. "The wealth-making mechanism of the Leavers is quite distinctly different."

"You're asking me to describe the wealth-making mechanism of the Takers?"

"That's right. It's not terribly obscure."

I gave it some thought and said, "I suppose it boils down to 'I've got something you want, you give me something I want.' Or is that too simpleminded?"

"Not for me, Julie. I'd always rather start with the bone than have to carve down to it." Ishmael said this while shuffling around his room to gather up a pad and felt-tip pen. He paged through it to a clean sheet, then spent three minutes making a diagram, which he flattened against the glass for my inspection.

"This schematic shows what your economy is all about: making products in order to get products. Obviously I'm using the word *product* in an extended sense, but anyone in a service industry will certainly know what I'm talking about if I refer to his or her product. And for the most part, what people get for their products is money, but money is only one step removed from the products it can buy, and it's the products people want, not the little pieces of paper. On the basis of our previous conversations, you'll have no difficulty identifying the event that got this product exchange rolling."

"Yeah. Locking up the food."

"Of course. Before that time, there was no point in making products. There was plenty of point in making a pot or a stone tool or a basket, but there was utterly no point in making a thousand of them. No one was in the pottery *business* or the stone-tool-making *business* or the basket-weaving *business*. But with food under lock and key, all this changed immediately. By the simple act of being locked up, food was transformed into a product—the fundamental product of your economy. All of a sudden it became true that someone with three pots could get three times as much to eat as someone with just one pot. All of a sudden someone with thirty thousand pots could live in a palace, while someone with three thousand pots could live in a nice house and someone with no pots at all could live in the gutter. Your whole economy fell into place once the food was put under lock and key."

"So you're saying that tribal peoples have no economy at all."

"I'm saying nothing of the kind, Julie. Here's the fundamental transaction of the tribal economy." He turned to a fresh page on his pad and produced a new schematic for me:

GIVE support
GET support

"It isn't products that make the tribal economy go round but rather human energy. This is the fundamental exchange, and it takes place so unobtrusively that people often mistakenly suppose that they have no economy at all, just as they often mistakenly suppose that they have no educational system at all. You make and sell hundreds of millions of products every year in order to build and equip and staff schools to educate your children. Tribal peoples accomplish the same objective through a more or less constant low-level exchange of energy between adults and youngsters that they hardly even notice. You make and sell hundreds of millions of products every year in order to be able to hire police to maintain law and order. Tribal peoples accomplish the same objective by doing it themselves. Maintaining law and order is never an agreeable chore, but it's not remotely the major concern for them that it is for you. You make and sell trillions of products every year in order to maintain governing bodies that are incredibly inefficient and corrupt—as you well know. Tribal peoples manage to govern themselves quite effectively without making or selling anything.

"A system based on exchanging products inevitably channels wealth to a few, and no governmental change will ever be able to correct that. It isn't a defect of the system, it's intrinsic to the system. This doesn't have anything to do with capitalism specifically. Capitalism is just the most recent expression of an idea that came into being ten thousand years ago in the founding of your culture. The revolutionaries of international communism didn't go nearly deep enough to effect the change they wanted to make. They thought they could stop the merry-go-round if they captured all the horses. But of course the horses don't make the carousel go round. The horses are just passengers like the rest of you."

"By horses, you mean rulers, governments."

"That's right."

"How *do* we stop the merry-go-round, then?"

Ishmael sorted through his tree clippings for a choice item as he thought about this. Then he said, "Suppose you'd never seen a merry-go-round and you came across one that was running out of control. You might hop on and try to stop it by pulling on the reins of the horses and yelling 'Whoa!'"

"I suppose I might, if I'd woken up kind of stupid that morning."

"And when that didn't work, what would you do?"

"I'd hop off and try to find the controls."

"And if no controls were in sight?"

"Then I guess I'd try to figure out how the damn thing works."

"Why?"

"Why? Because, if there's no on-off switch, you have to know how it works in order to make it stop."

Ishmael nodded. "Now you understand why I'm trying to show you how the Taker merry-go-round works. There is no on-off switch, so if you want to make it stop, you'll have to know how it works."

"A minute ago," I told him, "you said that a system based on exchanging products always concentrates wealth in a few hands. Why is that?"

Ishmael thought for a moment, then said, "Wealth in your culture is something that can be put under lock and key. Would you agree with that statement?"

"I think so. Except for maybe something like a piece of land."

"I'll bet the deed to the piece of land is under lock and key," Ishmael said.

"True."

"The owner of the land may never even set foot on it. If he has the deed, he can sell it to someone else who may never set foot on it."

"True."

"Because your wealth *can* be put under lock and key, it *is* put under lock and key, and this means that it accumulates. Specifically, it accumulates among the people who *have* the locks and the keys. Perhaps this will help. . . . If you imagine the wealth of ancient Egypt as a visible substance being drawn up atom by atom out of the land by farmers, miners, builders, artisans, and so on, you'll see it as a wide fog that spreads over the whole country at first. But this fog of wealth is in motion. It's being drawn steadily upward into a narrower and denser stream of wealth that flows directly into the storerooms of the royal family. If you imagine the wealth of a medieval English county as a visible substance in the same way, you'll see it being drawn steadily upward toward the local duke or earl. If you imagine the wealth of nineteenth century America in the same way, you'll see it being drawn steadily upward into the hands of railroad magnates, industrialists, and financiers. Each transaction at a lower level pushes a bit of wealth upward toward a Rockefeller or a Morgan. The miner who buys a pair of shoes enriches Rockefeller minutely, because part of his money finds its way to Standard Oil. Another minute part of it finds its way to Morgan through one of his railroads. In present-day America, the wealth streams upward toward the same sort of people, though now they're called Boesky and Trump instead of Rockefeller and Morgan. Obviously a great deal more could be said about this, but does this answer your question?"

"Yes. Maybe what I don't get is this. If there's going to be wealth, where could it go except to individuals?"

"I see where you're confused," he said with a nod. "Wealth must of course go to individuals, but that isn't my point. My point is not that product-generated wealth always goes to individuals but rather that it always goes to a *few* individuals. When wealth is generated by products, eighty percent of it will always end up being held by twenty percent of the population. This isn't peculiar to capitalism. In any economy based on products, wealth will tend to be concentrated in the hands of a few."

"I understand now. But I have a question."

"Proceed."

"What about people like the Aztecs and the Incas? From the little I know, I'd sure guess that they had the food under lock and key."

"You're absolutely correct, Julie. The idea of locking up the food was invented independently in the New World. And among peoples like the Aztecs and the Incas, wealth flowed inexorably into the hands of a wealthy few."

"Then were these people Leavers or Takers?"

"I'd say they were in between, Julie. They were no longer Leavers but not yet Takers, because they lacked one essential element: They didn't seem to think that everyone in the world should be made to live the way they lived. The Aztecs, for example, had territorial ambitions, but once they conquered you, they didn't care how you lived."

Wealth, Leaver Style

"Wealth generated in the tribal economy has no tendency to flow into the hands of a few," Ishmael said. "This is not at all because Leavers are nicer people than you are, but rather because they have a fundamentally different kind of wealth. There's no way to *accumulate* their wealth—no way to put it under lock and key—so there's no way for it to be concentrated in *anyone's* hands."

"I have no idea what their wealth *is*."

"I realize that, Julie, and I certainly intend to repair this deficiency. In fact, the easiest way to understand their economy is to start by looking at the wealth it generates. Of course when the people of your culture look at tribal peoples, they don't see wealth of any kind, they see poverty. This is understandable, since the only kind of wealth they recognize is the kind that can be locked up, and tribal peoples are not much interested in that kind.

"The foremost wealth of tribal peoples is cradle-to-grave security for each and every member. I can see that you're not exactly stunned by the magnificence of this wealth. It's certainly not impressive or thrilling, especially (forgive me for saying so) for someone your age. There are hundreds of millions of you, however, who live in stark terror of the future because they see no security in it for themselves anywhere. To be made obsolete by some new technology, to be laid off as redundant, to lose jobs or whole careers through treachery, favoritism, or bias—these are just a few of the nightmares that haunt your workers' sleep. I'm sure you've heard stories of dismissed workers returning to gun down former bosses and coworkers."

"Sure. One a week at least."

"They're not crazy, Julie. Losing their job looks like the very end of the world to them. They feel they've been dealt a mortal blow. Life is over, and nothing's left for them but revenge."

"I believe it."

"This is unthinkable in the tribal life, Julie—and not just because tribal peoples don't have jobs. As surely as any of you, each member of the tribe has a living to make. The wherewithal to live doesn't just fall out of the sky into their hands. But there is no way to deprive any member of the means to live. He or she has those means, and that's it. Of course this doesn't mean that no one ever goes hungry. But the only time anyone goes hungry is when *everyone* is going hungry. Again, this isn't because tribal people are more selfless and generous and caring—nothing of the sort. Do you think you can work this out?"

"You mean why no one goes hungry unless everyone is going hungry? I don't know. I can give it a shot."

"Please do."

"Okay. Well, it isn't like they have a store where they get the food. I'm not quite sure what I'm saying yet."

"Take your time."

"In the movies it happens this way. Let's say you've got explorers on an expedition to the North Pole or something. Their ship gets iced in and they can't get back on schedule. So the problem is how to survive. They've got to dole out the food very carefully and very fairly. But when they're on their last legs and ready to expire, guess what? The bad guy has a secret cache of food that he's been careful not to share with anyone."

Ishmael nodded.

"Now the reason this doesn't happen in a tribal situation is that they don't start out with a store of food. They go along and go along, and for some reason the food gradually starts to get scarce. There's a drought or a forest fire or something. On day one, everyone's out looking for food, and it's slim pickings for everyone. The tribal chief is as hungry as everyone else. Why wouldn't he be, since there's no store that he has first pick at? Everyone's out there scoring as much food as they can, and if someone makes a good score, the best thing he can do is to share it with others, not because he's a nice guy but because the more people who are on their feet and out there hunting for food, the better off they all are—including him."

"That's an excellent analysis, Julie. You have a distinct knack for this. . . . Of course there's nothing uniquely human about this. Wherever you find animals joined in foraging bands, you'll find them sharing food—not altruistically but in their own individual best interest. On the other hand, I'm sure there have been tribal societies that have departed from this way of handling hunger, societies in which the rule was 'If food is scarce, don't share it, hoard it.' But none in fact are seen. I'm sure you know why."

"Yeah. Because where a rule like that was followed, the tribe would fall apart. At least I think it would."

"Of course it would, Julie. Tribes survive by sticking together at all costs, and when it's every man for himself, the tribe ceases to be a tribe."

"I began this part of the conversation by saying that the foremost wealth of tribal peoples is cradle-to-grave security for each and every member. This is precisely the wealth that tribes stick together to have. And as you can see, it's impossible for one person to have more of this wealth than anyone else. There's no way to accumulate it, no way to put it under lock and key.

"I don't mean to say that this wealth is indestructible, of course. It remains intact only as long as the tribe remains intact, which is why so many Leaver tribes fought you to the death. As it looked to them, if the tribe was going to be destroyed, then they were dead anyway. I also don't mean to say that people can't be seduced away from this wealth. They certainly can be, and this is how it's done when for one reason or another you can't just send in the troops to kill them off. The young in particular are susceptible to the lure of Taker wealth, which obviously has much more glitter and flash than their own. If you can once get the young listening to you instead of to their own people, then you're well on the way to destroying the tribe, since whatever the elders can't pass on is lost forever when they die.

"To live and walk among your neighbors without fear is the second greatest wealth of tribal peoples. Again, this isn't very glamorous wealth, though certainly a great many of you wish you had it. I haven't made a study of this, but it seems to me a routine matter that every poll reveals fear of criminal attack to be either your greatest or second-greatest concern.

In Taker societies, only the rich live free of fear—or relatively free of fear. In tribal societies, everyone lives free of fear. But of course this doesn't mean that nothing bad ever happens to anyone. What it does mean is that it's sufficiently rare so that no one lives behind locked doors and no one carries weapons that they expect to have to use to defend themselves from their neighbors. Again, obviously, this isn't wealth that can be concentrated in anyone's hands. It can't be accumulated or put under lock and key.

"Equal to any of these is a form of wealth you lack so profoundly that you're truly pathetic. In a Leaver society, you're never left to cope with a crushing problem all by yourself. You have an autistic child, a disabled child. This will be perceived as a tribal burden—but (as always) not for altruistic reasons. It simply makes no sense to say to the child's mother or father, 'This is entirely your problem. Don't bother the rest of us with it.' You have a parent who is becoming senile. The rest of the tribe won't turn its back on you as you struggle with this problem. They know that a problem shared widely becomes almost no problem at all—and they know very well that each of them will someday need similar help with one problem or another. I find it truly heartrending to see the people of your world suffering without this wealth. One of a couple in late middle age contracts some horrible disease, their savings are wiped out in a matter of months, former friends shun them, there's no more money for medication, and suddenly their situation is completely desperate. Again and again the only solution they can find is to die together—a mercy killing and a suicide. Stories like this are commonplace in your culture but are virtually unheard of in Leaver societies.

"In the Taker system, you use your carefully accumulated product wealth to buy support wealth that is free to all in the Leaver system. When a tribal people has to deal with a troublemaker in their midst, the able-bodied band together to do whatever is necessary, and this, in fact, is highly effective. You, on the other hand, in order to avoid performing such a service, turn the service into a product. You build police forces, then compete to have the best (the highest-paid, the best-equipped, and so on). This is notoriously ineffective, despite the fact that you spend more and more money on it every year, but it does result in a situation in which the rich are much better protected than the poor. In Leaver societies, all adults take part in the education of the young, which happens painlessly and without fail. You, on the other hand, in order to avoid performing such a service, turn it into a product, building schools, then competing to have the best (best-staffed, best-equipped, and so on). This too is notoriously ineffective, despite the fact that you spend more and more money on it every year, but it does result in a situation in which the children of the rich are educated less badly and usually more pleasurably. Care for the chronically ill, the aged, the disabled, the mentally ill—all these services are dispensed cooperatively in Leaver societies, and in yours all are turned into products to be competed for, the rich getting the best, the poor lucky to get any at all."

There was one of those moments when neither one of us had anything to add. Then I said, "I need you to put this together for me, Ishmael. I'm not quite sure where we've been and where we are."

He scratched the side of his jaw for a bit before answering. "If you want to survive on this planet, Julie, the people of your culture are going to have to start listening to your neighbors in the community of life. Incredible as it may seem, you don't know it all. And, incredible as it may seem, you don't have to *invent* it all. You don't have to *contrive* things that work, you only have to visit the treasury around you. There's no reason to be surprised that Leaver peoples should enjoy cradle-to-grave security. After all, among your neighbors in the community of life, the very same security is enjoyed in every species whose members form communities. Ducks, sea lions, deer, giraffes, wolves, wasps, monkeys, and gorillas (to name just a few species out of millions) enjoy such security. It has to be assumed that the members of *Homo habilis* enjoyed such security—or how would they have survived? Is there any reason to doubt that the members of *Homo erectus* enjoyed such security or that they conferred it upon their descendants, *Homo sapiens*? No, as a species, you came into being in communities in which cradle-to-grave security was the rule, and the same rule has been followed throughout the development of *Homo sapiens* right up to the present moment—*in Leaver societies*. It's only in Taker societies that cradle-to-grave security has become a rarity, a special blessing of the privileged few."

Ishmael studied the look on my face for a few seconds and apparently realized that he still wasn't there.

"You daydreamed, Julie, of touring the universe to learn the secrets of how to live. I'm showing you where those secrets are to be found right here on your own planet, among your own neighbors in the community of life."

"I see. . . . I guess. There was a girl in my class last year who had a newsletter from some organization or other. I don't remember the name of the organization, but I remember its motto, at least approximately. It was 'Healing ourselves, healing the world.' Would you say that's what you're talking about?"

Ishmael gave that some thought and said, "I'm afraid I don't have much sympathy for the 'healing' approach to your problems, Julie. You're not ill. Six billion of you wake up every morning and start devouring the world. This isn't a sickness that you contracted one night while sitting in a draft. Healing is always a hit-or-miss proposition, I'm sure you know that. Sometimes aspirin fixes the headache and sometimes it doesn't. Sometimes chemotherapy kills the cancer and sometimes it doesn't. You can't afford to fool around with 'healing' yourselves. You've got to start living a different way, and you've got to do it very soon."

Less Is Not Always More

You know," I said, "there's something you could do that would help me a lot. I don't know if I have any business asking, but there it is."

Ishmael frowned. "Have I given you the impression that my program here is not subject to change? Do I really seem to you so rigid that I'm unwilling to accommodate you?"

Oops, I said to myself, but after thinking about it for a bit, I decided not to be apologetic. I said to him, "It's probably been a long time since you were a twelve-year-old girl talking to a thousand-pound gorilla."

"I don't see what my *weight* has to do with it," he snapped.

"Well, all right, a hundred-*year-old* gorilla."

"I'm *not* a hundred years old, and I weigh less than six hundred pounds."

"Good Lord," I said. "This is beginning to sound like something from *Alice in Wonderland*."

Ishmael chuckled and asked me what he could do that would be helpful.

"Tell me what you think the world would be like if we actually did manage to 'start living a different way.' "

"This is a very legitimate request, Julie, and I can't imagine why you hesitated to make it. I know from experience that, at this point, many people imagine that I'm thinking of a future in which technology has disappeared. It's all too easy for you to blame all your problems on technology. But humans were born technologists as they were born linguists, and no Leaver people has ever been discovered that is devoid of it. Like so many other facets of Leaver life, however, their technology tends to be almost invisible to eyes used to technology as furiously powerful and extravagant as yours. In any case, I'm certainly not envisioning a future for you devoid of technology.

"Very often people who are used to thinking in the Taker way will say to me, 'Well, if the Taker way isn't the right way, what *is* the right way?' But of course there is no one right way for people to live, any more than there is one right way for birds to build nests or for spiders to spin webs. So I'm certainly not envisioning a future in which the Taker empire has been overthrown and replaced by another. That's complete nonsense. What does Mother Culture say you have to do?"

"Oh my," I said. "I guess she'd say we don't have to do anything at all."

He shook his head. "Listen to her, don't try to second-guess her. You mentioned one of her teachings on this subject a minute ago. Here it is: 'You have some vague and probably incurable illness; you'll never figure out exactly what it is, but here are some cures you can try. Try this one, and if that doesn't work, try that one. And if that doesn't work, try this one.' Ad infinitum."

"Okay, I see what you mean. Let me think." I closed my eyes and after about five minutes began to get a glimmer. "This may be totally wrong," I told him. "This may just be the simple truth, but this is what I hear: 'Sure, you can save the world, but you're really going to hate it. It's really going to be painful.'"

"Why is it going to be painful?"

"Because of all the stuff we have to give up. But as I say, this may just be the simple truth."

"No, it's not the simple truth, Julie. It's Mother Culture's simple lie. Although Mother Culture is a metaphor, she really does behave uncannily like a real person sometimes. Why do you think she would tell this particular lie?"

"She wants to discourage us from changing, I guess."

"Of course. Her whole function is to preserve the status quo. This is not a peculiarity of *your* Mother Culture. In every culture, it's the function of Mother Culture to preserve the status quo. I don't mean at all to suggest that this is a wicked activity."

"I understand."

"Mother Culture wants to forestall you right at the outset by persuading you that, for you, any change *must* be a change for the worse. Why is it the case that *for you* any change must be a change for the worse, Julie?"

"I don't understand why you stress 'for you.'"

"Well, think about the Bushmen of Africa instead of about you. Would any change be a change for the worse for them?"

"Oh. I see what you mean. The answer is no, of course. For the Bushmen of Africa, any change would be a change for the *better,* according to Mother Culture."

"Why is that?"

"Because what they have is worthless. So any change would be an improvement."

"Exactly. And why must any change for *you* be a change for the worse?"

"Because what we have is perfection. It just can't get any better than this, so any change is ipso facto going to be a change for the worse. Is that right—ipso facto?"

"It's quite right, Julie. I've been surprised by how many of you actually seem to believe that what you have is perfection. It took me a while to realize that this results from the strange understanding you have of human history and of evolution. A great many of you consciously or unconsciously think of evolution as a process of inexorable improvement. You imagine that humans began as a completely miserable lot but under the influence of evolution very gradually got better and better and better and better and better and better and better and better and better and better and better and better until one day they became *you*, complete with frost-free refrigerators, microwave ovens, air-conditioning, minivans, and satellite television with six hundred channels. Because of this, giving up *anything* would necessarily represent a step backward in human development. So Mother Culture formulates the problem this way: 'Saving the world means *giving up things* and giving up things means reverting to misery. Therefore . . .' "

"Therefore forget about giving up things."

"And, more importantly, forget about saving the world."

"And what are *you* saying?"

"I too say 'forget about giving up things.' You shouldn't think of yourselves as wealthy people who must give up some of your riches. You should think of yourselves as people in desperate need. Do you understand the root meaning of the word *wealth*, Julie?"

"I'm not sure."

"What root word is the word *warmth* based on?"

"*Warm,* obviously."

"So take a guess. What root word is the word *wealth* based on?"

"*Well?*"

"Of course. In its root sense, *wealth* isn't a synonym for *money,* it's a synonym for *wellness.* In terms of products, you are of course fabulously wealthy, but in terms of human wealth, you are pathetically poor. In terms of human wealth, you're the wretched of the earth. And this is why you shouldn't focus on giving up things. How can you expect the wretched of the earth to give up *anything*? That's impossible. On the contrary, you must absolutely concentrate on *getting* things—but not more toasters, Julie. Not more radios. Not more television sets. Not more telephones. Not more CD players. Not more playthings. You must concentrate on getting the things you desperately need *as human beings.* At the moment you've given up on all those things, you've decided they can't be had. But my task, Julie, is to show you that this isn't the case. You don't have to give up on the things you desperately need as human beings. They're within your reach—if you know where to look for them. If you know *how* to look for them. And this is what you came to me to learn."

"But how do we *do* that, Ishmael?"

"You've got to be more demanding for yourselves, Julie—not less. This is where I part company with your religionists, who tend to encourage you to be brave and long-suffering and to expect little from life—and to expect better only in a next life. You need to demand foryourselves the wealth that aboriginal people all over the world are willing to die to defend. You need to demand for yourselves the wealth that humans had from the beginning, that they took for granted for hundreds of thousands of years. You need to demand for yourselves the wealth you threw away in order to make yourselves the rulers of the world. But you can't demand this from your leaders. Your leaders aren't withholding it. They don't have it to give to you. This is how you must differ from revolutionaries of the past, who simply wanted different people to be running things. You can't solve your problem by putting someone new in charge."

"Yeah, but who do we demand it of if we don't demand it from our leaders?"

"Demand it of yourselves, Julie. Tribal wealth is the energy that tribal members give each other in order to keep the tribe going. This energy is inexhaustible, a completely renewable resource."

I groaned. "You're still not telling me how to *do* that."

"Julie, the things you want as humans are *available*. This is my message to you over and over and over again. You can *have* these things. People you despise as ignorant savages have them, so why can't *you* have them?"

"But *how*? How do we go *about* having them?"

"First you have to realize that it's *possible* to have them. Look, Julie, before you could go to the moon, you first had to realize that it was *possible* to go to the moon. Before you could build an artificial heart, you first had to realize that it was *possible* to build an artificial heart. Do you see that?"

"Yes."

"At the moment, Julie, how many of you realize that your ancestors had a way of living that worked very well for people? People who lived this way weren't perpetually struggling with crime, madness, depression, injustice, poverty, and rage. Wealth wasn't concentrated in the hands of a lucky few. People didn't live in terror of their neighbors or of the future. People felt secure, and they *were* secure—in a way that's almost unimaginable to you. This way of living is still extant, and it still works as well as it ever did, for people— unlike your way, which works very well for business but very badly for people. How many of you realize all this?"

"None," I said. "Or very few."

"Then how can they begin? To go to the moon, you first had to realize that it was possible to go to the moon."

"So what are you saying? That it's impossible?"

Ishmael sighed. "Do you remember what I advertised for?"

"Of course. A pupil with an earnest desire to save the world."

"Then presumably you came here because you have that desire. Did you think I was going to hand you a magic wand? Or an automatic weapon with which you could gun down all the evildoers of the world?"

"No."

"Did you think there was nothing to be done? Did you think that you would come here, listen for a while, and then go home and do nothing? Did you think that doing nothing was my idea for saving the world?"

"No."

"On the basis of what I've been saying here, Julie, what *needs* to be done? What needs to be done first before people will begin figuring out how to get the wealth they so desperately need?"

I shook my head but that wasn't nearly enough. I popped up out of my chair and windmilled my arms. Ishmael looked at me curiously, as if I might have lost my mind at last. I said to him, "Look! You're not talking about saving the world. I can't figure you out! You're talking about saving *us*!"

Ishmael nodded. "I understand your puzzlement, Julie. But here is how it is. The people of your culture are in the process of rendering this planet uninhabitable to yourselves and millions of other species. If you succeed in doing this, life will certainly continue, but at levels you (in your lofty way) would undoubtedly consider more primitive. When you and I speak of saving the world, we mean saving the world roughly as we know it now—a world populated by elephants, gorillas, kangaroos, bison, elk, eagles, seals, whales, and so on. Do you understand?"

"Of course."

"There are only two ways to save the world in this sense. One of them is to destroy you immediately—not to wait for you to render the world uninhabitable for yourselves. I know of no way to accomplish that, Julie. Do you?"

"No."

"The only other way to save the world is to save *you*. Is to show you how to get the things you so desperately need— *instead* of destroying the world."

"Oh," I said.

"It is my bizarre theory, Julie, that the people of your culture are destroying the world not because they're vicious or stupid, as Mother Culture teaches, but because they're terribly, terribly deprived—of things that humans absolutely must have, simply cannot go on living without year after year and generation after generation. It's my bizarre theory that, given a choice between destroying the world and having the things they really, deeply want, they'll choose the latter. But before they can *make* that choice, they must *see* that choice."

I gave him back one of his own bleak stares. "And I'm supposed to show them that they have that choice. Is that it?"

"That's it, Julie. Isn't that what you wanted to do in your daydream? Bring enlightenment to the world from afar?"

"Yeah, that's what I wanted to do in my *daydream,* all right. But in real life, gimme a break. I'm just a kid wondering how I'm gonna make out when I finally get to high school."

"I realize that. But you're not going to remain so forever. Whether you know it or not, you came here to be changed, and you've been changed. And whether you know it or not, the change is permanent."

"I *do* know it," I told him. "But you know, you didn't answer my question. I asked you to tell me what the world would be like if we actually did manage to start living a different way. I think we need to have something to shoot for. *I* sure need it anyway."

"I'll do that, Julie, but next time. I think for today it's time to quit. Can you come on Friday?"

"Yeah, I guess. But why Friday in particular?"

"Because I have someone I want you to meet. Not Alan Lomax," he added in a hurry when he saw my face. "His name is Art Owens, and he's going to be helping me make my getaway from this place."

"I could help you."

"I'm sure you could, Julie, but he has a vehicle and a place to take me, and it will all be done in the dead of night. Not a time when you should be out and about."

I thought about it some. "He could pick me up. If he's coming here, he could come there."

Ishmael shook his head. "A forty-year-old African-American man picking up a twelve-year-old white girl in the middle of the night would be an invitation to catastrophe."

"Yeah. I hate to say it, but you're right."

My God, It Isn't Me!

There was a second chair in place when I arrived on Friday, and I didn't like it one bit—not the chair itself, of course, but rather the very idea of sharing *my* Ishmael with anyone, selfish minx that I am. But at least it was not as nice as the friendly old broken-down one I was used to. I pretended it wasn't there, and we got started.

"Among her friends in college," Ishmael began, "my benefactor, Rachel Sokolow, counted a young man named Jeffrey, whose father was an affluent surgeon. Jeffrey became an important person in many lives at this time and later, because he presented people with a problem. He couldn't figure out what to do with himself. He was physically attractive, intelligent, personable, and talented at almost anything he turned his hand to. He could play the guitar well, though he had no interest in a musical career. He could take a good photograph, produce a good sketch, play the lead in a school play, and write an entertaining story or a provocative essay, but he didn't want to be a photographer, an artist, an actor, or a writer. He did well in all his classes but didn't want to be a teacher or a scholar and wasn't interested in following his father's footsteps or in pursuing a career in law, the sciences, mathematics, business, or politics. He was drawn to things of the spirit and was an occasional churchgoer but didn't care to become a theologian or a clergyman. In spite of all this, he seemed 'well-adjusted,' as it's called. He wasn't notably phobic or depressive or neurotic. He wasn't doubtful or confused about his sexual orientation. He figured he'd settle down and marry one day, but not until he'd found some purpose in life.

"Jeffrey's friends never tired of finding new ideas to present to him in hopes of awakening his interest. Wouldn't he enjoy reviewing films for the local newspaper? Had he ever thought of taking up scrimshaw or jewelry making? Cabinetry was put forward as a soul-satisfying occupation. How about fossil hunting? Gourmet cooking? Maybe he should get into Scouting. Or wouldn't it be fun to go on an archaeological dig? Jeffrey's father was completely sympathetic with his inability to discover an enthusiasm and ready to support him in whatever exploration he might find worthwhile. If a world tour had any appeal, a travel agent would be put to work on it. If he wanted to try the life of an outdoorsman, equipment would be supplied, gladly. If he wanted to take to the sea, a boat would be made ready. If he wanted to try his hand at pottery, he'd have a kiln waiting for him. Even if he just wanted to be a social butterfly, that would be fine. He shrugged it all off, politely, embarrassed to be putting everyone to so much trouble.

"I don't want to give you the impression he was lazy or spoiled. He was always at the top of his class, always held a part-time job, lived in ordinary student housing, didn't own a car. He just looked at the world that was on offer to him and couldn't see a single thing in it worth having. His friends kept saying to him, 'Look, you can't go on this way. You've got too much going for you. You've just got to get some *ambition,* got to find *something* you want to do with your life!'

"Jeffrey graduated with honors but without a direction. After hanging around his father's house for the summer, he went to visit some college friends who had just gotten married. He took along his knapsack, his guitar, his journal. After a few weeks he set out to visit some other friends, hitchhiking. He was in no hurry. He stopped along the way, helped some people who were building a barn, earned enough money to keep going, and eventually reached his next destination. Soon it was getting on for winter and he headed home. He and his father had long conversations, played gin rummy, played pool, played tennis, watched football, drank beer, read books, went to movies.

"When spring came, Jeffrey bought a secondhand car and set out to visit friends in the other direction. People took him in wherever he went. They liked him and felt sorry for him, he was so rootless, so ineffectual, so unfocused. But they didn't give up on him. One person wanted to buy him a video camera so he could make a film of his wanderings. Jeffrey wasn't interested. Another person volunteered to send his poetry around to magazines to see if anyone would publish it. Jeffrey said that was fine, but personally, he didn't care one way or the other. After working at a boys' camp for the summer, he was asked to stay on as a permanent member of the staff, but it didn't appeal to him that much.

"When winter came, his father talked him into seeing a psychotherapist he knew and trusted. Jeffrey stuck with it throughout the winter, going three times a week, but in the end the therapist had to admit that, apart from being 'a little immature,' there was nothing whatever wrong with him. Asked what 'a little immature' meant, the therapist said Jeffrey was unmotivated, unfocused, and lacked goals—everything they already knew. 'He'll find something in a year or two,' the therapist predicted. 'And it'll probably be something very obvious. I'm sure it's staring him in the face right now, and he just doesn't see it.' When spring came, Jeffrey went back out on the road, and if something was staring him in the face, he went on being unable to see it.

"The years drifted by in this way. Jeffrey watched old friends get married, raise children, build careers, build businesses, win a little fame here, a little fortune there . . . while he went on playing his guitar, writing a poem now and then, and filling one journal after another. Just last spring he celebrated his thirty-first birthday with friends at a vacation cottage on a lake in Wisconsin. In the morning he walked down to the water, wrote a few lines in his journal, then waded into the lake and drowned himself."

"Sad," I said after a moment, unable to think of anything more brilliant.

"It's a commonplace story, Julie, except for one fact—the fact that Jeffrey's father made it possible for him to drift, actually supported him while he did nothing for nearly ten years—put no pressure on him to shape up and become a responsible adult. That's what made Jeffrey different from millions of other young people in your culture who in fact have no more motivation than he did. Or do you think I'm mistaken in this?"

"I don't understand you well enough to say whether you're mistaken."

"Thinking of the young people you know, do you find them burning to be out there becoming lawyers and bankers and engineers and cooks and hairstylists and insurance agents and bus drivers?"

"Some of them, yeah. Not especially to be the things you

mentioned, hairstylists and bus drivers, but *some* things. I know kids who wouldn't mind being movie stars and professional athletes, for example."

"And what are their chances of becoming these things, realistically speaking?"

"Millions to one, I suppose."

"Do you think there are eighteen-year-olds out there dreaming of becoming cabdrivers or dental technicians or asphalt spreaders?"

"No."

"Do you think there are a lot of eighteen-year-olds out there who are like Jeffrey, who are not really attracted to anything in the Taker world of work? Who would be glad to skip it entirely if someone gave them an annual stipend of twenty or thirty thousand dollars?"

"God yes, if you put it like that, I'm sure there are. Are you kidding? Millions of them."

"But if there isn't anything they really want to do in the Taker world of work, why do they enter it at all? Why do they take jobs that are clearly not meaningful to them or to anyone else?"

"They take them because they have to. Their parents throw them out of the house. They either get jobs or starve."

"That's right. But of course in every graduating class there are a few who would just as soon starve. People used to call them tramps or bums or hobos. Nowadays they often characterize themselves as 'homeless,' suggesting that they live on the street because they're forced to, not because they prefer to. They're runaways, beachcombers, ad hoc hookers and hustlers, muggers, bag ladies, and Dumpster divers. They scrounge a living one way or another. The food may be under lock and key, but they've found all the cracks in the strongroom wall. They roll drunks and collect aluminum cans. They panhandle, haunt restaurant garbage cans, and practice petty thievery. It isn't an easy life, but they'd rather live this way than get a meaningless job and live like the mass of urban poor. This is actually a very large subculture, Julie."

"Yeah, I recognize it now that you put it this way. I actually know kids who talk about wanting to go live on the street. They talk about going to specific cities where there are already a lot of kids doing it. I think Seattle is one."

"This phenomenon shades off into the phenomena of juvenile gangs and cults. When these street urchins are organized around charismatic warlords, they're perceived as gangs. When they're organized around charismatic gurus, they're perceived as cults. Children living on the street have a very low life expectancy, and it doesn't take them long to realize that. They see their friends die in their teens or early twenties, and they know their fate is going to be the same. Even so, they can't bring themselves to rent some hovel, collect some decent clothes, and try to get some stupid minimum-wage job they hate. Do you see what I'm saying, Julie? Jeffrey is just the upper-class representative of the phenomenon. The lower-class representatives don't have the privilege of drowning themselves in nice clean lakes in Wisconsin, but what they're doing comes to the same thing. They'd as soon be dead as join the ranks of ordinary urban paupers, and they generally *are* soon dead."

"I see all that," I told him. "What I don't see yet is the point you're making."

"I haven't really made a point yet, Julie. I'm drawing your attention to something the people of your culture want to pretend is of no importance, is irrelevant. The story of Jeffrey is terribly sad—but he's a rarity, isn't he? You might be concerned if there were thousands of Jeffreys walking into lakes. But young riffraff dying on your streets by the thousands is something you can safely ignore."

"Yes, that's true."

"What I'm looking at is something the people of your

culture feel sure doesn't need to be looked at. These are drug addicts, losers, gangsters, trash. The adult attitude toward them is, 'If they want to live like animals, let them live like animals. If they want to kill themselves off, let them kill themselves off. They're defectives, sociopaths, and misfits, and we're well rid of them.' "

"Yeah, I'd say that's how most grown-ups feel about it."

"They're in a state of denial, Julie, and what is it they're denying?"

"They're denying that these are *their* children. These are somebody *else's* children."

"That's right. There is no message for you in a Jeffrey drowning himself in the lake or a Susie dying of an overdose in the gutter. There's no message for you in the tens of thousands who kill themselves annually, who disappear into the streets, leaving behind nothing but faces on milk cartons. This is no message. This is like static on the radio, something to be ignored, and the more you ignore it, the better the music sounds."

"Very true. But I'm still groping for your point."

"No one would think of asking themselves, 'What do these children *need*?' "

"God no. Who cares what they need?"

"But *you* can ask yourself that, can't you? Can you bring yourself to it, Julie? Can you bear it?"

I sat there for a minute, staring at nothing, and suddenly the goddamnedest thing happened: I burst into tears. I exploded into tears. I sat there completely overwhelmed in great, huge racking sobs that wouldn't go away, wouldn't go away, until I began to think I'd found my life's work, to sit in that chair and sob.

When I began to settle down, I stood up, told Ishmael I'd be back in a while, and went out for a walk around the block—around a couple blocks, in fact.

Then I went back and told him I didn't know how to put it into words.

"You can't put the emotions into words, Julie. I know that. You put those into sobs, and there are no words equivalent to that. But there are other things you *can* put into words."

"Yeah, I suppose that's true."

"You had some sort of vision of the devastating loss you share with the young people we've been talking about."

"Yeah. I didn't *know* I shared it with them. I didn't know I shared *anything* with them."

"The first day you visited me, you said you're constantly telling yourself, 'I've got to get out of here, I've got to get out of here.' You said this meant 'Run for your life!' "

"Yeah. I guess you could say that's what I was feeling as I sat here crying. *Please! Please let me run for my life! Please let me out of here! Please, let me go! Please don't keep me penned up here for the rest of my life! I've GOTTA run! I can't STAND this!*"

"But these aren't thoughts you can share with your classmates."

"These aren't thoughts I could have shared with *myself* two weeks ago."

"You wouldn't have dared to look at them."

"No, if I'd looked at them, I would've said, 'My God, what's *wrong* with me? I must have a disease of some kind!' "

"These are exactly the kinds of thoughts that Jeffrey wrote in his journal again and again. 'What's *wrong* with me? What's wrong with *me*? There must be something terribly wrong with *me* that I'm unable to find joy in the world of work.' Always he wrote, 'What's wrong with *me*, what's wrong with *me*, what's wrong with *me*?' And of course all his friends were forever saying to him, 'What's wrong with *you,* what's wrong with *you,* what's wrong with *you* that you can't get with this wonderful program?' Perhaps you understand for the first time now that my role here is to bring you this tremendous news, that *there's nothing wrong here with YOU.* You are not what's wrong. And I think there was an element of this understanding in your sobs: 'My God, it isn't *me!*' "

"Yes, you're right. Half of what I was feeling was a tremendous sense of *relief.*"

Revolutionaries

You want to know how the world would be if you started living a different way. Now you have a better idea of what a different way would be *for*. I told you that you had to stop thinking of giving up things and be more demanding, but I don't think you understood what I meant."

"No, I didn't, not really. But I thought I did."

"But now you really understand. You fell apart when you finally realized that I would actually *listen* to your demands, that I actually wanted to *hear* your demands—that you even deserved to have your demands *met*."

"Yes, that's right."

"That's how we'll design a world for you, Julie. By listening to your demands. What is it you want? What would you die to have?"

"Wow," I said. "That's quite a question. I want a place to be where I'm not always saying, *I've gotta get out of here, I've gotta get out of here, I've gotta get out of here, I've gotta get out of here.*"

"You and the Jeffreys of the world need a cultural space of your own."

"Yeah, that's right."

"Cultural space isn't necessarily geographic space. The kids who live on the streets of Seattle and places like that aren't looking for a thousand acres of their own. They're perfectly happy to share your domain and in fact would probably starve to death if they had to live in a separate domain of their own. They're saying, 'Look, we're content to live on what the rest of you throw away. Why can't you just let us do that? Just give us enough room to be scavengers. We'll be the tribe of Crow. You don't kill the crows that are taking care of your roadkills, do you? If you kill the crows, then you have to scrape off the roadkills yourselves. Let the crows do it. They're not taking anything you want, so what's the problem with crows? We're not taking anything you want either, so what's the problem with us?' "

"That actually sounds pretty neat—not that it will ever happen."

"But what about you, Julie? Would you like to belong to the tribe of Crow?"

"Not especially, to be honest."

"Well, why should you? There's no one right way for people to live. But suppose the people of Seattle actually said, 'Let's try this. Instead of fighting these kids and trying to change these kids and making life hell for these kids, let's give them a hand. Let's give them a hand to become the tribe of Crow. What's the worst that could happen?' "

"That would be terrific."

"And if you knew there were people like that in Seattle— people willing to take a risk like that—where would you want to live if you were looking around for a place to live?"

"I'd want to live in Seattle."

"Could be an interesting place, Julie. A place where people *try* things." Ishmael fell silent for several minutes, and I had the feeling he'd sort of lost his place. Finally he went on. "No matter how thorough I think I've been, at this stage students say to me, 'Yes, but what are we actually supposed to *do*?' And I say to them, 'You Takers pride yourselves on being inventive, don't you? Well, *be inventive*.' But this doesn't seem to do much good, does it?"

I didn't know whether he was talking to himself or to me, but I just went on sitting there and listening.

"Tell me about being inventive, Julie."

"What do you mean?"

"When was your greatest period of inventiveness? The greatest period of inventiveness in human history."

"I'd have to say *this* was. Is. This is it."

"The period of the Industrial Revolution."

"That's right."

"How did it work?"

"What do you mean?"

"Your greatest task in the decades ahead is to be inventive—not for machines but for yourselves. Does that make sense to you?"

"Yes."

"Then maybe there are some things we can learn about inventiveness from the greatest outpouring of inventiveness in human history. Does that sound plausible?"

"Yes, absolutely."

"So, once again, how did it work?"

"The Industrial Revolution? God, I don't know."

"Did an Industrial Revolutionary Army move into the capital and seize the reins of power? Did it round up the royal family and guillotine them?"

"No."

"Then how did it work?"

"God . . . Are you asking me about cartels and monopolies?"

"No, nothing of the sort. I'm not looking into money, I'm looking into inventiveness. Try it this way, Julie. How did the Industrial Revolution start?"

"Oh. Okay. I remember that. It's all I *do* remember. James Watt. The steam engine. Seventeen hundred and something."

"Excellent, Julie. James Watt, the steam engine, seventeen hundred and something. James Watt is often credited with inventing the steam engine that started it all, but this is a misleading simplification that misses the whole point of this revolution. James Watt in 1763 merely improved on an engine designed in 1712 by Thomas Newcomen, who had merely improved on an engine designed in 1702 by Thomas Savery, who doubtless knew the engine described in 1663 by Edward Somerset, which was only a variation of Salomon de Caus's 1615 steam fountain, which was in fact very like a device described thirteen years earlier by Giambattista della Porta, who was the first to make any significant use of steam power since the time of Hero of Alexander in the first century of the Christian era. This is an excellent demonstration of how the Industrial Revolution worked. But I don't imagine you see it quite yet, so I'll give you another example.

"Steam engines wouldn't have had much utility without coked coal, which is flameless and smokeless. The coking of coal produces coal gas, which originally was simply vented as worthless. But by the 1790s it was beginning to be burned in factories, both to run equipment and to produce light. But coking coal to produce coal gas generated another waste product, coal tar, a nasty, smelly sludge that was especially difficult to get rid of. German chemists reasoned that it was foolish to work to get rid of it when there might be something useful to *do* with it. Distilling coal tar, they produced kerosene, a new fuel, and creosote, a tarry substance that was found to be a wonderful wood preservative. Since creosote kept wood from rotting, it seemed reasonable to suppose that similar results might be obtained from other coal-tar derivatives. In one such experiment, carbolic acid was used to inhibit putrefaction in sewage. Hearing of this effect of the material in 1865, the English surgeon Joseph Lister wondered if it might prevent putrefaction in human flesh wounds (which at that time made all surgery life-threatening). It did. Still another derivative was carbon black, the residue left by the smoke of burned coal tar. This found one use in a kind of carbon paper invented by Cyrus Dalkin in 1823. It found another use when Thomas Edison discovered that he could amplify telephonic sound by inserting a pellet of carbon black in the receiver."

Ishmael looked at me hopefully. I told him coal tar was a lot more useful than I'd imagined. "I'm sorry," I added. "I know I'm missing the point."

"You've asked me what to do, Julie, and I've given one blanket directive: Be inventive. Now I'm trying to show you what it means to be inventive. I'm trying to show you how the greatest period of human inventiveness worked: The Industrial Revolution was the product of a million small beginnings, a million great little ideas, a million modest innovations and improvements over previous inventions. These millions aren't exaggerations, I think. Over a period of three hundred years, hundreds of thousands of you, acting almost exclusively from motives of self-interest, have transformed the human world by broadcasting ideas and discoveries and furthering these ideas and discoveries by taking them step-by-step to new ideas and discoveries.

"I know that there are Luddite puritans among you who

think of the Industrial Revolution as the work of the devil, but I'm certainly not one of them, Julie. Partly because it didn't proceed according to any theoretical design, the Industrial Revolution was not a utopian undertaking—unlike things like your schools, your prisons, your courts, your governmental structures. It didn't depend on people being better than they are. In fact, it depended on people being just what they've always been. Give them gaslight and they'll abandon candles. Give them electric light and they'll abandon gaslight. Offer them shoes that are attractive and comfortable and they'll abandon shoes that are ugly and uncomfortable. Offer them electric sewing machines and they'll abandon foot-driven sewing machines. Offer them color television and they'll abandon black-and-white television.

"It's tremendously important to notice that the wealth of human inventiveness that was generated by the Industrial Revolution was broadcast and not concentrated into the hands of a privileged few. I'm not referring to the products that were turned out but rather to the intellectual wealth that was generated. No one could lock up either the inventive process itself or the discoveries it produced. Every time some new device or process came out, everyone was free to say, 'I can do something with that.' Everyone was free to say, 'I can take this idea and build on it.' Everyone was free to say, 'I can use this idea in a way its inventor never dreamed of.' "

"Well," I told him, "it certainly never occurred to me to think of the Industrial Revolution this way."

"It's important to note that I'm not proposing it as a candidate for sanctification. I'm not recommending its goals or its shameful features—its relentless materialism, its appalling wastefulness, its enormous appetite for irreplaceable resources, its readiness to flow wherever greed took it. I'm recommending only its mode of operation, which released the greatest and most democratic outpouring of human creativity in human history. Far from thinking about 'giving up' things, you've got to be thinking now about releasing just such another outpouring of human creativity—one that is not directed toward turning out product wealth but rather turning out the kind of wealth you threw away to make yourselves the rulers of the world and now so desperately crave."

"Give me an example, Ishmael. Give me an example."

"The Seattle project that we just discussed is an example. This would be the equivalent of Salomon de Caus's 1615 steam fountain, Julie. Not a last word, just a beginning. People in Los Angeles would look at their experiment and say, 'Yes, that's not bad, but we can do something better here.' And people in Detroit would look at the Los Angeles effort and find a different angle of attack to use in their own city."

"Give me another example."

"The people of Peoria, Illinois, say, 'Look, maybe we could head toward the tribal model by building on the Sudbury Valley School in Framingham, Massachusetts. We could pension off our teachers, close the schools, and open up the city to our children. Let them learn anything they want. We could take that risk. We believe in our kids to that extent.' This is an experiment that would draw national attention. Everyone would be watching to see how well it worked. I personally have no doubt that it would be a tremendous success—provided they really let the kids follow their noses instead of subverting the project with curricula. But of course the Peoria model would just be the beginning. Other cities would see ways to enrich it, surpass it."

"Okay. One more example, please."

"You know, Julie, health-care workers aren't universally overjoyed to be part of the moneymaking machine that health care has become in this country. Many actually went into health care for entirely different reasons than to get rich. Maybe in Albuquerque, New Mexico, they could get together and take the system in a whole new direction. Maybe it will occur to them that there's already a sort of James Watt in this field, a physician by the name of Patch Adams, who started the Gesundheit Institute, a hospital in Virginia where people are treated free of charge. But maybe they need the additional inspiration of seeing similar things happening elsewhere—things like the Seattle project and the Peoria project. This is how the Industrial Revolution worked, Julie. People saw other people figuring out how to make things work and were inspired to try it themselves."

"I think the biggest obstacle to all these things would be the government."

"Of course, Julie. That's what governments are there for, to keep good things from happening. But I'm afraid I have to say that if you can't even manage to force your own presumably democratic governments to allow you to do good things for yourselves, then you probably deserve to become extinct."

"I agree."

"I've opened the tribal treasury for you, Julie. I've shown you the things you threw away for the sake of making yourselves rulers of the world. A system of wealth based on an exchange of energy that is inexhaustible and completely renewable. A system of laws that actually helped people live instead of just punishing them for doing things that people have always done and always will do. An educational system that cost nothing, worked perfectly, and drew people together generationally. There are many other systems worthy of your study there, but you'll find none that encourages people to build creatively off each other's ideas the way you've done during your Industrial Revolution. There was no prohibition against such creativity in the tribal life—but there was also no demand or reward for it."

He fell silent for a moment. I opened my mouth to speak, and he held up a hand to stop me.

"I know I haven't yet given you what you asked for. I'm getting there. You'll just have to be patient and let me get there my own way."

I batted my eyelashes and held my peace.

A Look into The Future

For you, it's just another bit of ancient history, like Reconstruction or the Korean War, but twenty-five years ago many thousands of children your age knew that the Taker way is a way of death. They didn't really know much more than that, but they knew that they didn't want to do what their parents had done—get married, get jobs, get old, retire, and die. They wanted to live a new way, but the only real values they had were love, good fellowship, emotional honesty, drugs, and rock 'n' roll—not bad things by any means, but not enough to found a revolution on, and a revolution was what they wanted. Just as they had no revolutionary theory, they had no revolutionary program. What they had was a slogan—'Tune in, turn on, drop out'—and they imagined that if *everyone* would just tune in, turn on, and drop out, then there'd be dancing in the streets and a new human era would begin. I tell you this because it's as important to know why a thing fails as why a thing succeeds. The children's revolt of the sixties and seventies failed because it had neither a theory nor a program. But they were certainly right about one thing: It's time for something new for you people.

"You *must* have a revolution if you're going to survive, Julie. If you go on the way you're presently going, it's hard to imagine your living through another century. But you can't have a negative revolution. Any revolution that thinks of 'going back' to some 'good old days' of imagined simplicity when men tipped their hats, women stayed home and cooked, and no one got divorced or questioned authority is founded on dreams. Any revolution that depends on people voluntarily giving up things they want for things they don't want is mere utopianism and will fail. You must have a positive revolution, a revolution that brings people *more* of what they *really* want, not *less* of what they *don't* really want. They don't really want sixteen-bit electronic games, but if that's the best they can get, they'll take it. You won't get far in your revolution by asking them to give up their sixteen-bit electronic games. If you want them to lose interest in toys, then you must give them something *even better* than toys.

"That must be the watchword of your revolution, Julie— not voluntary poverty, but rather voluntary wealth. But *real* wealth this time. Not toys, not gadgets, not 'amenities.' Not stuff you can put in bank vaults. Real wealth of the kind that humans were born with. Real wealth of the kind that humans enjoyed here for hundreds of thousands of years—and continue to enjoy wherever the Leaver life is still intact. And this is wealth you can enjoy without feeling guilty, Julie, because it isn't something stolen from the world. It's wealth that is entirely the product of your own energy. Are you with me?"

"I'm with you."

"Now let's see if we can find a reasonably plausible way of looking at the future of your revolution. Back around 1816 the Baron Karl von Draise of Karlsruhe, Germany, thought he'd try his hand at inventing (the Industrial Revolution really has reached into every class, high and low, for its talent). What he had in mind was a self-propelled wheeled vehicle, and what he came up with was a pretty good design for a first try: a bicycle propelled by pushing on the ground with your feet. Now if he'd been able to look seventy years into the future, he could have seen a bicycle that worked *really* well—the one built by the Englishman James Starley, which, except for refinements, is still in use today, a century later.

"Just like the Baron, you and I can't look into the future to see a global human social system that works really well. Such a system may well come into being—but we can no more imagine it than the Baron could imagine James Starley's bicycle. Do you see what I'm saying?"

"I think so."

"All the same, we're better off than the Baron. The Baron not only couldn't look into the future for guidance (because no one can), he couldn't look into the past either, because there were no bicycles there to look at. We're better off than he was, because, while we can't look *forward* to see a global human social system that works really well, we can look *back* to one that worked really well. It worked so well that we can say with some confidence that it was a final, unimprovable system for *tribal peoples*. There was no complex organization. What you had was just independent tribes playing the Erratic Retaliator strategy: 'Give as good as you get, but don't be too predictable.' "

"Right."

"Now what principle or law did the Erratic Retaliator strategy enforce or protect for tribal peoples?"

"Well . . . it protected tribal independence and iden-
tity."

"Yes, that's true, but those are things, not principles or
laws."

I worked on it some but in the end had to admit I didn't
see it.

"It doesn't matter. The Erratic Retaliator strategy en-
forced this law: *There is no one right way for people to live*."

"Right, I see it now."

"This is something that is as true today as it was a million
years ago. Nothing can render it obsolete. This law is something we can count on, Julie. At least you and I can, speaking
as revolutionaries. Opponents of the revolution will insist
that there is surely *some* one right way for people to live, and
they'll generally insist that they know what it is. That's all
right, so long as they don't try to impose their one right way
on us. 'There is no one right way for people to live' is where
we begin, as 'I think therefore I am' was where Descartes
began. Both statements must be accepted as self-evident or
otherwise simply rejected. Neither is capable of proof. Both
can be opposed by other axioms, but neither can be dis-
proved. Are you following me?"

"I think so, Ishmael. At a distance."

"So we have a motto for our banner: 'There is no one
right way for people to live.' Shall we have a name for the
revolution itself?"

After giving this some thought, I said, "Yeah. We could
call it the Tribal Revolution."

Ishmael nodded. "That's a good name, but I think we'd
better make it the *New* Tribal Revolution, Julie. Otherwise
people will think we're talking about bows and arrows and
living in caves."

"Yeah, you're right."

"Here are some things we can expect of the New Tribal

Revolution, based on the experience of the Industrial Revolution. We can call it the Seven-Point Plan.

"One: *The revolution won't take place all at once.* It's not going to be any sort of coup d'état like the French or Russian revolutions.

"Two: *It will be achieved incrementally, by people working off each other's ideas.* This is the great driving innovation of the Industrial Revolution.

"Three: *It will be led by no one.* Like the Industrial Revolution, it will need no shepherd, no organizer, no spearhead, no pacesetter, no mastermind at the top; it will be too much for anyone to lead.

"Four: *it will not be the initiative of any political, governmental, or religious body*—again, like the Industrial Revolution. Some will doubtless want to claim to be its supporters and protectors; there are always leaders ready to step forward once others have shown the way.

"Five: *It has no targeted end point.* Why should it have an end point?

"Six: *It will proceed according to no plan.* How on earth could there be a plan?

"Seven: *It will reward those who further the revolution with the coin of the revolution.* In the Industrial Revolution, those who contributed much in the way of product wealth received much in the way of product wealth; in the New Tribal Revolution, those who contribute much in the way of support will receive much in the way of support.

"Now here's a question for you. What do you think will happen to the Takers in this revolution, Julie?"

"What do you mean 'happen'?"

"I want you to begin thinking like a revolutionary now. Don't make me do all the work. The first thing people will want to do is outlaw the Taker way. Isn't that right?"

I stared at him blankly. "I don't know."

"Think, Julie."

"How can they outlaw the Taker way?"

"I suppose the same way they outlaw anything."

"But I mean . . . if there's no one right way for people to live, how can you outlaw the Taker way? Or any way?"

"That's better. If there's no one right way for people to live, then of course you can't outlaw the Taker way. The Taker way is going to continue, and the people who follow it are going to be the people who really *like* having to work to eat. They really like keeping the food locked up so they can't get at it."

"The Takers are going to lose a lot of people in this case, because the rest of us are going to want the food to be out there free for the taking."

"Then that's what'll happen, Julie. You don't have to outlaw the Taker life to make it disappear. You just have to open the prison door, and people will start pouring out. But there'll always be some who prefer the Taker way, who really thrive on that lifestyle. Maybe they can all get together on the island of Manhattan. You can declare it a national park and send your kids there to study the inhabitants on field trips."

"But how will the rest of it work, Ishmael?"

"Under the original system, tribal membership was determined by birth. That is, you were born a Ute or a Penobscot or an Alawa, you couldn't become one by choice. I suppose it was possible, but it was certainly a rarity. Why would a Hopi want to become a Navajo, or vice versa? But in the New Tribal Revolution, tribal membership will have to be by choice exclusively, at least at first. Imagine a world in which Jeffrey, instead of traveling from one set of Taker friends to another, had been able to travel from one tribe to another— every tribe different, every tribe with its doors open for people to come in or to leave. Do you think he would have ended up walking into that lake?"

"No, I don't. I think he would have ended up in a tribe

where folks like to sit around playing the guitar and writing poetry."

"They probably wouldn't get much 'accomplished,' would they?"

"Probably not, but who cares? But aren't there a lot of intentional communities like this out there right now?"

"Yes, more than ever. Unfortunately, they all operate inside the Taker prison. They pretty much have to do that, because the Taker prison *has* no outside. The Takers long ago claimed the entire planet for themselves, so it's all *inside*."

"What's this have to do with it?"

"Inside real-life prisons, the inmates form groups for various purposes, some of them sanctioned by the prison authorities and some not. For example, some cliques exist for protection; the members watch each other's backs. These cliques have no official status. They're unsanctioned, even outlawed. And if they became sanctioned, they'd actually be worthless, because they wouldn't be able to take actions that the prison authorities couldn't condone. To perform the function they exist to perform, they *must* remain unsanctioned—free to break the rules. Once they become sanctioned, they become like a chess club or a book-discussion group—obedient to the prison rules and so of very marginal importance to the inmates' real concerns."

"What's this got to do with intentional communities?"

"Intentional communities almost always start out with the goal of being sanctioned by Taker law. This keeps them from being hassled by the police, but limits the amount of importance they can achieve in their members' lives. This is the difference between intentional communities on one hand and cults and gangs on the other. Intentional communities want to be officially sanctioned, whereas cults and gangs never do—and this explains how cults and gangs can come to have tribal importance in their members' lives."

"What do you mean by 'tribal importance'?"

"I mean that belonging to the cult or the gang takes on the same importance as belonging to a Leaver tribe. Basically, I mean that membership becomes worth dying for, Julie. When the followers of Jim Jones realized that Jonestown was doomed, they saw no point in living. Jones told them, 'If you love me as I love you, then we all must die together or be destroyed from the outside.' I realize this happened a year or so before you were born, but I thought you might have heard of it."

I told him I hadn't.

"Nine hundred people committed suicide with him. Leaver tribes have done the same when they knew there was finally no hope of being allowed to go on as a tribe."

I shook my head doubtfully, and he asked what was wrong. "I'm not sure. Or maybe I am. I'm used to thinking of gangsters as animals. I'm used to thinking of cultists as lunatics. Putting Leaver tribes in with gangs and cults leaves me feeling distinctly . . . confused."

"I understand. As you move out into the world, you'll find that the intellectually insecure often bolster their confidence by maintaining subjects in solid, impermeable categories of good and evil. The Industrial Revolution is *evil,* and nothing should be seen in it that might be construed as *good.* Gangs and cults are *evil,* and nothing should be seen in them that might be construed as *good.* Tribes, on the other hand, are *good,* and no connection must be seen between them and evil things like cults and gangs. It's permissible to note that Leaver tribes do very well without classes and private property, but you should be careful to emphasize that they haven't been reading naughty books by Marx and Engels."

"Yeah, I can believe that. But I'm still not quite sure what this has to do with intentional communities."

"When government officials began to look into his People's Temple, Jim Jones took it to Guyana. He did this because he knew it would cease to function if it fell under government oversight. To move to a different example, a recovered alcoholic by the name of Charles Dederich started a drug rehabilitation center in Santa Monica in 1958. It was called Synanon. It wasn't exactly a community to begin with, because addicts naturally came and went, but as time went on Dederich became dissatisfied with this model. He wanted a community, and before long he was encouraging recovered addicts to stay on as subsistence employees. Next Dederich opened up the community to outsiders—professionals and businessmen who were willing to turn over real estate, cars, bank accounts, and stock holdings to Synanon for the sake of belonging to a unique community and having what they expected to be a home for life. Step-by-step, Synanon gradually went from being a treatment center to being a cult—and an embattled cult, armed not only for defense but offense, engaging in attempted murder and brutal assaults on perceived enemies in the surrounding community. The cults of Bhagwan Shree Rajneesh, the Hare Krishna, and the Alamo Christian Foundation were all embraced by people who were similarly willing to turn over their worldly possessions and to work for nothing in order to *belong*—to have membership and all that comes with membership—food, lodging, clothing, transportation, health care, and so on. Security, in a word."

"Again, I'm not quite sure why you're telling me all this."

"I'm trying to make you see that these people are not *crazy*. They desperately want something that humans had here for hundreds of thousands of years and still have wherever the Leaver life survives. They want to be taken care of *in the tribal way,* Julie. They're perfectly willing to give to the cult their total support—in return for *its* total support, which means food, lodging, clothing, transportation, health care, and so on—everything it takes to live as a human. They didn't seek out these cults because they perceived them as tribal. They sought them out because they perceived them as offering something they desperately wanted—and still *do* want, I guarantee it, Julie. In the years to come, you're going to see more and more completely ordinary and intelligent people being drawn into cults, not because they're crazy but because the cult offers them something they deeply want and can't get in the Taker world. The support-for-support paradigm is more than just a way of staying alive, it's a profoundly satisfying human style. People really *like* living this way."

"All right, I understand this. Now tell me what I'm supposed to do about it."

"Right now, Julie, who is permitted to start cults in the sense we're talking about here?"

"I guess I'd have to say no one is."

"And since no one is permitted to start cults, who in fact *do* start cults?"

"Crazy people," I said. "People with delusions of grandeur. Also con artists."

"Julie, here's what I'm trying to make you see. Since no one but lunatics and con artists is *allowed* to start cults among you, why are you surprised to find that all your cults *are* started by lunatics and con artists?"

"That's a helluva good question."

"Here's another one for you. What would you do with a cult that *wasn't* started by a lunatic or a con artist?"

"What do you mean, what would I do with it?"

"Well, would you suppress it?"

"I don't know."

"Do you know who the Amish are?"

"Yeah. A couple years ago Harrison Ford hid out with the Amish in a movie."

"Don't you think the Amish should be suppressed?"

"No. Why would I?"

"Because they live just like a cult that isn't centered on a lunatic or a con man."

I closed my eyes and shook my head. "Ishmael," I said, "you're really confusing me."

"Good. That's progress. I must make you stumble over your cultural taboos. I know of no other way to break down the way you've been conditioned to respond to *words*. When you hear the word *gang,* you've been conditioned to think, 'Bad—must not think about.' When you hear the word *cult,* you've been conditioned to think, 'Bad—must not think about.' When you hear the word *tribe,* you've been conditioned to think, 'Good—okay to think about.' "

"What am I supposed to think about when I hear the words *gang* and *cult?*"

"You can start by thinking, 'The word is not the thing.' You can start by thinking, 'The thing does not become bad by being called a bad name.' You can start by thinking, 'The fact that this thing has been called a bad name doesn't mean I can't think about it.' "

"Okay. But what should I think about here?"

"You should think about the fact that there's no *operational* difference between a tribe and a cult, Julie. There's no operational difference between a carburetor built by a church-going Republican and a carburetor built by an atheistic anarchist. Both work the same way. That's what I mean when I say there's no operational difference between them."

"I understand that."

"The same is true here. Perhaps it will help if I point to another example of tribal life that has survived (and even thrived) in your own culture: the circus. You might call the circus a business run on tribal lines, but of course no circus owner ever sat down and deliberately crafted the business that way. Rather, circuses came into being as tribes and would cease to be circuses if they ceased to be tribes. Their legendary tribal solidarity, so unlike the society through which they move, makes them an irresistible lure, and people of all ages 'run off to join the circus' to be part of that solidarity. They're especially important as models for our revolution, because, unlike aboriginal tribes, they're seldom exclusive along ethnic lines. The border around them is solid against the general public but will open to any circus person from anywhere. The tribe, the cult (and of course the circus) all operate on this principle: You give us *your* total support and we'll give you *our* total support. Total—both ways. Without reservation—both ways. People have died for that, Julie. People *will* die for that—not because they're crazy but because this is something that actually *means* something to them. They *will not* exchange this total support for nine-to-five jobs and Social Security checks in their old age."

(Naturally, I'd remember this conversation three and a half years later when the mighty U.S. government found it necessary to obliterate a tiny sect of cultists outside Waco, Texas. It mattered not that the Branch Davidians had been convicted of no crime—and not even *charged* with a crime. They were deluded, and this meant they could be destroyed without a trial—evidently on the principle that *our* delusions are okay, but *their* delusions are inherently evil and must be expunged from the face of the earth, whatever they might actually turn out to be.)

I said, "It almost sounds like you're urging me to start a cult."

He sighed and shook his head. "You're my message-bearer, Julie, and this is my message: Open the prison gates and people will pour out. Build things people want and they'll flock to them. And don't flinch from looking with wide-open eyes at the things people *show you* they want. Don't look away from them just because Mother Culture has given them bad names. Instead, understand *why* she's given them bad names."

"I *do* understand. She's given them bad names because she wants us to recoil from them in horror."

"Of course."

As if on cue, a good-looking, compact man sat down in the chair next to me—and I knew instantly that my course of studies with the ape was over.

The Man from Africa

Ishmael said, "Julie, this is Art Owens," and I gave him a more careful look. Ishmael had said he was forty, but I would have thought he was younger—I'm not great at ages. He was a richer shade of black than I was used to seeing in African-Americans, probably (I later realized) because there were no white folks in his ancestry anywhere at all. He was beautifully dressed, in a fawn-colored suit, olive shirt, and paisley tie. We took some time to look each other over, so that's why I'm giving you all this here.

He was built like a Tyson-style fighter, short and blunt and powerful, like a heavy wrench. I don't know what to say about his face. He wasn't handsome or hideous. He had a face that made you think again about what can be done with faces. It was a face that belonged to someone who, if he said it was going to rain for forty days and forty nights again, starting tomorrow, you'd remember you always sort of wanted to own a boat.

"Hello, Julie," he said, in a rich, dark voice. "I've heard a lot about you." From anyone else, I would have taken it as nothing more than the usual cliché. I told him I hadn't heard word one about him, and he repaid me with a modest smile—not a big dazzler, just an acknowledgment. Then he looked at Ishmael, obviously expecting him to tell me what he wanted me to know.

"You have in fact heard word one about Art, Julie. I told you he has a vehicle and is going to help me make my getaway from this place."

"Yeah," I said. "Okay."

"You offered to help—and now your help is needed."

I looked at Art Owens, I suppose because I figured he must have slipped up somehow or promised something he couldn't deliver. He too nodded. "Something fell through that we thought we had figured out." Then he asked Ishmael how much he'd told me of the plan.

"Nothing at all," Ishmael said.

"Ishmael's going back to Africa," Art said. "There's no support for him here, now that Rachel's gone."

"What's in Africa?"

"A rain forest in the north of Zaire."

"You're joking," I told him. Art frowned and looked at Ishmael.

"She thinks you mean a few thousand acres with a fence around it," Ishmael explained.

"I'm talking about a virgin rain forest—thousands of square miles."

"You both misunderstand me," I said. "When I say you're joking, I mean, are you telling me that Ishmael is going to go out and live like a *gorilla*?"

Briefly, they both looked like I'd reached out and socked

them on the jaw. Art recovered first, saying, "Why *shouldn't* he go out and live like a gorilla? He *is* a gorilla."

"He's not a gorilla, he's a goddamned *philosopher*."

They exchanged baffled glances.

Ishmael said, "Believe me, Julie, there are no chairs of philosophy open for me anywhere in the world, and there never will be."

"That's not the only choice." Ishmael raised a brow at me, challenging me to name some others, but I said I didn't see why he should expect *me* to come up with alternatives. I'd only been working on the problem for thirty seconds.

"I've been working on it for months, Julie, and you'll just have to trust me when I say that this is the best that can be managed. I don't regard it as a defeat or a last resort. This offers me a condition of freedom I can achieve in no other way."

I looked from one to the other and back again. There was no doubt that it was a settled thing, so I shrugged and asked what they needed me for.

They visibly relaxed, and Ishmael said, "How do you imagine such a thing would be managed, Julie?"

"Well, I don't suppose you can just book a first-class seat on an airplane."

"That's certainly true. But working out the details of transportation is the easy part. The first eight thousand miles, from here to Kinshasa, is nothing. The next five hundred miles, from Kinshasa to a point where I can be released, couldn't be organized by any travel agent or shipping agent in the world. They present problems that can only be solved by someone on the ground in Africa who can command cooperation and assistance at the highest levels of government."

"Why is that?"

"It's because Zaire is not Kansas or New Jersey or Ontario or England or Mexico. It's because Zaire is utterly beyond your experience. It has achieved a level of corruption and organized chaos beyond anything you can imagine."

"Then why go there, for God's sake? Go someplace else."

Ishmael nodded and gave me a ghostly smile. "There are certainly easier places to get to, but not many where lowland gorillas are an expected sight, Julie. Only getting to the wilderness is a problem. Once I *am* there, Zaire's corruption will be left far behind, as least for the near future. Under Taker rule, there's ultimately no place in the world where gorillas have an assured future forever. Besides, Zaire recommends itself because we *have* someone on the ground there who can command cooperation and assistance at the highest levels of government. That's something we have no place else."

Obviously, I thought, this had to be Art Owens, and I looked at him to get the story.

"I don't suppose you know anything about Zaire," he said.

"Nothing at all," I admitted.

"Briefly, Zaire won its independence from Belgium thirty-one years ago, when I was five years old. After an initial period of chaos, the reins of power fell into the hands of Joseph Mobutu, a vicious and corrupt strongman who has held them ever since. My real name is Makiadi Owona. My younger brother, Lukombo, and I hung out with Mokonzi Nkemi, another boy our age. All three of us were dreamers, but with different kinds of dreams. I was a naturalist at heart and wanted nothing more than to live in the bush and learn. Nkemi was an activist who wanted to free Zaire not only from Mobutu but from the insidious influence of the white man. Luk was born to be a right-hand man. He thought of me as the Africa that Nkemi wanted to save, and that made us both people he worshiped. Does that make any sense to you?"

"I think so," I said.

"When we were in our teens, Nkemi began to argue that

we owed it to ourselves and to the people of Zaire to beat the white man at his own game, which meant getting the best education we could. It just wasn't going to be good enough for me to live in the bush and play at being a naturalist. I had to go to school and study botany or zoology. He had to go to school and study public affairs and government, which would not be a bad thing for Luk to do either. This is how it played out. With a lot of hard work and determination, we all ended up at the university in Kinshasa. Then, with some more hard work and determination, Nkemi and I managed to get to Belgium to study in the early eighties. That's where Makiadi came to be shortened to Adi. After two years I was eligible for Belgian citizenship, and I took it. I eventually worked my way to the United States, where I studied rainforest resource management at Cornell. That's where Adi eventually became Artie, and Artie became Art. While at Cornell, incidentally, I met Rachel Sokolow and was given the first hints of her relationship to a gorilla named Ishmael. Meanwhile, Nkemi, back in Zaire, was elected to the local urban zone caucus in Bolamba, where he began to build a power base, with Luk at his right hand, where he'd always intended to be.

"I returned to Zaire in 1987 with a head full of dreams of wildlife preservation in the north—our part and the least heavily inhabited part of the country. That was the year Nkemi attempted his first big move into national politics, making a bid for election to the National Legislative Council. But his ideas were too radical, and Mobutu cut the ground from under him. Nkemi returned to Bolamba, a virtual exile, and the three of us—but mostly Nkemi, of course—began to plan our own breakaway revolution."

Art paused to gaze at me thoughtfully, as if to gauge how much of all this I was actually taking in. I gazed back steadily, and he went on.

"Any vision would have been an improvement in Zaire,

which is just a chaos that everyone's used to, with corruption and bribery the only things you can count on from one day to the next. But Nkemi actually had a marvelous vision. The north had long been a stepchild of the more 'civilized' central portion of the country around Kinshasa. Mobutu wanted foreign currency, which meant he wanted the north to produce cash crops for export. Since the farmers were growing crops for export, they had to buy food to eat. This made life very difficult." He paused, stuck, and looked to Ishmael for help.

"Imagine that you're a cobbler with a big family," Ishmael said. "You're a cobbler, but you can only make shoes for export, you're not allowed to make shoes for your own family. You sell your shoes to a distributor for five dollars a pair. The distributor sells them to a retailer for ten dollars a pair. And the retailer sells them to the public for twenty dollars a pair. This means you have to make and sell four pairs of shoes in order to buy one pair of shoes at the shoe store for your own family."

"It's even worse than that, Ishmael, because the shoes you buy in the store are imported shoes, so they cost forty dollars a pair. You have to make and sell eight pairs of shoes to buy one pair at the shoe store."

"I get the drift," I told them.

"That was the cornerstone of Nkemi's revolution. The people were going to take care of the people first. We had to stop looking toward Kinshasa, because Kinshasa was looking toward Paris and London and New York. We had to look toward ourselves, toward traditional village life, toward tribal values. We had to get rid of outsiders trying to focus our attention elsewhere—missionaries, Peace Corps workers, and foreign merchants with their surrounding flocks of servants, shopkeepers, tavern owners, and prostitutes. All the outsiders had to go, and the people loved the idea of getting rid of them. They loved all of Nkemi's ideas.

"On March the second, 1989, we seized control of the

governmental compound of Bolamba and proclaimed the Republic of Mabili—a name referring to an inspiring east wind that draws people together. As is always the case in these situations, there was a lot of confusion and disruption at first as the haves fought to hold on to what they were used to having. I won't go into all that. Our real concern was Mobutu. It would take him three or four weeks to move troops to our position, but we didn't doubt that he would do it. Even though we represented an unimportant and remote section of the country, he couldn't afford to let us break away without a fight. Practically overnight, arms were pouring into our hands across the border from the Central African Republic, north of us. It seemed that André Kolingba, the dictator of that nation, was delighted with our naive little enterprise.

"We braced ourselves for attack. When it finally came, in mid-April, it was surprisingly halfhearted. Mobutu's troops shelled a few villages, executed a few rebels, burned a few fields, and then went home. We were stunned. Was Mobutu ill? Was he being distracted by unrest in some other part of the country? Isolated as we were, we couldn't know for sure. Another possibility was that he meant to lull us asleep. Without anything like a regular army or military discipline, Kolingba's arms would soon be gathering dust and rust. A well-planned secret attack in a year would be devastating. We tried to keep people in a defensive frame of mind, but ordinary citizens thought we were being needlessly cautious.

"There was a Nkemi-type agitator named Rubundo who was trying to unite the Zande tribes in the region to the east of us. He came to say that his followers were ready to secede from Zaire to join the Mabili Republic if we'd let them. Nkemi told him that this was exactly the opposite of what we wanted, and he was right in that respect. Rubundo said he could understand that—but would we at least agree to support them in their own breakaway revolution? Nkemi hemmed and hawed and finally told him he'd think about it. He thought about it and thought about it, and Luk and I watched him think about it, and Rubundo kept calling and sending messages, and weeks went by. Then one day in November we got word that Rubundo had been assassinated. The second I heard that, I understood it all. Nkemi had made a secret deal with Mobutu: *Let us break away, and we'll keep all the other tribes in the north in line for you.* This was the only way to explain why Mobutu had let Mabili go with only token opposition. When I brought this out into the open, there was no doubt that I'd hit on the truth. Luk hadn't seen it any more than I had, but he thought the deal was a good one—just ordinary, practical politics. Since I didn't agree, Nkemi asked me what I intended to do.

"I said, 'Do you expect me to keep quiet about it?'"

"He said, 'Only if you want to go on living,' and I left Bolamba that night. I was back in the United States by Christmas."

I thought about it for a minute, then said, "I'm groping to understand why you're telling me all this. You said you had someone on the ground in Zaire. Is that the person you call Luk?"

"Yes, that's right. My brother."

"Okay. Then I'm still groping. Why have you told me all this?"

"So you'd understand the situation."

"Yeah, I've got that. But why should I understand the situation?"

Art Owens shot the gorilla a look, then went on. "Getting Ishmael to Kinshasa is relatively easy. Getting him the rest of the way will require a network of people—cooperation, collusion, bribery amounting to thousands of dollars. Luk can handle all that, but only by the authority of Mokonzi Nkemi. In other words, he not only needs Nkemi's permission to do it, he needs Nkemi's direct *order* to do it."

"Okay. So?"

"So how is Luk to get Nkemi to order him to handle this matter?"

"I don't know. Ask?"

Art shook his head. "Luk would have no reason to ask such a thing. I don't mean he'd be unwilling. I mean he would arouse suspicion by asking such a thing."

"Suspicion of what?"

"It's enough that he would arouse suspicion, Julie. It needn't be suspicion of anything in particular."

"You mean it would be dangerous for him to go to Nkemi and say, 'I want to import a gorilla from the United States.' "

"If he were to go to Nkemi and say this, Nkemi would assume that he had lost his mind. He would have no doubt of it whatever."

"I see. So?"

"So someone else must ask Nkemi to order Luk to handle this matter."

And Ishmael and Art looked at me. When I finally figured out why, I laughed out loud. "Is that really it? You want *me* to ask Mokonzi Nkemi to order Luk to get Ishmael from Kinshasa to Mabili?"

"No, you wouldn't have to mention Luk at all. All you'd have to do is ask Nkemi to help you get Ishmael to Mabili. He would automatically turn the matter over to Luk."

I looked from one to the other in utter disbelief. They were not kidding.

"You're crazy," I told them.

"Why, Julie?" Ishmael asked.

"First, because why on earth would Nkemi do something just because I asked him to?"

Art nodded. "You must trust me that I understand Nkemi. You'd be asking him to do something that no other person on earth could do. It would please him very much to think that it was in his power to do something no one else could do."

"That's not a very good reason."

"All you'd be asking him to do, Julie, is to lift a finger. That's all it would take for him to grant the wish of a young woman from the most powerful nation in the world. President Bush himself could not grant you this wish, but Nkemi can, simply by turning to Luk and saying, 'Make this happen.'"

"In other words, he'd do it out of sheer . . . what's the word I want, Ishmael?"

"Vanity."

"Yeah. You're saying he'd do it just to please himself."

"He can *afford* to please himself, Julie," Art said.

"Okay. But that's only the first part. The second part is, are you saying I'd actually *go* there?"

"Oh yes. Nothing less than that kind of effort and expense would persuade him of your seriousness."

"And how long would this take?"

"The ordinary traveler would have to go by boat from Kinshasa to Bolamba, a journey that could easily take two weeks each way. You'd go by helicopter. With luck, the whole trip—from here to there and back—would not take more than a week."

"A week! Good Lord, that's completely out of the question! I mean, if you could get me there and back in time to go to school Monday morning, that would at least be in the realm of the possible."

Art shook his head. "Even the president of the United States, with all his resources, would have a hard time meeting that schedule."

"Well, a week is just impossible. Why don't you get Alan Lomax to do it, for God's sake? He's a grown-up. He can do anything he pleases."

There was a moment of dead silence. Art shifted uncomfortably in his chair, crossed one leg over the other, and waited, along with me.

"Alan is not a candidate for this mission, Julie," Ishmael said at last. "He couldn't do it."

"Why not?"

Ishmael frowned—scowled, really. He obviously didn't care to have his word questioned on this point, but he pretty well had to put up with it, didn't he? "Let me put it this way, Julie. Whatever you think, whatever opinion you may have in the matter, I *will not* ask Alan. But I *am* asking you."

"Well, I'm flattered, I really am, but that doesn't change the fact that it's impossible."

"Why is it impossible, Julie?"

"Because my mother wouldn't let me go."

"Would she let you go if you could be back by Monday morning?"

"No . . . but I could do a little fiddling with that. I could tell her I was spending the weekend with a friend."

"I would never permit you to do that, Julie," Art said solemnly. "Not because I'm so moral but because it would be too risky."

"It doesn't matter anyway," I said, "since I certainly can't tell her I'm spending a week with a friend."

"Suppose we tell her something nearer the truth, Julie. Suppose we tell her you're visiting an African head of state on an important mission."

"Then she'll just send for the police."

"Why?"

"Because you're obviously a lunatic. No one sends twelve-year-old girls on missions to heads of state."

Art turned slowly to Ishmael and said, "You led me to expect someone brighter than this, Ishmael."

I sprang up out of my chair and zapped him with a thunderbolt from my eyes that reduced him to a small mound of smoldering ashes.

Ishmael chuckled and waved me down. "Julie's bright enough. She's just not an experienced intriguer and confidence trickster." Turning to me, he went on: "Since reality is not quite going to measure up to our needs in this situation, Julie, we're going to have to help it along. In fact, you might say that we have to create a reality of our own, in which there are certain missions that can *only* be entrusted to twelve-year-old girls."

"And who's supposed to sell this reality to my mother?" I asked.

"If you agree, then the minister of the interior of the Republic of Mabili will sell it to her, Julie—Makiadi Owona, known to you as Art Owens. His passport still lists him as holding this rank. It's an impressive one, don't you think?"

Getting Me Ready

I'm not going to go into it.

What we finally ended up telling my mother was not very far from the truth, but the *way* it was told was a complete lie. As I say, I'm not going to go into it. Between them, Art Owens and Ishmael constructed a piece of reality so seamlessly cogent that all she could do was nod and say, "Well, good God Almighty, if Julie's the only person on the planet who can do this thing, then I guess she's got to do it." Her only proviso was that I never be put in a position where I was on my own to get from one place to the next or from one plane to the next. I was to be met coming off every flight and constantly chaperoned till boarding the next flight.

Naturally she knew the mission had to do with returning a gorilla to its original habitat. This was all Luk was going to know as well. It was all that either one of them *needed* to know. Anything more than that they would have rejected anyway. Why it was so all-fired important to return a gorilla to Africa was just not going to be discussed nohow. It was an act of cosmic symbolic importance, so forget it.

Ishmael made his getaway from the Fairfield Building at three o'clock Sunday morning. I wasn't involved in that.

Art and Ishmael were obviously uneasy about disclosing his immediate destination to me, but in the end there was just no way around it. Naturally they had to preface the information with some history. The years Art spent playing at being a naturalist in the bush provided him with a way of supporting himself during his years at school in Brussels and America. He worked as an animal handler at menageries, zoos, and circuses, and gained a reputation as the man to call in on problem cases—animals that couldn't settle down to life behind bars, animals that wouldn't eat, animals that were unusually hostile or that developed strange, self-destructive habits like opening up wounds in their skin and perversely keeping them open. When he returned to America at the end of 1989, he had his pick of jobs, and he took one with the Darryl Hicks Carnival, then wintering in Florida. As it turned out, Hicks was experiencing some health problems and had been planning to lighten his load by liquidating the menagerie attached to the carnival. Instead, he sold it to Art, who was not by any means destitute. He'd made some shrewd investments while in America and had left them in the hands of a friend he knew he could trust—Rachel Soko-low. Within a year Hicks was ready to get out of the business entirely and offered Art a deal on the whole carnival. Art had enough capital to take it off his hands, though he couldn't buy it outright. It was during the second half of

1990 that he got to know Rachel really well—along with Ishmael, at long last. In January 1991 Rachel tested HIV-positive. Evidently she'd been infected during an operation to correct a heart problem of some kind. Rachel, Art, and Ishmael soon began to formulate the plans that were now involving me.

On leaving the Fairfield Building, Ishmael would be moved to a cage in the menagerie of the Darryl Hicks Carnival during its weeklong gig in our town. From that point on, till the Zaire transfer was arranged, Ishmael would go where the carnival went. Naturally I had some questions, like, *Why a cage, for God's sake?* Because there'd be a panic if anyone caught sight of a gorilla that wasn't behind bars; the local law would be down on them in a flash, bristling with weapons. And, *If they could afford all this other stuff, why not leave him at the Fairfield Building until it was time to put him on a plane?* Because the carnival had all the various licenses, permits, and connections that were ultimately going to be needed to put him on a plane—and Ishmael not only didn't have them, he couldn't get them.

"You're going to have to trust us on this, Julie," Ishmael said. "None of this is perfect, but it's the best that can be done under the circumstances." I had to settle for that. But the first time I went to the carnival, set up on an empty lot at the edge of town, and saw Ishmael in his cage, it nearly broke my heart. Though I had to eventually, I couldn't face him that way yet. I was embarrassed—not for him, for me. Even knowing it was irrational, I felt personally guilty for his being there.

A lot had to be done—that's an understatement. The plan was that I would leave at the crack of dawn on Monday, October 29, and (all going miraculously well) get back around midnight on Friday, November 2. This meant I was going to miss a week of school, and the school had to be cooled out on this. This departure date gave us time to:

Organize plane reservations;

Get passport photos;

Get passport;

Get visa application;

Get shots—tetanus-diphtheria booster, hepatitis-A immune globulin, yellow fever, cholera (not all on the same day!);

Begin taking antimalaria tablets (two weeks before leaving);

Get medical and dental checkups;

Get tickets and travel insurance (including medical);

Get international health certificate;

Get French phrase book;

Get medical supplies: aspirin, antihistamine, antibiotics, stomach aids, diarrhea medicine, salt tablets, calamine lotion, sunscreen, Band-Aids, bandages, scissors, antiseptic, mosquito repellent, water purification tablets, lip balm, facecloth and hand towel, moist-towelette packs, Swiss army knife with scissors, tweezers, and nail file;

Get a backpack and a tummy pack to put it all in.

Now if you happen to have lost your mind and are planning to vacation in Zaire this year, you can follow the above list right down the line, except that now you'll need a currency declaration form (which was eliminated in 1980 and reinstated in Kinshasa in 1992).

I needed an eight-day transit visa, but they wouldn't issue

one by mail to someone my age. I'd have to visit the Zairean
embassy in Washington when I was actually on the way.

More important than all the stuff I needed to get and get
done, were all the instructions I received from Art, repeated
almost daily for three weeks.

"You'll be met at the gate at the end of every flight. Stay
put till your escort arrives. Don't wander off. Stand out in
the middle of the gate area in plain sight."

"You'll be taken care of at every destination from the time
you arrive till the time you leave, so you don't need to take a
lot of money."

"Travel as light as possible."

"In the air, sleep whenever you can, as much as you can.
When you arrive in Zurich, it'll feel like the middle of the
night to you, but it'll be the beginning of the workday for
them. When you arrive in Kinshasa, you'll just be getting
ready to face the day, and they'll be getting ready for dinner
and bed. In the short amount of time you have, there's nothing you can do about this except sleep as much as possible."

"Don't get involved with the people you meet on the
airplane. Be polite but have a book with you that you're
interested in."

"Go into Kinshasa knowing it's probably the most crimi-
nally dangerous city in the world. People are routinely
robbed and killed in the street in broad daylight—especially
foreigners. You won't be, because you'll be heavily protected,
but you have to understand why you *need* that protection.
Don't get cute. Don't play games." (This aspect of the journey is one we hadn't stressed to my mother, needless to say.)

"There'll be no signs at the airport, no announcements on
an intercom. Follow the crowd toward the terminal, but my
brother Luk should meet you before you get there. Remember that you'll be met by Luk and no one else. He doesn't

look like me (we had different fathers). In fact, we hardly look like brothers at all. He's tall and gawky and wears thick glasses. If you have any doubt that it's him, make him tell you your name and his brother's name, and if he can't do that, it isn't Luk and you shouldn't talk to him or have anything to do with him. Stay with the crowd from the airplane and talk to no one but Luk."

"Luk will have two people with him—a bodyguard, who'll be armed to the teeth, and a driver, who'll stay with the car (otherwise it'd be stripped or stolen). The bodyguard will stay with you while Luk takes your bags and passport through customs."

"Don't wear sunglasses. They signal 'big shot'—a target. Don't carry a purse or wear jewelry—they'll be ripped right off of you, bodyguard or no bodyguard. And don't stuff pockets to bulging—someone with a razor will open them right up and be gone with their contents before you can even open your mouth. Compared to Kinshasa, Times Square in New York City is as safe as a Sunday-school picnic."

"Have copies of all your documents and keep them with you at all times in a traveler's belt under your shirt."

"Don't expect the police to protect you—even in the airport. There's nothing like airport security. Nobody is making this place safe for tourists. Roaming bands of kids and beggars will grab whatever they can and take off with it."

"People who flash police IDs are not necessarily police. Even if they are police, they're not necessarily your friends. They'll detain you for any minor infraction—or for no reason at all—until a bribe is paid."

"Don't bring a camera—taking photos of the wrong things can land you in jail. Don't expect your tender age to protect you. No one in Kinshasa will think you're too young to be a criminal—or a whore. You should be aware that a lot of Africans, especially under Muslim influence, think all American girls are more or less whores."

"While you're waiting for Luk to get finished, a stranger could walk up and stick a package or a sack in your hand and walk away without a word. He's hoping you'll carry it through customs and no one will notice. Believe it or not, people do this all the time. They're so stunned that they actually carry the contraband through customs for him. Afterward, of course, he walks over and relieves them of it."

"Obviously none of this applies to the people I'm sending you to. Anyone Luk introduces you to is someone you can trust completely, and they'll be very flattered if you're as friendly to them as you are to me."

"A good way to catch a case of worms is through the soles of your feet, so don't walk around barefoot anywhere. Don't go swimming. Wash your hands often. Drink only beer or purified water. Drink more water than you think you need—but only purified water. And don't let anyone put ice in your drinks, unless it's made with purified water. Use only purified water for brushing your teeth. If someone offers you ice cream as a special treat, you'll have to say no to that also."

"When you get to Bolamba, be prepared to eat with your fingers. This is perfectly respectable and well mannered. Also be prepared to eat strange food. People may offer you Zairean delicacies, especially out in the bush—fried grubs or termites. Shut your eyes if you have to and pretend to like them. The termites are crunchy and taste like popcorn. I promise you it won't kill you to eat these things."

"Don't draw attention to yourself. And be respectful to everybody!"

I especially liked that last one!

En Route

Damned if the very first minder didn't fail to show up at the Atlanta airport to help me connect to Washington. I hung around till I had only fifteen minutes to make the next flight—leaving from another concourse, naturally!—then I took off, following the signs downstairs to some kind of goddamned train station. It's my experience of trains that you're not at liberty to get off of them once they get started. Was I going to get on one here at this juncture of my life and maybe wake up three days later somewhere in Montana? No, I definitely wasn't.

I ran. I'm no connoisseur, God knows, but it's my opinion that whoever designed that airport had to be someone with a deep-seated grudge against travelers. Maybe my way wasn't the most elegant way, but I got there.

I hoped this wasn't going to be the pattern for the whole trip, but I needn't have worried. At Dulles Airport my minder was right there waiting for me at the gate, a competent-looking woman in her forties, dressed like a lawyer in a movie. I felt like an orphan in my jeans and T-shirt (but then I was going to Zaire and she wasn't). We got a cab, and on the way I asked her if she was a friend of Art Owens. She smiled at that—but in a friendly way. She explained that she was a professional escort; this is what she did for a living, meeting people at trains and airports and getting them wherever they needed to be. She explained that in other cities escorts spend most of their time shepherding authors on book tours. In Washington they're expected to serve as bureaucratic pathfinders and trailblazers as well.

At the Zairean embassy they had no record of my visa application or of the letter they'd written saying they'd hand over my visa as soon as I proved I wasn't indigent. I hauled out all my papers plus the copy of their letter plus my wad of traveler's checks totaling the required $500 and waved them at the clerk. He agreed it was all in order and invited me to fill out another application and come back in two days. At that point my escort stepped in and very politely explained that if they didn't stop horsing around, she was basically just going to rip out their lungs and sell them for dog food. She didn't put it in exactly those terms, but that was the general idea. They stopped horsing around, and fifteen minutes later I walked out with my visa. On the basis of this experience, I added "professional escort" to my list of attractive future career choices.

Between there and Kinshasa it was just air travel and plenty of it, with boredom, movies, sleep, snacks, and boredom. Kinshasa from the air surprised me. I was expecting a smoking, postapocalyptic ruin. Instead, it was just an ordinary-looking big city, with office buildings, skyscrapers, and everything. There was even sunshine.

Njili Airport at six P.M. was hot and muggy and did not come equipped with nice air-conditioned passenger-loading bridges moved up to the door. We didn't have to wait to go outside to know what Kinshasa smelled like, because as soon as they cracked the door, Kinshasa came right in and gave us a sample, and it wasn't pleasant.

We climbed down to the tarmac and shuffled off toward the terminal building. An aging hippie with a gray ponytail and beard stepped forward with a smile and said, "Julie?" I ignored him and kept shuffling. Puzzled, he scanned the crowd again, looking for other twelve-year-olds to accost. Finding no others to choose from, he said again, "Julie?"

I told him firmly, "I'm here to meet Lukombo Owona and no one else, and if you're not him, I'd appreciate it if you'd get away from me."

He cackled with laughter. "You're gonna have a long wait, kiddo. Luk Owona's five hundred miles away in Bolamba."

I just kept shuffling forward as I tried to work this out. Not a single thing had been made clearer than that I was to accept no substitute for Lukombo Owona. Luk was it—Luk and absolutely no one but Luk. This guy had done his looking around. I now did mine, looking for a tall, gawky black guy that might be Art Owens's half brother. Standing by the doorway of the terminal was a black guy who was a sort of bigger, meatier version of Art—neither tall nor gawky, but definitely interested in me. I went up to him and said, "Luk?"

He frowned and turned to the hippie, and the two of them exchanged some words in French. When they were finished, the hippie looked down at me and said, "I explained to Mafuta here that you were expecting to meet Luk Owona at the airport, and Mafuta said, 'Luk Owona is the prime minister of Mabili. He doesn't meet people at the airport.' Which is the way it is, Julie. He *sends* people to meet people. He sent Mafuta and he sent me, and I'm afraid you're just gonna have to live with that. Either that or turn around and go home."

So, there went one prime directive down the drain.

Mafuta went to get my stuff through customs while the aging hippie stood guard over me in a waiting room that was like a bus station from hell, with people sitting on the floor, propped against the wall, sleeping, looking bored, tired, and resigned as they waited for flights that would arrive sometime, someday, or maybe never. The hippie was Glen, or rather Just Glen, as he was known. As a pilot in Vietnam, he abandoned his last name in exchange for the helicopter that was sitting out on the tarmac waiting to take us to Bolamba—in other words, he deserted in a stolen helicopter full of spare parts and fuel, spent the next few years running guns and contraband wherever there was money to be made, and finally settled down to a semirespectable life in Zaire.

As Glen talked, just killing time till Mafuta managed to distribute all the necessary bribes, I began to conceive a hope that we would fly directly to Bolamba and not have to spend a night in Kinshasa as planned. But this was not to be. Air travel in Africa, he explained, was not to be confused with air travel in the U.S. In the U.S. you can track your position constantly, day or night, by loran—long-range navigation by way of a network of ground radio stations—and you always know what weather you're flying into. In Africa you fly by sight and by guesstimate, and heading out to cross five hundred miles of wilderness after dark is strictly an enterprise for heroes and lunatics.

Half an hour later we were outside and piling into a car of a make I'd never seen, certainly not American. Mafuta sat in front, beside the driver, a carbine propped up conspicuously inboard of his left knee. This, Glen explained, let all the riffraff know that we would not take kindly to being messed with. In case of actual trouble, Mafuta would be much more likely to use a handgun.

We set out on a long drive through La Cité, the vast slum where two-thirds of the city's population lives—block after block of low hovels with lean-to kitchens, where meals were being cooked over open fires. It didn't take me long to realize that this was the wellhead of the ghastly smell that had greeted us at the airport. When I asked Glen what caused it, he asked if I'd ever visited a big garbage dump. I had to admit that this was a treat I'd missed so far.

"Well, to put it simply," he said, "garbage burns."

"So?"

"In La Cité garbage is cooking fuel. A whole lotta people cooking food over burning garbage makes a stench that stays with you a long time."

I had nothing to say to that—I was concentrating on swallowing.

Oddly enough, there were tons of bars and nightclubs in La Cité—many of them operating in open air and almost all of them throbbing with live music that, to my ears, sounded like the very hottest hot salsa. I wondered how people living in such soul-crushing squalor could produce music that is just purely wild, exciting fun—then I decided maybe the music is their *antidote* to soul-crushing squalor. Seeing that I was taking it in, Glen noted (with a touch of irony, I thought) that Kinshasa is the live-music capital of Africa. I wasn't tempted to pause for a closer look and listen.

After driving half an hour we were still nowhere near the city center, where the government buildings, museums, and European-style shops are, but were in a better class of slum, which is where Glen lived and where I'd spend the night. He and his girl, Kitoko, had an apartment in a house dating from the colonial era, once elegant but now pretty bedraggled. Even here, there were people scattered around cooking

over open fires, and we had to climb over some to get to the
outside staircase that led to Glen's apartment on the second
floor.

I liked Kitoko as soon as I saw her. She was about
twenty-five, skinny, no great beauty, but with a huge,
friendly smile. Like Mafuta, she spoke only Lingala and
French, but she didn't need me to draw pictures to know
that I craved a bathroom, which, luckily, they had. I was
relieved to learn they had a kerosene stove—no cooking with
garbage here! The place was also equipped with kerosene
lamps (and plenty of kerosene smell) for when the electricity
went off, which was often.

Kitoko was cooking *moambé*—chicken and rice with a
peanut- and palm-oil sauce that filled the tiny kitchen with a
wonderful fragrance. Glen showed me his collection of cassettes—half rock 'n' roll, half current Zairean music—and
invited me to make a choice. I always hate it when people do
this, so I just grabbed some cassettes at random and handed
them over.

As we listened to music and waited for the *moambé,* Glen
explained that he'd met Kitoko while flying and doing other
odd jobs for the Republic of Mabili. Turns out she is the
daughter of Luk's wife's cousin—a relation I have to admit
is way beyond my comprehension. She worked downtown
for an import-export firm and also served as Luk's fixer,
arranger, and eyes and ears in Kinshasa.

Art was right about one thing. I'd slept all the way to
Zurich and most of the way to Zaire, and by nine o'clock
Kinshasa time I was just perking up for an all-night poker
game or something. However, after downing a couple of
giant bottles of the local beer with dinner and after, I started
to mellow out, so that by one in the morning I was ready for
a nap. Eight hours later we breakfasted on bananas from
their stash and Oreo cookies from mine, and Kitoko gave
each of us a hug good-bye. Mafuta was waiting for us down-

stairs with the car, and we made it back to the airport with-out getting mugged, stoned, shot at, pounced on, bombed, shelled, garroted, gassed, pitched into, caught in a cross fire, sniped at, blockaded, napalmed, or trip-wired. No one even hit us with a water balloon.

All the same, overnight someone had siphoned off the gas from the helicopter, parked in plain view at the airport *under guard the whole time* by an airport mechanic specially bribed for that purpose. Just business as usual as far as Glen was concerned, and he had us under way after an hour's delay.

Once we were in the air and stabilized, Glen remarked that I was now in a position to tell my friends back home that I'd met a real, live spy.

At first I thought he was referring to himself, but that didn't make any sense. After thinking about it for a second, I said, "Oh—you mean Mafuta."

"No, not Mafuta. He's just muscle. I'm talking about Kitoko. Most spies that operate in real life are nothing like the ones you read about in spy novels."

Lukombo Owona

The general route to Bolamba was simple enough: Follow the Zaire River northeast for five hundred miles, turn left at the Mongala, and after fifty miles there you are. The Zaire part would be easy enough—it's a huge river, as big and muddy as the Mississippi. Turning left at the Mongala would be easy too—if it were marked by some nice monument like the World Trade Center. It wasn't my problem to worry about. Obviously Glen had some way of knowing how to pick the Mongala out of all the other tributaries that wander off and disappear into the rain forest every few miles.

Even if we could have taken a direct beeline route, I'm glad we didn't, because then I would have missed seeing one of the coolest things in the world, a sort of floating village that travels back and forth between Kinshasa and Kisingani. From what I could make out, it's a steamboat pushing a collection of barges so totally loaded with trade goods and people that you can't actually see the barges at all. There were live crocodiles, chickens, and goats, an overstuffed sofa and chairs being transported upriver (and meanwhile providing seating for a dozen people), boxes, bundles, crates, bales of clothes, a rusty Jeep, a stack of coffins, an upright piano, people everywhere, babies and children everywhere, women pounding something I later learned was manioc in big enamel tubs, people cooking, people trading, people gambling, people scrambling from barge to barge. Every barge has a bar, and music and dancing are nonstop day and night. Traders from interior villages paddle down tributaries to reach the river and meet up with the steamer—it can take them days. Along the way, folks paddle out and tie up to the barges to sell stuff like bananas, fish, monkeys, and parrots and buy stuff like enamel pots and bowls, razor blades, and cloth to take back to their villages. Glen said it almost *is* a village, with kids being born and growing up seldom setting foot off this steamer barge-train that shuttles perpetually between Kinshasa and Kisingani. I wished Ishmael could see it, it was such a great demonstration of the idea that there is no one right way for people to live—certainly not to everyone's taste, but I have to admit it had a powerful attraction for me.

It wasn't until we were actually racketing along half a mile above the Zaire that I understood what Glen had been telling me about night flight over the rain forest without loran or weather forecasts. The forest is just solid from horizon to horizon, and it grows right up to the river's edge. Caught in a thunderstorm and forced to land, you'd have only two choices—to consign yourself to the forest canopy or go straight into the river itself. The first would be almost certain death and the second not too much more promising for survival. In daylight the problem could be solved easily enough by landing in the clearing of any riverside village; at night those clearings would be all but invisible.

We were in the air about three hours, I guess, when we turned north to follow the Mongala. On this tributary we saw a trio of dugouts being poled downriver toward the Zaire, where they would hook up to the floating village when it came abreast of the Mongala early the next morning. Glen said they were carrying yams and dried manioc, which he explained is a root that is pounded into flour and cooked into a sort of tropical equivalent of potato dumplings.

After another half an hour we were in sight of Bolamba. At first I thought Glen was putting me on, and that the *real* Bolamba was probably another thirty or forty miles upriver. But no, he was perfectly serious. This crummy little village, about the size of a baseball field, was the capital of the Republic of Mabili. I know it sounds stupid, but I felt insulted. Like, if I'd known this was all there was to it, I would have said, "Hey, look, don't send me over to Bolamba, send Bolamba over to me."

Sensing my outrage, Glen explained that it had been a much larger town during the colonial era and in spite of its unimpressive appearance was still a major trading center for the entire region. We landed in the school playground—and dozens of kids and grown-ups showed up to see who or what Glen was bringing in. Among them was a youngster who stepped forward to introduce himself as Lobi, the minister's assistant, and to invite me to follow him to the official residence a block away. He grabbed my suitcase and my backpack before I could get it on and said, "Is this all you brought?"

I admitted it was, and we got under way. He asked politely, in heavily accented English, if I'd had a pleasant flight and if my stay in Kinshasa was "satisfactory." I assured him I had and it was, and that was it, so far as conversation went.

The official residence was a collection of buildings known

as the Compound, left over from colonial days—very pleasant looking from the outside, with nothing but a bronze plaque at the gate to indicate its governmental function. The building at the front actually looked like a less well-kept version of the Zairean embassy in Washington. We went in and Lobi nodded to someone at the front desk, took me up to the second floor, showed me the location of a bathroom, and sat me down on a bench.

"The minister knows you're here," he said, "and will come for you soon. Meanwhile I'll take your things to your room. Is that all right?"

I said that was fine, and he nipped off down the hall. Ten minutes later he was back, looking surprised to see me still sitting there.

"Hasn't the minister come for you?" he asked, rather unnecessarily, I thought.

I told him he hadn't.

He said he'd see what was keeping him and disappeared through a door down the hall. After about three minutes he stuck his head out into the hall and beckoned me over.

"He was on the phone," Lobi said, "but he's ready for you now."

He led me through an outer office—like, designed for a receptionist but presently empty of receptionists—and into the inner sanctum, where a man who was unmistakably Luk Owona unfolded himself from his chair and rose to give me a formal bow. "Welcome to Bolamba, Miss Gerchak," he said, in a not-very-welcoming tone, and invited me to sit down. Without showing much interest, he went through the usual rigmarole of hoping I'd had a pleasant flight and a satisfactory stay in Kinshasa, then got right down to business.

"I understand," he said, peering at me disdainfully through his thick glasses, "that you are looking for some help in finding a home for a lowland gorilla."

Sitting there listening to him go through all this, I finally realized how far off base Art Owens was in his estimate of this situation. I might have worked it out from the fact that Luk didn't meet my plane in Kinshasa (and probably never had any intention of doing so). I might have worked it out from the fact that he didn't walk a block down the street to meet the helicopter—or stick his head out into the hallway or even move out from behind his desk to greet me. But I had certainly worked it out by now.

Contrary to everything Art took for granted, his brother Luk was not our friend. I didn't know if he was an enemy, but he was certainly not an ally.

In about three seconds flat, I was thoroughly pissed off—partly at Art for being so blind and partly at Luk for being whatever he was being. I totally lost my temper, and when that happens, I'm capable of doing very stupid things. What I did next may look spunky and courageous to some people, but I don't have any such illusions. It was stupidity, plain and simple.

I said I understood that he and his brother had different fathers.

He was clearly disconcerted by my introducing this personal element into our conversation, but he admitted it was true.

I said, "Art's father must have taught him manners."

Luk sat absolutely still for about twenty seconds as he tried to get the right of this remark, then, when he did, his black face turned ashen, like dead coals.

Instantly I wished I was dead. Instantly I wished I was back home, or at least back on that helicopter. Instantly I imagined being taken away and shot. He glared at me as if he too was imagining me being taken away and shot. I glared back—at least I know that much. If you run, that's when people attack.

"How dare you," he finally said coldly, "come into my office and insult me."

"How dare *you*," I said icily, "be so inhospitable to a friend of your brother who has traveled eight thousand miles to ask a favor."

Was I really inspired to the extent that I used the word *inhospitable*? I won't swear to it, but I was certainly inspired.

He stared at me and I stared back. Soon the feeling grew in me that our positions had reversed. It was now he who was gradually beginning to wish he was dead.

He dropped his eyes, and I knew that, incredibly, I'd won. I may not have made a friend for life, but I'd pushed him harder than he'd pushed me.

We sat there. Clearly he didn't know what to do, and certainly I didn't have the vaguest idea what to do. I had just delivered a mortal insult to a man powerful enough to have me killed—and forced him to swallow it. And neither one of us knew how to proceed from there.

Finally, desperately, I said, "Your brother asked me to tell you that he misses you—and Africa." This was a total fabrication, of course. He had never expressed such a sentiment or anything remotely like it.

"That," Luk said, "is hard to believe."

I shrugged as if to say, "What can one do with someone so stupid?"

"He is well?"

"He's doing well," I replied ambiguously. His question and my reply meant that outright war had been averted.

After another longish pause, he said, "Please accept my apology . . . and do me the favor of explaining to me what this business with the gorilla is all about." I thought it was neatly done, to put the apology together with the request this way. It spared him the additional humiliation of having to sit there and receive my forgiveness.

All the same, it was clear from his tone that he assumed "this business with the gorilla" was camouflage for some more important matter. This forced me to shift slightly from the ground I'd come to Bolamba to occupy. If I told Luk the truth, that Art's interest was nothing more than resettling a gorilla, Luk might well shrug it off as unworthy of his attention. That was certainly the impression I was receiving. In order to avoid this outcome, I turned everything around and explained that it was *I* who was interested in resettling the gorilla. In other words, instead of making myself out to be a tool Art was using to achieve *his* purpose, I made Art out to be a tool I was using to achieve *my* purpose. It was a bold and potentially disastrous move, since I had no more than five seconds to wonder if it made any sense at all.

It made a kind of sense to Luk that I couldn't have predicted if I'd had six months to wonder about it. I saw it leap into his eyes. I saw it flash across the surface of his whole body as every molecule in his body realigned itself to this new reality. Art, he saw in this electrifying instant, had gone crazy. Specifically, Art had gone crazy over *me*. In a split second I had been transformed in Luk's imagination from a grubby, travel-worn kid into an alluring nymphet.

There was nothing I could do about this—and nothing I particularly wanted to do about it. It clarified everything in Luk's mind. I had a gorilla (God knows how or why) that I wanted to resettle in the rain forest of central west Africa. Art was powerless to resist helping me get what I wanted. Art couldn't come to Zaire in person to make the arrangement, so here I was. All this tremendous fuss and expense was not for the sake of a gorilla—that would be absurd. It was for the sake of me. This was something Luk could understand . . . so I let him understand it.

After my meeting with Luk, I was shown to my room, which was nothing to write home about either way. I hung up the dress I'd be wearing the next day to meet Mokonzi Nkemi and tried to brush out some of the more obvious wrinkles. It was a pretty dressy little thing, a type I'm not big on, but I was told (again and again) that jeans and T-shirt would be hideously *mal à propos* for meeting the president of the republic. There was a bathroom down the hall with a tub almost deep enough to swim in, and I took a wonderful long bath, followed by a nap.

Since there were not that many English speakers on the premises, Just Glen had appointed himself my mentor for the evening. There would be a vast buffet dinner in what passed for a ballroom, but I was relieved to hear this wasn't in my honor. On the contrary, it was just Nkemi's style to provide a nightly blowout for what was basically the whole government. He and Luk were seldom on hand, as it was felt that the presence of the big bosses might put a damper on the lower orders. Tonight (as on most nights) thirty or forty people were expected to show up—workers and their families, from infants to great-grandparents.

Glen warned me that, like it or not, my entrance would create a sensation, and it did, especially among the kids and young adults. A solid wall of questioners formed around me, and Glen told me I might as well satisfy their curiosity as a group or they'd pursue me individually all night, asking the same questions over and over.

Naturally they wanted to know why I was there, and I explained that I was there to see the president. Naturally they next wanted to know what I was seeing him about. After translating the question, Glen advised me to say I couldn't discuss it, and I took the advice. They wanted to know exactly where I was from and what it was like there, with all the details. They wanted to know what I thought of Zairean food and Zairean music and Zairean roads and Zairean weather. They wanted to know what could be seen on American television, and I got stuck trying to explain what a situation comedy is. I asked them what could be seen on Zairean television, and that got a big laugh. Glen explained that Mobutu was crazy about professional wrestling, so that's what's mainly seen on television. Some of the older questioners wanted to know if I approved of U.S. policies in places like Libya and Israel and Iran. When I said I was keeping an open mind and told Glen to explain that I was joking, he said they wouldn't get it, and he was right, they didn't. I made up for it by being (for a visitor) unusually knowledgeable about the history of the Republic of Mabili, which obviously pleased them very much.

After an hour or so Glen called a halt so we could get something to eat. He took me around the tables, where there looked to be about fifty different dishes—most of it being stuff even Glen couldn't identify. He picked out five or six things that he recognized and thought I'd like, then made me take dabs of another five or six, just to try—nothing weird or terribly exotic, so I didn't get to find out if fried termites really taste like popcorn. All of it was very tasty. I mean it was unusual to encounter food that actually has a taste, as opposed to most American food, which has no taste of its own, so you make it taste like something else—salt or pepper or soy sauce or mustard or lemon juice. One of the things I took on Glen's recommendation turned out to be smoked monkey, which I guess he thought would freak me out. It was nothing to rave about, but it didn't freak me out.

Mokonzi Nkemi

The purpose of my interview with Luk Owona on Wednesday afternoon had been clear enough. In the fiction we were trying to sell here, it was his role to "find out what I wanted" so he could prepare Mokonzi Nkemi for our meeting Thursday morning. As far as Nkemi would know, my request had not the remotest connection to Art Owens, who was persona non grata and not to be mentioned by anyone. The meeting with Nkemi was supposed to be very simple. I'd walk in, exchange a few pleasantries, and explain what I wanted. Nkemi would say, sure, why not, then I'd say thanks, good-bye, and be on my way home. It made perfect sense to everyone that it would happen this way.

Nkemi had a reception area with an actual receptionist in it. After being delivered there by my faithful Lobi (whose name, Glen claimed, was a Lingala word meaning both "yesterday" and "tomorrow"), I sat down for a ten-minute wait and then was shown into the presence. Nkemi's office was suitably bigger and more elegant than Luk's, but the real surprise for me was the man himself. For no good reason, I'd been expecting someone upright, short, and blocky—a generalissimo, in other words. On the contrary, Nkemi was a tall, lanky, slope-shouldered scholar in a dark suit, white shirt, and dark tie. He too wore glasses, but he took them off to wave me to a chair in front of his desk.

"Will you join me in some coffee?" he asked. Then, seeing my hesitation, he assured me that it would be made with purified water. I said that would be very nice, though to be honest I would rather have skipped it. He asked in even greater detail about the pleasantness of my journey and the satisfactoriness of my stay in Kinshasa. To these inquiries, he was able to add new ones about my quarters in the Compound and my dinner the previous night, which for some reason he called a reception. Soon there was the coffee and the drinking of coffee. Then at last there was the getting down to business. He explained that he was sorry to seem to hurry me, but he was expecting a phone call from Paris in a few minutes. I said I understood and didn't mind at all. He said that Mr. Owona had outlined my project to him. He asked me to present it in detail.

It was show time at last.

The gorilla Ishmael, I explained, was a celebrity in America, much the way the gorilla Gargantua had been in a previous generation. Gargantua had eventually died in captivity, but many things had changed among American animal lovers since that time. There was a strong desire to see Ishmael released in the wild, and his owners were willing to cooperate in effecting this outcome—not only to give up an animal that was worth a lot of money but to expend a lot of money to return him to his homeland in the rain forest of central west Africa. All we needed was assistance in moving Ishmael from the point of his arrival in Kinshasa to the point of his release in the Republic of Mabili.

Nkemi demonstrated a polite interest by asking if I thought an animal that had spent its life in captivity would be able to survive in the wild. This was one of many questions on which I'd been coached.

"If he were a predator, no," I replied. "A full-grown lion, kept in a cage all its life, would almost certainly not have the hunting skills to stay alive in the wild. But a foraging animal like a gorilla will have no difficulty surviving in an appropriate habitat. Even so, his handlers will stay with him in the bush until they're certain he's successfully established. If he fails to become established, they'll have to choose between bringing him back or giving him a painless death." I didn't much like mentioning this last point, but it had to be there.

Nkemi next wanted to know if the venture was being sponsored or at least endorsed by some international wildlife protection group like the World Wildlife Fund. I scored one for Art, who had predicted that this question would be asked. What Nkemi was angling for was the possibility of winning some nice headlines for himself in the world press. I told him we hadn't as yet asked for such sponsorship or endorsement but would be glad to do so if that were an issue.

Nkemi asked why a child had been sent on this mission. This, in my opinion, was one of the weak elements in our fiction, but my only choice was to rattle off what we'd worked out. A national competition had been held in the schools, to be won by the student who wrote the best essay advocating Ishmael's return to his homeland. I was the winner, and the prize was this journey and this responsibility of asking the president of the Republic of Mabili for his help. Nkemi's opinion of this feeble tale didn't seem much higher than mine, but he let it pass without comment.

"Tell me this, Miss Gerchak," he said after a bit. "What

reason do you think I would have for obliging you in this matter?".

"I'd hope that the opportunity to do a good thing would be reason enough."

He nodded his approval of this diplomatic reply, but that wasn't the end of it. "But suppose," he went on, "that the mere opportunity to do a good thing were *not* sufficient."

"Okay," I said. "I can suppose that. Please tell me what *would* be sufficient."

He shook his head. "I'm not fishing for a bribe, Miss Gerchak. I want you to find something in this venture that will make it worth my doing, for, to be quite honest, I don't as yet see it. To be completely blunt, what's in it for me? Or if there's nothing in it for me, what's in it for Mabili—or for Africa? I'm not a terribly greedy man, but I certainly expect to be paid in some coin or other for my cooperation. You're getting something *you* want. The owners of this animal are getting something *they* want—or they would not be doing it, I can assure you. And if what you tell me is true, then all the animal lovers of America will get something they want. Out of all these people, why should I be the only one who doesn't get something he wants?"

This was without doubt one helluva point, and since I hadn't a ghost of an idea how to answer it, I could see nothing ahead but the failure of my whole mission. I was in the clutch of pure terror, and my brain locked up. "The trouble is," I said, "I don't know what you *do* want."

He shook his head again, exactly the same way—painfully, sorrowfully. "The things I want are not the issue, Miss Gerchak. If, hearing of your desire to resettle this animal, I had invited you to come here so I could persuade you to allow me to help you, then you'd certainly expect to hear me explain why I should be granted this opportunity—rather than someone else. You'd want to know how giving me the nod (rather than someone else) would benefit you. And I would *tell* you that, because I would have worked that out at the very beginning, before inviting you here."

I sat there gaping at him like a bumpkin.

"You're a charming young person," Nkemi went on, "and doubtless wrote a charming essay, but I'm afraid the organizers of this affair would have been wiser to send someone who actually knows how these things are done."

"Many people will be disappointed," I offered weakly.

"Making them happy is not my job."

"But we're asking for so little!" I bleated.

He shrugged. "If you only ask for a little, then of course you need only offer a little. But asking for little hardly justifies offering nothing."

Luckily, it was at that moment that Nkemi's secretary came in to tell him that his call to Paris had gone through. He asked if I'd mind waiting outside for a few minutes. Mind? I made for the door as if my shoes were on fire.

You'll have some idea of my frame of mind if I tell you that I considered trying to reach Art by phone. I figured it was four-thirty in the morning where he was, so at least he'd be home. The trouble was, I didn't know how long I had and I didn't know how long it would take to get a call through. I decided the time would be better spent beating back my panic and coming up with some brilliant reply that was for the moment unimaginable to me.

Besides, I'd already heard what Art had to say on this subject. He was the author of the basic argument I'd just presented: *We aren't asking for very much, so why not give it to us?* This argument had proved to be a washout. Ishmael had offered no argument on the point, but if he had, what would it be? Oddly enough, I didn't know what argument he'd make, but I knew *how* he'd make it. He'd tell a story—a fable. A fable about a king and a foreign supplicant . . .

About a king who is asked to assist in a restoration of some kind, but who somehow misses the point that this restoration is its own reward . . .

I'd seen Ishmael come up with a serviceable fable in a matter of minutes. It could be done. The problem was finding the right elements and getting them to work together. . . . I thought of a pearl. I thought of a gold coin. After getting warmed up on these, I ventured onward to the structure of the inner ear that controls equilibrium; if I'd known what the damn thing is called, I might have stuck with it. Finally I got an idea that I thought would be as good as any I was likely to get, and I went to work on it. After about five minutes I was ready for Nkemi, and Nkemi was ready for me.

"I'd like to tell you a story," I said when I was again seated in his office. Nkemi gave me a little quirk of the head to indicate that this was an interesting and novel approach and that I should proceed.

"One day a prince was interrupted at court by a foreign visitor who had come to ask a favor. The prince drew the visitor into an inner chamber and asked what favor he wanted.

" 'I'd like you to open the gate of your castle so I can bring in a horse to lodge in your stable,' the stranger said.

" 'What kind of horse?' the prince asked.

" 'It's a gray stallion, Your Highness, with a black star on its forehead.'

"The prince frowned and said, 'There was a horse like that in my father's stable when I was a boy. Then there was a disastrous fire, and it disappeared along with several others.'

" 'Will you open the gate, then, and let me lodge the horse in your stable?'

" 'I don't understand why I should do that,' the prince replied. 'Forgive me if I'm blunt, but how would I benefit from doing this favor for you?'

" 'I thought you understood, Your Highness,' the stranger said. 'This is the very horse that disappeared from your father's stable when you were a boy. I'm only bringing back something that shouldn't have left here in the first place.' "

Nkemi smiled and gave me a nod that seemed to say, "Carry on."

"We're not asking you to look after something that belongs to *us*," I told him. "We're trying to restore something that belongs to *you*."

Nkemi nodded, still smiling. "You see? I could have discovered this benefit for myself with a little thought. But it was your obligation to show it to me, not mine to discover it. By expecting me to find whatever benefit I could in your proposal, you were being quite disrespectful to me—though I understand perfectly that you personally meant no such disrespect."

"I understand," I said, "and I agree completely."

"I will of course be glad to cooperate with you in this odd little venture. Mr. Owona will see to all the arrangements that must be made at this end."

With that, he stood up and extended his hand to me to say farewell.

Eight hours later I was in the air headed back to Zurich.

Feats of Timing

After a long, boring layover in Atlanta, I was home before midnight on Friday—home but virtually comatose. Mother shoveled me into bed. I wasn't too friendly when she woke me at eight the next morning to say that Mr. Owens was on his way to pick me up. I could have used another six hours of unconsciousness, but I got up, got showered, got dressed, and got fed in time to be out on the street to meet him so that he didn't have to come in and make polite talk with my mother. We would have about a ninety-minute drive to get to the carnival, which had moved two towns northward by this time.

After giving him a fairly blow-by-blow account of my African adventure, I asked him what was up.

"Two things have happened since you left," he said. "One is that Ishmael has caught a terrible cold that I'm afraid may turn into pneumonia. There aren't many vets who're capable of treating a gorilla or set up to treat a gorilla, but I've located one, and an ambulance is on its way to the carnival grounds right now."

All I wanted to say about this was: "He'll be all right, won't he?" But I knew Art well enough to know that if he had any reassurance to give me, he would already have given it. He didn't *look* terribly worried, and I had to make do with that.

"What's the second thing?"

He gave a brief, bitter laugh. "The second thing is that Alan Lomax has tracked us down."

"Listen," I said, "you've got to tell me what this thing with Alan is all about. I know Ishmael doesn't want to talk about it, but that shouldn't stop *you* from talking about it."

Art drove for a while as he gave the problem some thought. Finally he said, "Every once in a while Ishmael will encounter a pupil who just won't let go. Who gets . . . possessive. This just scares Ishmael to death—for good reason, actually."

"Why do you say that?"

"Think about it. Once you *own* an animal, well, let's face it, you control it absolutely."

"Yes, but Alan doesn't own *Ishmael*."

"The point is, Alan *wants* to own him. Day before yesterday, he offered me a thousand dollars for him."

"Oh, Christ Almighty," I groaned. I wanted to scream. I wanted to bite hunks out of the dashboard. "What did you tell him?"

Art grinned. "That I might take twenty-five hundred."

"Why did you do *that*?" I inquired indignantly.

"What would you have me do? I had to preserve the

fiction that, as far as I'm concerned, Ishmael's just another animal in my collection."

"Yeah, I can see that."

"You have to keep in mind that, from Alan's point of view, he's doing something completely admirable. He's trying to rescue Ishmael from a desperate situation."

"Hasn't Ishmael told him he doesn't *need* to be rescued?"

"I'm sure he has. But he doesn't dare explain *why* he doesn't need to be rescued."

"Why not?"

"Think about it, Julie. You can work that out for yourself."

I gave the problem some thought but didn't get anywhere with it. I asked, "How does Alan think Ishmael got to the menagerie in the first place?"

"I have no idea."

We rode in silence for a while. Finally I said, "What'll he do next, do you think?"

"Alan? My guess is he'll go home and try to raise as much money as he can. Once he's able to flash the cash before my very eyes, greed will make me putty in his hands."

"But Ishmael will be gone by then, won't he?"

"Oh yes—unless Alan's able to move very quickly. Ishmael will be gone in a few hours, and the carnival itself will be gone by this time on Monday."

At that moment we came to a little town about halfway there, and damned if I didn't catch sight of Alan Lomax himself pulled into a service station. He and a mechanic were poking around under the hood of a Plymouth that had been around since the Carter administration.

"Looks like engine trouble," Art observed.

"Yeah."

"Probably just a little grit in the radiator fan."

"Do you really think so?"

"Well, it could be," Art replied.

I looked at him curiously. "Will he need a new one?"

"Oh yes, eventually," he said. "Unfortunately, it's not easy to get parts out here in the boondocks, especially on a Saturday. If he takes it easy, he can probably limp home without a fan, but he'll be too late to get it fixed today."

"A bad break," I noted.

Farewell, My Ishmael

Sitting in that goddamned cage, he looked terrible and he looked miserable, snuffling and groaning, his fur sticking up every which way, but he wasn't prostrate, and he certainly showed no signs of fading away. In fact, he was thoroughly grumpy and bad-tempered, which he wouldn't have been if he was ready to breathe his last.

After hearing all the details of my African adventure, he was irked that he and Art had misread Luk Owona and Mokonzi Nkemi so badly. "The rule has to be 'Hope for the best, but plan for the worst,' and we just hoped for the best," he said. "A month away from my office, and I'm already losing my touch."

On the other hand, he was clearly tickled by the fable of the gray horse that I'd made up for Nkemi. "You said something about an idea you worked on involving the inner ear. What on earth was that?"

"Well, you know, there's this little gizmo floating around in the inner ear that helps you keep your balance. I was thinking . . . the wicked sorcerer sneaks it out of the ear of the prince at his christening or something, so he grows up lurching—and all his children and grandchildren grow up lurching as well. Then one day the grandson of the sorcerer shows up at the castle and says to the then-reigning king, 'Look, I'd like to turn this gizmo over to you.' And the king says, 'What would I want with such a thing? What's in it for me to take this gizmo off your hands?' Then the sorcerer's grandson explains."

"A bit . . . convoluted," Ishmael said doubtfully.

"Exactly. That's why I went with the horse."

"You'll be a good teacher," Ishmael said, taking me by surprise.

"Is that what I should be?"

"I don't mean a *professional* teacher," he said. "All of you must be teachers, whether you're lawyers, doctors, stockbrokers, filmmakers, industrialists, world leaders, students, fry cooks, or street cleaners. Nothing less than a world of *changed minds* is going to save you—and changing minds is something every single one of you can do, no matter who you are or how you're situated. I told Alan to reach a hundred, but to tell the truth I was getting a little impatient with him. Of course there's nothing wrong with reaching a hundred, but if you can't reach a hundred, then reach ten. And if you can't reach ten, then reach one—because that one may reach a million."

"I'll reach a million," I told him.

He gazed at me for a while and said, "I believe you will."

· · ·

"Will you try to teach in Africa?" I asked him.

"No, no, not at all. Perhaps someday I'll write you a letter, but otherwise I won't be involved in anything like that."

"Then what will you do?"

"I'll journey to the darkest, leafiest, most remote section of the rain forest, and try to find a tribe of my own kind that will let me forage with them. I don't mean to worry you, but it's pointless to disguise the fact that we're not likely to survive as a species in the wild for very much longer. But of course I bring new tools to the problem."

"Meaning what?"

"Meaning that if you hear that there's still one wily old silverback out there that no one seems to be able to throw a net over, you'll know that's me."

Before long, Art dropped by to say that the ambulance had arrived.

I asked Ishmael if I could come with him.

"I'd really rather you didn't, Julie. It won't be a bit easier to say good-bye tomorrow than it is today."

I reached in through the bars, and he took my hand as if it were as fragile as a soap bubble.

Life Goes On

Incredible as it may seem, on Monday morning I got up, ate breakfast, and went to school. On Tuesday morning I did the same damn thing.

It wasn't really possible for me to stay in touch with Art. He had to stay in touch with me, and he did. Through him, I learned that Ishmael gradually recovered and one day in January 1991 set off on his own journey to Africa. I didn't ask what the travel arrangements were; it was not going to be a fun trip, and the less I knew about it the better. In March Art called to let me know that the whole mission had been accomplished. Ishmael was home, and if he didn't like it, he'd have to lump it.

By some mysterious process, my mother seemed gradually

to come to the realization that the reality of the Zairean thing was different from what she'd been told. She didn't challenge me about it or demand an explanation or anything like that. Instead, she developed a mild sort of grievance about it, making dark comments like, "I know you have your secrets. Well, I have mine too."

In September the Darryl Hicks Carnival came back to town, and Art and I spent some time together. I told him that, looking back on it from the distance of a year, I found it hard to believe that the two of them had been unable to find any way of setting up the transfer except through me.

Art grinned and said, "I thought you would have figured this out by now, a smart girl like you."

"What do you mean?"

"We had two other plans worked out for setting up the transfer. Either one would have been cheaper—and a whole lot easier to manage—than sending you."

"Then for God's sake, why *did* you send me?"

"Ishmael insisted on it, of course. He wanted *you* to do it, and no one else."

"But why?"

"I guess you could say it was all he had left to give you. This was his last gift: the knowledge that you had played a key role in his life. And there's no doubt that you did. The fact that we could have done it another way doesn't change that."

"But I might have failed!"

Art shook his head. "He knew you wouldn't fail. That was part of the gift, of course. He wanted you to know that he trusted you with his life."

"Did Alan show up again?"

"Yes, actually he did, just about when I figured he would.

We were all packed up and on the road by dawn, and I left a man behind to intercept him if he showed up, which he did, around noon."

"Why did you do that?"

"Because it had to be ended."

"I don't understand."

"I know you don't. Ishmael was in a difficult position when it came to discussing Alan with you."

"Why is that?"

Art paused and gave me a speculative look. "What did you think of Alan?"

"To tell the truth, I thought he was a creep."

"That's exactly why Ishmael couldn't talk to you about him. You weren't disposed to listen."

"True, I guess."

"There's no guesswork to it, Julie. For some reason, when it came to Alan, your mind was closed."

"Okay, you're right. I know that. Go on."

"Most of Ishmael's pupils have been like you in this one way, that when the time came to let go of him, you let go. Do you know what I'm talking about?"

"I'm not sure. I didn't really have a choice in the matter anyway. I *had* to let him go."

Art disagreed. "No, you didn't, Julie. You could've said, 'If you don't let me go with you, I'll slash my wrists.'"

"True."

"Alan was one of those pupils who simply *would not* let go. Ishmael saw the signs early on, and this became a necessary element of his planning."

"How do you mean?"

"When it became clear that Ishmael was going to have to abandon the Fairfield Building, he could involve you in his plans, but he couldn't involve Alan. This being the case, Ishmael had no choice but simply to disappear. All Alan was going to see was that one day Ishmael was there in his office and the next day he wasn't. He was gone, vanished into thin air."

"You mean Alan had no advance notice at all that Ishmael was leaving?"

"That's right. What would you have thought if one day you'd walked into Ishmael's office and found it empty?"

"Wow, I don't know. I guess I would've thought, 'Well, kiddo, you're on your own.'"

"That's the way most people would take it—but not Alan. Alan reasoned this way: 'If Ishmael has disappeared, then I've got to *find* him!' Which is what he then set out to do."

"I see. It didn't occur to him that Ishmael *wanted* to disappear."

"I doubt if he gave any thought to what Ishmael wanted. The overwhelming fact was what *Alan* wanted, which was to have Ishmael *back*."

"Yes, I see."

"Now, you've got to understand that Ishmael wasn't just trying to ditch Alan. He was trying to wake Alan up. He was trying to shatter Alan's dependence on him. Otherwise Alan was going to remain a pupil forever."

"What do you mean by that?"

"Ishmael doesn't just want pupils, he wants pupils who are going to become teachers themselves. Didn't he make this clear to you?"

"Yes. He said all his pupils are message-bearers. That's why it's important for them to have 'an earnest desire to save the world.' Without that desire, they might do nothing with what they learned."

"That's right. But here's what Ishmael was hearing from Alan: 'I'm never going to pursue my desire to save the world—never going to become a teacher like you, never going to carry your message out into the world—because I'm going to stay here and be your pupil *forever*.' And this is what Ishmael was trying to shatter."

"I understand now."

"When Alan tracked Ishmael to the carnival, the situation became even more desperate, because Alan wasn't just saying, 'I want to stay here and be your pupil forever,' he was now saying, 'I want to buy you and take you home with me and be your pupil forever.' We really had to bring this to a complete and definitive halt."

"Yes, I can see that."

"But how were we going to do that, Julie? How would you have done it, knowing what our situation was? Alan has gone home, presumably to raise enough money to buy Ishmael outright. Ishmael is suffering from a bad cold, bad enough that I want him hospitalized. When Alan returns on Monday, both Ishmael and the carnival will be gone. But I can leave someone behind with a message for Alan."

"Okay."

"What message do I leave behind for him?"

" 'Go home and leave us alone.' "

Art shook his head. "That's not going to work, Julie. Alan is rescuing his teacher from the forces of evil. 'Go home and leave us alone' just isn't enough."

"True." I shrugged. "I know how *I'd* do it, but I don't think Ishmael would approve."

"Ishmael wanted Alan to give up all hope of ever resuming his career as a pupil. He wanted Alan once and for all to say to himself, 'I'm on my own—completely and forever. Ishmael is never again going to be there for me to lean on.' He wanted Alan once and for all to say to himself, 'Ishmael's gone, so I have to become Ishmael myself.' "

"Then maybe he *would* approve."

"So what message would you leave behind for Alan?"

"I would leave this message behind: 'Ishmael is dead. His condition got worse and worse, and he died of pneumonia.' "

"That was the message I left for him, Julie."

"Jesus." Though I didn't say it, I remembered wondering: *Will it work?*

Five months later I had my answer.

Alan's Ishmael

In Alan Lomax's account of his experience with Ishmael,* he admits to protesting that he was "not the kind of writer" who could bring Ishmael's message to the world. But when faced with Ishmael's death, he evidently went home and found a way to *become* that kind of writer. I salute him for this.

I've talked to many people who have read Alan's book, and not a single one has commented on the very odd fact that when it came time for Ishmael to leave the Fairfield Building, he left without saying a word to Alan about it. (Alan doesn't comment on it either!) Similarly, no one seems to notice that Ishmael is very far from delighted when Alan

---

* *Ishmael,* Bantam Books, 1992.

finally shows up at the Darryl Hicks Carnival. (And while Alan notices it, he shies away from looking at it very closely.)

I'm sure everyone will be relieved to hear that I don't intend to produce a point-by-point comparison between what Ishmael said to me and what he said to Alan. To my mind, the only real discrepancy occurs on the subject of Ishmael's other pupils. If Alan is reporting truthfully (and why wouldn't he be?), Ishmael gave him the impression that he'd had very few pupils in the past—and had failed with all of them. This is very strange, since he gave me the opposite impression—that he'd had many pupils and succeeded with all of them to some extent. This indicates that Ishmael was shading the facts for one of us, though I can't imagine why.

Is Alan's Ishmael *my* Ishmael? I personally don't think so, but then I'm hardly in a position to be objective about it. Alan's Ishmael seems to me a bit dour and gloomy, and rather uncomfortable with this particular pupil. But how will *my* Ishmael seem to people who read *this* account? I have no idea.

I learned something very important from reading Alan's book—besides what Ishmael had to teach him. I mean I learned something from Alan himself. It's not easy to put into words, partly because it means admitting I was wrong. From reading Alan's book, I learned how easy it is first to leap to a false conclusion about someone and then to view everything he does in light of that conclusion. Once I'd made up my mind that Alan was a jerk, everything he did looked to me like the work of a jerk. Reading his book made me see that this was not only grossly unfair, it was completely untrue. Art Owens was guilty of the same fault to some extent—but not Ishmael. Ishmael consistently defended Alan to me, was clearly irritated by my prejudice against him, and refused to contribute to that prejudice by discussing with me his worries about Alan's possessiveness. I once saw Sigmund Freud quoted as saying, "To understand is to forgive." In Alan's case, after living with his book for four years, I'd revise that maxim to read, "To understand is to understand."

People also ask me about my reaction to the teachings of the person known as B—Charles Atterley, another pupil of the gorilla.* What I think is this: Ishmael wasn't training parrots, and B is certainly no parrot. He took what he learned from Ishmael and carried it in the direction of his own passion, and I'm sure this is exactly what Ishmael wants to see happen. Are the teachings of B authentic—meaning, do they derive in any way from the teachings of Ishmael? I would certainly have to say so, based on intimations to be found in Alan's book. The fact that these same intimations are not to be found in my book means nothing. Ishmael made it very clear that each of his pupils receives "a different telling" of his message.

As I've written this book, I've known all along that I was eventually going to have to justify my opening line about waking up at age sixteen and knowing I've been screwed. I guess now's the time.

When Alan's book came out, I told Art I intended to write one of my own. His reply was: "Ishmael would certainly want you to do that—but you'll have to wait for a while."

Naturally I asked why.

"You'll have to trust me about this," he said.

"I trust you," I said, "but that doesn't mean I can't ask why."

* *The Story of B,* Bantam Books, 1996.

"In this case it does, Julie. You're just going to have to take it on faith."

"Okay. But what am I waiting *for*?"

"I can't tell you that either."

"Is this some instruction from Ishmael?"

"No."

"How *long* am I supposed to wait?"

"Until I tell you to go ahead."

"Yes, but how long will that be? One year? Two years? Five years?"

"I'm sorry, Julie, I just don't know."

"This isn't fair."

"I know it's not fair. I'm not doing it because it's fair. I'm doing it because it's necessary."

That conversation took place in the summer of 1992. I figured he'd relent sometime during the following year, but he didn't. In 1993 I figured he'd *surely* relent during the following year—but again he didn't.

In the fall of 1994 I took a world-history course in which Alan's book was read by the entire class as a sort of introduction. The effort it took to hold my peace nearly killed me. Otherwise it wasn't a bad year. My mother turned some sort of corner in her life and cut out the booze cold turkey. She started losing weight, joined a women's group, and remembered how to smile.

When I got together with Art in the summer of 1995, I said, "Look, there can't be any harm in my *writing* the book, can there? Can't I write it if I promise to hold on to it?"

He said, yes, I could write it, provided that I swore on a stack of Bibles that I'd show it to no one.

So I started writing—but I did indeed feel that I'd been screwed.

I started writing and finished most of it in six months—all of it but this chapter.

I sent Art a copy of it. He said, "It's terrific—but you've got to wait."

I waited another year, then I wrote this chapter.

Art says . . . wait.

The date is November 28, 1996 . . . and I'm waiting.

The Waiting Ends

On February 11, 1997, two weeks before my eighteenth birthday, Art telephoned to give me the green light. He said, "Mobutu's days are numbered. He'll be out of power in a matter of weeks."

"For Christ's sake, is that what I've been waiting for?"

"That's what you've been waiting for, Julie. Because if Mobutu's days are numbered, then so are Nkemi's."

"You mean you wanted Nkemi to be out of power before I revealed where Ishmael is?"

"That's not quite the point. Until Nkemi was out of power, I didn't want him to know what kind of gorilla he'd given shelter to. Remember that you *named* Ishmael to him."

"True. But Alan names him too. Nkemi could have

known from Alan's book what kind of gorilla he was sheltering."

"No, he couldn't have known this from Alan's book, because, according to Alan's book, Ishmael's dead."

"Okay, I see that. But what would Nkemi have done if he'd known?"

"I have no idea, but I certainly didn't want to find out the hard way, by watching him do it."

"True." I thought about this for a minute, then asked if he was sure that Nkemi's days were numbered.

"Take my word for it, Julie. I have information that even the State Department doesn't have at this point. By summer, Nkemi and his republic will be history."

"I sort of liked Nkemi—and your brother too."

"Don't worry about those two. Before Halloween, they'll both have good jobs teaching political science and African history in Paris or Brussels—though they'll probably make their real money advising businessmen on who to bribe in the new regime."

"Why couldn't you have told me what I was waiting for all these years?"

"If I'd done that, you would have asked how long Mobutu was going to be in power, and I would have had to say, 'Who knows? He might live to be a hundred.' I didn't think you'd like to hear that."

"True."

So the waiting's over, and I'm two years older and wiser than the girl who wrote most of this book. I could easily go back and smooth over some of the rough spots that I know must be there.

But I think I'd better just leave it the way it is.

AUTHOR'S NOTE

Many readers have written to ask, "What can I do to help?" I'd like to encourage you to support a very admirable enterprise, mentioned in the text of this book: Gesundheit Institute, 6855 Washington Blvd., Arlington VA 22213.

In early editions of *Ishmael,* I included a note that began, "*Ishmael* has always been much more than a book to me. It's my hope that it will be much more than a book to many of those who read it. If you are one of this number, I hope you'll do me the favor of getting in touch."

    I'd like to renew that invitation here, adding only that, while I look forward to receiving your letters (and each one will be read!), please understand that it's not possible for me to answer each one personally.

Regular mail: P.O. Box 66627, Houston TX 77266-6627

Email: danielquinn@ishmael.org

You can also contact other readers of my books at
http://www.ishmael.org

ABOUT THE AUTHOR

Daniel Quinn's first book, *Ishmael,* won the Turner Tomorrow Fellowship, a prize for fiction presenting creative and positive solutions to global problems. He is also the author of *Providence, The Story of B,* and (with Tom Whalen) *A Newcomer's Guide to the Afterlife.*